RED CICADA

OTHER BOOKS AND AUDIOBOOKS

BY GREGG LUKE

The Survivors

Do No Harm

Altered State

Blink of an Eye

Bloodborne

Deadly Undertakings

"The Death House" in *Twisted Fate*

The Healer

Infected

The Hunter's Son

"Insidious" in *Entangled*

Plague

RED CICADA

A SUSPENSE NOVEL

GREGG LUKE

Covenant Communications, Inc.

Cover image courtesy shutterstock.com

Published by Covenant Communications, Inc.
American Fork, Utah

Printed in the United States of America
First Printing: May 2022

28 27 26 25 24 23 22   10 9 8 7 6 5 4 3 2 1

ISBN 978-1-52441-864-9

To my brother, C. Lemar Luke Jr.—
my exemplar, my technical advisor, and one of my best friends ever

PRAISE FOR GREGG LUKE

"An edge-of-your-seat suspense-filled ride!"

—*InD'tale Magazine*

"Gregg Luke presents a delightful mystery full of twists and turns that compel a reader to turn to the next page, with *Red Cicada*. Superbly written . . . Gregg Luke slowly builds tension as Lana's past is revealed in its shocking truth in a satisfying climax. Readers will enjoy moments of flirtation between Lana and Lance, which will bond them into the story. An excellent book."

—Readers' Favorite five-star review

"Fans of government conspiracies, medical thrillers, witty banter, and heart-pounding suspense will love *Red Cicada*."

—Jennifer Moore, The Blue Orchid Society series

"I can always depend on Gregg Luke to tell a well-written story with a fascinating premise and white-knuckle suspense. *Red Cicada* was no exception. This novel grabbed my interest quickly and held on for the entire story. Fans of suspense will not want to miss this intriguing, absorbing read."

—A. L. Sowards, award-winning author of *Before the Fortress Falls* and the Duchy of Athens series

"When you pick up *Red Cicada* by Gregg Luke, you are in for a wild ride full of intrigue, suspense, and one surprise after another. The protagonist, Lana Baker, learns that everything she thought she knew about the person closest to her was wrong. And the hero, Lieutenant Lance Kipling, helps her wade through the dangerous waters of espionage to keep her alive. Together they uncover a deadly secret from Lana's past that could have global repercussions. So buckle up and fasten your seat belts. You're in for a great ride reading this book."

—Kathi Oram Peterson, Whitney Award–winning author of *A Stranger Watches*

"With twists and turns around every corner and surprises galore, Gregg Luke's *Red Cicada* is a definite page turner. A must read."

—Ronda Gibb Hinrichsen, author of *A Revolution of Hearts*

"You know that kind of book you can't put down in order to fix dinner? You stand there stirring the gravy with one hand while holding the book with the other, or 'just one more chapter' takes you to 2:17 a.m. and the final page? Yeah, Gregg Luke's *Red Cicada* is that kind of book. Mystery/suspense readers will love this one! The characters are easy to love or despise. The action is exciting. It packs a strong emotional punch, and there are elements that easily alert the reader's attention to possibilities that might be linked to today's problems and headlines. A low-key romance is an added bonus."

—*Meridian Magazine*

"Luke's suspense novels unravel like a medieval tapestry, mesmerizing with their accurate attention to medical and scientific research. He keeps you guessing until the very end."

—Paige Edwards, 2021 Readers' Favorite Book Award Finalist for *Danger on the Loch*

ACKNOWLEDGMENTS

I HAVE A GREAT GROUP of beta readers whose contributions are priceless when it comes to primary editing, content review, and plot-hole discovery. I feel comfortable relying on them again and again whenever I finish a new manuscript. They are Melissa Duce, Erika Luke, and Lemar Luke. I would also like to thank my amazing editor, Kami Hancock, who performs miracles equal to the precision of a surgeon when applying her skills to my writing.

Ofttimes, I will also enlist the help of experts in a particular field for technical advice. In this novel, the following experience was all the expert advice I needed:

Not long ago, I had my knees scanned to see if I qualified for knee-replacement surgery. After the MRI was taken, the technician asked me when I had had my previous knee surgery. I hadn't. Ever. She asked if I'd been in an accident that banged up my left knee. I hadn't. Ever.

"Are you certain?" she asked in a disbelieving tone. "Because you have a piece of metal just below your kneecap," she said, pointing to a bright mark on the image.

I gawked. Sure enough, there was a spot about the size of an eraser tip just below my left kneecap. I wracked my brain trying to remember when that could have happened. When the radiologist entered, he identified it as a shadow that sometimes occurs because of the positioning of the patella. There was no foreign piece of metal in my knee.

But . . . what if there were? What if, unbeknownst to me, some ne'er-do-well had implanted it in my leg—or, better yet, my skull—for sinister reasons?

And that, dear reader, is how the mind of an author works.

CHAPTER 1

Fort Collins, Colorado, July 2011

Pulsing bright lights zigzagged across Lana Baker's field of vision. She shut her eyes, but that didn't stop the intense auras. She groaned. *Not again!*

The afternoon was overcast, so no sun glare made it to her section of the office floor. Her cubical was adequately lit, but not to any extreme. Her computer screen was set to low illumination. She'd even made sure she didn't have any office implements with highly reflective surfaces, knowing such glinting flares often triggered her migraines.

Narrowing her eyes, she reached for her top drawer. Inside was a bottle of Excedrin. She popped three into her mouth and washed them down with Dr Pepper. Continuing to squint, she switched off her desk lamp and forced herself to ignore the warning signs. If she ignored them, they might go away. But within two minutes of the first flashes, Lana felt the all-too-familiar pressure form in her forehead and creep down to her temples, where it pooled and throbbed. Massaging the sides of her head, she silently begged, *Not now. Please, not again.*

Ignoring her plea, harsh zigzags sparked a second time, like horizontal lightning strikes. She squeezed her eyes shut and grimaced at the rapidly building pressure and prayed the headache would at least not fully manifest until she finished her shift. If she could make it home, she'd be okay. But when Lana reopened her eyes, clear, jagged lines formed crenellated edges in her vision, as if she were looking through the notched parapet of a fractured glass castle.

Nothing she did was going to stop the impending misery.

Lana's coworker Camry Ellis stopped at the entrance of Lana's cubical. "Hey, bestie, you okay? Your face is all scrunched like you're in pain."

"I'm fine," Lana lied feebly.

"Headache again?"

She resisted nodding. It would tip the pain over the edge. "Yeah."

"Then, go home."

"I can't," she said. "I've already had two sick days this month and it's only the seventeenth. HR has me on slacker alert as it is."

"But you look miserable," her friend argued.

"I'll be okay. I took some Excedrin. They'll kick in in a minute."

Camry gave her a skeptical look. "If they don't kick in soon, I'm calling HR myself and telling them I'm taking you to the hospital. Look at your hands—they're shaking. HR can't say you're a slacker if you go to the hospital."

Lana was touched. "Thanks, Cams. But I'll be fine. I'm used to this."

"How can you be *used* to a migraine? That's not a good thing. I read online that regular migraines can be a sign of meningitis or a brain tumor. You get your migraines way too often."

"If it were either of those, I'd already be dead. I've had these since childhood."

"That's what I'm saying."

Lana grimaced against another jolt of pain. She took a stuttered breath and said, "Okay. I promise I'll get it checked out tomorrow."

"You'd better. I don't take no for an answer."

"So I've learned," Lana said with a forced smile.

Camry patted the edge of the cubical and walked away.

As Lana turned back to her computer, a brutal wave of nausea rushed up her throat. She stood to run to the restroom, but lightning again flashed behind her eyes, accompanied by a disorienting *whoosh* in her ears. She staggered and collapsed. White-hot spikes strobed throughout her head. She twitched on the floor. Her stomach emptied violently through her throat. The floor tipped back and forth like a Tilt-A-Whirl before all went black.

Δ

Lana awoke to orchestrated busyness around her. The overhead lights were blinding. Painful, glaring brilliance penetrated her lids. She reflexively squeezed her eyes tighter, but it did little good. Caustic bile coated her mouth; each swallow burned intensely. She inhaled deeply, and a strong disinfectant odor assaulted her sinuses. She heard urgent voices and sneakers chirping against linoleum flooring.

Panic clenched Lana's throat as she realized she was in a hospital. *No!*

"Lana? Lana Baker, can you hear me?" It was a female voice, insistent but caring. A hand pressed gently against her shoulder.

"Yeah," Lana croaked, keeping her eyes closed.

"You passed out at work. You're in Poudre Valley Hospital. Are you in any pain?"

"Headache. Migraine."

"Okay. That's what your friend said. You vomited and passed out at work. Your friend said you were seizing too. Are you on any medicines for your headaches and seizures?"

"Just Excedrin. I've never had seizures."

"Are you allergic to any medications?"

"No."

"Okay, good deal. We've got you cleaned up and are prepping you for a CT scan now."

Lana's breathing faltered. "No," she whimpered, wishing she could have screamed it. "No scans."

A second female voice joined in. "Hi, Lana. I'm Dr. Amelia Perkes. A CT is a routine exam for someone with seizures. It's perfectly safe, I promise."

"No," Lana insisted, feeling her strength wane. "No X-rays."

"No X-rays? Do you have a pacemaker or thyroid disease?"

"No."

"Are you pregnant?"

"No."

"Are you currently on any prescription medication or recreational drugs?"

"No. Never."

"Do you have any stents or piercings, any pins or bone screws or extra-sensitive skin?"

"No, none of that. Just . . . please don't."

There was a pause before the doctor continued. "Who is your primary care provider?"

"I don't have one. But I don't want X-rays either," she repeated.

"No X-rays, yes, okay. Can you give me a reason I can note in your chart?"

Lana didn't know how to answer that question. She didn't have a specific *physical* reason not to get an X-ray; it was just a warning her dad had given long ago. He'd said X-rays were a common medical tool, but they could be dangerous for her. "If you break a bone, X-rays are fine. Just don't ever X-ray your head," he'd told her.

As far back as Lana could remember, she'd never been to a doctor—except maybe when she was an infant. While she was growing up, her father had taken care of any acute medical needs, which weren't many.

"Lana?" Dr. Perkes prompted.

"My father told me never to get a head X-ray. I think it has something to do with my migraines."

"I see. Do you know what triggers your migraines?"

"Bright lights. Chocolate sometimes. But not always. Sometimes they just come randomly."

"Do you always pass out from them?"

"No." She swallowed hard, fearing where this line of questioning was headed. "This was the first time."

The doctor paused briefly before saying, "Lana, here's the thing: If I had a medical history to work from, I'd consider a different approach. But we can't seem to find any medical information on you. That's why we need tests—to establish a foundation before I can begin to assess how to treat you. In your particular instance, passing out from a headache and subsequent seizures can indicate a serious brain disorder, and a basic CT scan is the best diagnostic tool we have to address it. It's quick and painless and very safe, I assure you."

Lana opened her eyes a slit and looked at the doctor's ID badge. Brightly colored, it listed the doctor's name and position and the name of the hospital. The badge swung gently from a clip securing it to the doctor's lab coat. The motion caused another wave of nausea to assault Lana, cramping her stomach muscles involuntarily. She turned her head and vomited onto the gurney and ED floor. She sucked in a few panicked gulps of bile-tinged air before her stomach convulsed again. Serrated blades of pain slashed through her skull. Every sound threatened to burst her eardrums. The urge to vomit was unstoppable. The entire room seemed to pulse.

"Take deep breaths, Lana," Dr. Perkes urged.

She was trying! But she couldn't stop retching. Even with her stomach empty, her abdominal muscles seized with crippling spasticity. The pain in her head was unrelenting. She felt her whole body spasm and cramp, spasm and cramp in violent repetition.

"She's seizing again," the doctor announced. "Push two milligrams of diazepam and fifty milligrams of promethazine, stat."

Hot tears streamed down Lana's cheeks.

"Just try to stay calm, Lana. I'm gonna give you something to relax your muscles and stop your vomiting."

"Please—help—me," she begged between gasps.

"We're going to help you, Lana. Just focus on breathing slowly. Deep and slow. And . . . there you go. The meds are on their way."

A warm prickling rushed into Lana's arm, followed by a tingling sensation of lightness. It quickly filled her head.

"You should begin to relax in a few seconds. Just listen to my voice and try to stay calm. Let the meds do their work. I'll keep talking you down until you drift off."

Lana's body continued to convulse, but it was a distant, hollow thing. Soon, the cramps dwindled. The pain lessened. Then darkness enveloped her.

CHAPTER 2

Lana plummeted through heavy mist; moisture streaked across her face, stinging her eyes and whipping her hair. Then, breaking through the mist, she found herself high in the air, plummeting toward a large city. Lifeless gray buildings covered the ground, offering no promise of a soft landing. Rotating her arms wildly, Lana screamed until she tasted blood. Rooftops raced toward her. Radio towers atop the buildings threatened to impale her. Before she could draw a breath, she slammed into an asphalt terrace with bone-snapping force.

△

Lana jolted awake. Her bed shook as if she'd impacted with it. She instantly felt hands firmly grip her shoulders. Someone was calling her name, pleading. Camry's voice.

"Lana. Lana, wake up. It's just a bad dream. You're safe, I promise."

Trembling uncontrollably, Lana opened her eyes. Camry was leaning in, her face contorted with worry and fright. She released Lana's shoulders and tenderly blotted her damp forehead with a tissue.

"Shh. There now, Miss Blue Eyes. See? Everything is okay."

Lana swallowed hard. Her throat seared with caustic pain. "Was I screaming again?"

"Like a banshee," Camry said with a sympathetic smile.

"Oh. Sorry."

Camry's eyes narrowed. "What do you mean 'again'?"

"Nothing," Lana said, looking past her friend. "I'm still in the hospital?"

"Obviously."

Lana tried to sit up, but her head felt like it weighed a ton. Her entire body ached. "What happened?"

"You don't remember? Wow. Um, okay. You started seizing, so they gave you a sedative or something. It knocked you out cold. In fact, this is the first you've been fully awake in a day and a half. Snored completely through Wednesday, Sleeping Beauty. I should have found a handsome prince to kiss you awake yesterday."

Lana cringed. "No thanks. Can I have some water, please?"

Camry handed her a plastic mug with a flexible straw.

She took a sip and cringed even more. "My throat is on fire."

"I don't doubt it. You were making enough noise to wake the dead clear in the next county."

Lana abruptly remembered that the attending doctor had insisted on running a scan of some kind. "Did they take X-rays?"

"They did something," Camry said, then huffed. "Why didn't you tell me you'd had brain surgery?"

What? She must not have heard her friend correctly. Lana frowned and tried again to sit up. Camry pressed the remote on the bed to raise her into an upright position and stuffed a pillow behind her neck.

"Did you say brain surgery?"

"Yeah. When they wheeled you back here, the doc asked me if I knew anything about the plate in your skull. Obviously, I didn't have a clue. Why didn't you tell me?"

Lana's frown deepened. "I've never had brain surgery—or *any* surgery, for that matter."

"Seriously?"

"Yeah. This is the first time I've ever been in a hospital."

"Right. You're pulling my leg." Camry again huffed. "You *had* to have been in a hospital. Why else would you have a metal plate in your skull?"

"But I don't." Lana gently probed the top of her head but felt nothing unusual. "I've never had brain surgery or a fractured skull or anything. They must have confused me with someone else."

Camry stood and stuck her head out the door. "I need the doctor in here right away!"

Someone answered, but Lana couldn't understand the response.

"I don't care!" Camry yelled. "I need the doctor now. That's not a suggestion."

"I'm sure it's no big deal," Lana said, embarrassed by her friend's outburst.

"No big deal?" Camry cried, returning to her bedside. "Either they switched your chart with someone else's or there's a chunk of metal in your skull you don't know about. Either way, it's a *very* big deal."

Lana's hand moved from her head to the back of her neck. Feeling nothing, her fingers frantically searched the front of her neck and chest. "My amulet! Where's my necklace?"

"Here is it, sweetie," Camry said, reaching for a paper cup on the bedside tray. "They must have removed it before they examined you. Your dad gave you this, right?"

"Yes. He said—"

A middle-aged nurse entered the room, interrupting her. "What seems to be the problem?" she asked, glancing over the top of her narrow reading glasses.

"The problem is I asked for a doctor," Camry snipped.

"The doctor is with another patient. She—" The nurse stopped mid-phrase, seeing Lana awake. "Well, hello there. I'm glad to see you're finally up. How you feeling, hon?"

"Like I just went skydiving without a parachute," she said, securing her pendant around her neck.

"You still have a headache?"

Camry cut in. "My best friend has a metal plate in her skull, and she has no idea how it got there—or that it even existed. Of course she still has a headache."

"It's down to a dull thrum," Lana answered. "Whatever you got in this IV seems to be working."

The nurse adjusted her glasses to examine the IV bag. Her badge read *Trina*. "You're on a saline drip right now to keep you hydrated. Any nausea or vertigo?"

"No nausea. A little dizziness."

"Blurred vision?"

"Not really. My throat is very sore."

"I can get you some ice chips or a popsicle."

"A popsicle sounds great."

"You can have any flavor except cherry or grape. Can't have the dark coloring stain your throat."

"Banana?"

"Sure thing, hon."

The nurse pressed the call button on the monitor attached to Lana's bed.

Camry placed her fists on her hips and glared. "Great. Let's all have a popsicle party instead of learning what's up with the plate in her skull."

The nurse flashed Camry a look of censure. "We *are* still looking into that. It may take some time."

"How long?" Lana asked.

"Not sure. We still need to get your medical history. Now that you're awake, what can you tell me about your past?"

Lana's eyes dropped. "Nothing. I don't have a record from my early childhood. It was lost in an apartment fire. But I'm certain I've never been in a hospital or had surgery of any kind. My dad would have told me if I had."

"Ever?"

"Not that I can remember."

An orderly entered the room and raised his eyebrows expectantly.

Trina said, "Hey, Ryan, can you bring Lana a banana popsicle?"

"Two," Camry added.

The young man nodded and left.

"Now then," the nurse continued, using a stylus to bring up data on an electronic tablet. "Let's see—boy, there're a lot of blanks here. I guess we need to start from square one. Your driver's license says your birth date is August 29, 1981. That makes you, what, thirty?"

"Twenty-nine. Don't push it."

She made a notation. "Who is your primary care physician?"

"I don't have one."

"Gynecologist?"

"No. I've never been to any doctor. I've always been very healthy. I do have a dentist, but that's about it."

Trina looked up from the tablet. "Your parents never took you in for a well-child exam or tonsillitis or an ear infection?"

"No. My mom died right after childbirth and my dad never remarried. He was a marine corps medic before he joined special forces, so he always took care of my medical concerns."

"O . . . kay," Nurse Trina murmured as she wrote something on the tablet. "Are you on any medications, prescription or over the counter?"

"Excedrin Migraine, sometimes three to four times a day."

"That's a lot of aspirin. Do you ever have stomach pain or reflux?"

"No."

"Huh. Do you smoke, vape, drink alcohol, or use recreational drugs?"

"I have an occasional glass of wine, but that's it."

"Do you know if you were vaccinated as a child?"

"I think so. Maybe. Except for headaches, I guess I was always a healthy kid."

For as long as Lana could remember, she'd had headaches. At first, she thought everyone did. They became much worse when she entered her teens. Dad had figured they were part of her becoming a young woman. Hormones were tricky things. Everything she'd read confirmed his diagnosis, so she simply learned to tolerate the pain.

But her migraines were a different story. Blinding, excruciating, incapacitating, they'd started in her early twenties. And they seemed to come more often during times of stress. Her worst ones had begun right after her dad's death. Was there a connection between a loved one's passing and the intensity of migraines? In spite of hours of searching, she'd never found a single article on *Father's death increases intensity of daughter's migraines*.

She doubted the hospital staff would find any connection either. That was one of the reasons Dad had cautioned her to avoid hospitals. They'd just run a dozen expensive tests and end up giving her a drug that would only mask the pain—not eliminate it. Painkillers were just Band-Aids with side effects.

The nurse continued. "Your address is local. How long have you lived in Fort Collins?"

"I moved here about two months ago from Gilbert, Arizona. Got a job with the Fort Collins Comptroller's Office."

"We both work in the auditing department," Camry joined in.

The nurse asked for Lana's cell phone, work phone, and Social Security number, which she entered in the tablet. She verified Lana's height and weight with the measurements taken during admission.

"But no primary doctor, huh?"

"No. I'm pretty sure I've made that clear."

Nurse Trina released a frustrated sigh and logged off the chart. "You aren't giving us much to work with, Lana. The more information you share with us, the easier it is to treat you. Can't do much about your present without knowing about your past. Still, we'll get to the bottom of your headaches." She patted Lana on the knee as if she were suddenly a dear friend. "I'll see what's keeping those popsicles. Try to remember more about your medical history. Anything you can come up with may help."

As soon as Trina left the room, Camry huffed. "Thanks for nothing, Nurse Nosey."

Lana exhaled. "She's just doing her job."

"Not very well. She thought you were withholding information. People like that make me want to chew off my arm and beat myself with it."

When Lana chuckled, a tiny spike of pain flashed up the back of her head. She drew a quick breath between her teeth. Seeing the look of concern on her friend's face, she said, "It's nothing. Just an aftershock. It happens sometimes."

Camry frowned. "Well, I do agree with Nurse Nosey on one thing. We need to get to the bottom of this. You *can't* do squat about your future without knowing about your past."

CHAPTER 3

THAT EVENING, LANA AND CAMRY were discussing events at work when Dr. Perkes entered the room. The doctor was medium height and had perfectly arched eyebrows and rounded cheekbones. Lana didn't remember that about her. She usually had a pretty good memory for faces. Her dad had taught her little tricks to memorize features that make people unique—the shape of each eye, the contour of the nose, the width of the mouth, their posture, and so on. *Don't focus on eye and hair color. Those are easily changed.*

The doctor looked poised but exhausted, as if her day had been a soul-crusher.

"Are you okay?" Lana asked.

Dr. Perkes forced a smile. "That's the question I'm supposed to ask you."

"I agree with Lana," Camry joined in. "You look pretty beat."

"It's been a long day. How's the migraine?"

"All but gone. I actually feel much better, thanks. When can I go home?"

"Not for a while, I'm afraid. We still need to figure out what's going on in your skull."

"Not much brain activity," Camry quipped. "Just kidding, Lana."

Clearly unamused, Dr. Perkes pinched the bridge of her nose and sighed. Then, reading from the electronic tablet, she said, "I had a colleague in radiology look at your CT scan. He isn't sure—"

"You took an X-ray?" Lana cut across. "Why did you take an X-ray?"

Dr. Perkes frowned. "It's standard procedure in a case like yours."

"I said no X-rays!"

"Lana," the doctor said in a work-weary tone. "A CT scan is a specific type of X-ray focused on an isolated section of the body—in this case, the brain. It's not an overall image. There's minimal radiation. It's a standard procedure for any patient presenting with seizures of unknown origin. It's actually *required* by this hospital. You won't suffer any ill effects from it, I assure you."

Lana fumed, fixating on her clenched fists instead of the doctor. She couldn't believe they'd gone against her wishes.

"I'm sorry that upsets you, Lana," the doctor continued, "but it was necessary. There's no mistaking you have what looks to be a disk about the size of a nickel, made from a dense material, implanted in your skull."

Still angry, Lana refused to make eye contact, refused to acknowledge anything the doctor was saying.

Camry gently rubbed Lana's foot through the blanket. "What's done is done, Lana. Let's just figure this out so you can go home."

She huffed in resignation, then probed the top of her scalp. "Where?"

The doctor guided Lana's fingers to the back of her head. "Do you feel that little bump at the base of your skull? It's called the external occipital protuberance."

Lana felt the familiar bony knob. "Yeah, but that's always been there. I thought everybody has one."

"True. Now, just below it, on either side of the bump, is where your trapezius muscles connect to your skull. Those are the big neck muscles that help you look up and down and that get sore from too much desk work. The disk is just to the left of the indentation created by those muscles, just below where the tendons connect to the skull. Right . . . there," she said, pushing Lana's index fingertip into the depression.

Lana pressed deeply into the dent between the muscles. "I . . . I can't feel anything. Are you sure there's something there? I swear I've never had surgery on my head."

"The image isn't perfect—CTs are notorious for not being very clear around the base of skull—but I'm quite confident."

"Is there a scar?"

Dr. Perkes set her tablet on a tray and began meticulously searching through Lana's hair, seemingly strand by strand.

Camry snorted. "Why am I reminded of Jane Goodall right now?"

"I'll save the fattest ticks for you," the doctor retorted smoothly.

"Hey," Lana cried. "I am not a chimpanzee, and I don't have ticks."

After a minute, Dr. Perkes said, "Well, if there *is* a scar, it's so fine I can't see it. Even so, this is precisely where the CT shows the disk."

Lana bit her lower lip. “Should I be worried?”

“Seriously?” Camry scoffed. “They’ve discovered a mysterious piece of alien alloy in your skull. For all you know, your body’s already been snatched. Yeah, you should be worried.”

Dr. Perkes raised a calming hand. “We really can’t answer that without getting a clearer idea of what it is. I’d like to schedule an MRI, but before I do that, I need to make sure it isn’t an iron-based metal.”

“Ooh, good idea, Doc,” Camry said, glancing at Lana, “or you’d end up with a jagged hole in your head.”

Lana’s face paled. “What?”

“I read it online. If you have any metal in your body, the MRI will rip it out, right through your skin. If you have tattoos that used a metal-based ink, you’ll end up with horrible bloody scabs instead of skin art. There was this one Vietnam vet who had a metal plate in his head, and an MRI about ripped his whole head clean off—”

“You’re not helping,” the doctor interrupted.

“Do I really have to get an MRI?” Lana asked, horrified.

Dr. Perkes sat on the edge of Lana’s bed. “I think it would be for the best. You experienced a seizure of unknown origin—one possibly caused by the foreign object in your skull. And, except for the mysterious disk, your CT was otherwise inconclusive.”

Lana stared at her hands and softly said, “They’re not totally unknown. The seizures, I mean. They happen sometimes . . . when I get a migraine.”

“You said this was the first time.”

Her voice softened even more. “I was scared.”

“And you never thought to see a doctor about them?”

She shrugged. “They’ve never been too bad.”

“Lana,” Dr. Perkes said firmly. “Your seizure was massive. It didn’t fully stop until I gave you a second dose of diazepam—which is unusual. Benzodiazepines typically work faster.”

“Which means what?” Camry asked.

“Which means we’re still not sure of anything. Migraines don’t usually cause seizures. More importantly, there’s the unknown disk—which may or may not be associated. I hope to have that particular mystery figured out tomorrow morning.”

Lana swallowed hard. She squeezed her hands tightly together to stop her trembling. “Dare I ask how you’re going to see if it’s made of metal?”

"Oh, that's super easy. We're mostly concerned about iron-based metals, so I'll simply hold a magnet to it. If it reacts, then we need to do something other than an MRI. Perhaps exploratory surgery."

Lana closed her eyes. "Do you think the disk *is* linked to my migraines?"

"I still don't know. Migraines are primarily a prefrontal presentation. In other words, the pain radiates from your brow to your temples. It's doubtful a piece of dense alloy at the base of your skull is linked, but I haven't entirely ruled it out either."

"Can't you just cut it out?" Camry asked. "Make a little slit and squeeze it out like a zit?"

The doctor shook her head, not so much in answer to the question as in exasperation. "I might be able to determine the external characteristics of the disk if I incise the area, but I probably won't be able to tell if it's attached to any brain tissue or dura mater unless I do an exploratory operation."

"If it's not metal, you gotta get the MRI, Lana," Camry affirmed.

"She's right, Lana. You'll be okay. You have my word on that."

Lana struggled to compose herself. Neither option sounded good. She gripped the amulet on her necklace and focused on breathing slowly and deeply. She let her mind retrieve her favorite childhood memory: Late summer in Rhinelander, Wisconsin. Lake Julia. She couldn't remember how old she was. Ten? Maybe eleven?

A wooden pier extended into the lake about twenty yards. She sat on the end of the pier, her legs dangling over the edge. Only a couple of boats could be seen in the distance. The muggy end-of-summer heat was being gently pushed away by a subtle north breeze. A select few trees surrounding the lake had already donned their brilliant fall colors. Her dad sat by her side. Neither of them spoke. They simply soaked in the quietude and serenity of the moment.

At length, Dad said, "You're getting older now." He spoke facing the lake. As always, his words were soft but also carried hard truths. "You have a sharp mind, and I know you have questions." He turned to her. "There're a few things I need to tell you. You see, life comes down to a matter of trust."

Remembering his voice, Lana felt her trembling subside. If the doctor said she'd be okay, she needed to trust that she'd be okay. She had to believe that. Nothing had happened with the CT scan—and it was a type of X-ray.

"Okay. I'll go get the magnet first." The doctor stepped outside for a brief minute before returning with what looked like a ballpoint pen. "We sometimes use this to extract small metal toys from kids' noses or ears," she said with a grin. "It should be strong enough to let us know whether or not the disk is metal."

Dr. Perkes rolled Lana onto her side and held the magnetic pen over different sections around the small bump on the back of her head.

"Getting anything?" Camry asked.

"Not . . . yet," Dr. Perkes said, continuing to probe, pushing deeper and deeper around the area in question.

Lana felt a twitch underneath her skin. "Wait. Go back. I felt something."

The doctor moved the magnet back and forth very slowly across the area.

The minuscule twitch happened again. "There!"

"Did you feel it move?"

"Not sure. It wasn't a movement so much as a tiny twinge."

"That's what I was afraid of." Dr. Perkes slipped the magnetic pen into her pocket.

"That rules out the MRI, right?" Camry said.

"It does until I get a better look."

That meant surgery. Lana wanted to feel confident about the procedure, but she hated the idea of her head being sliced open. "Is there any way you can take a look at the disk without major surgery?" Lana asked softly.

Dr. Perkes stood. "Well, it's near enough to the surface. I suppose I can make a preliminary slit like your friend suggested and take a peek."

Lana hesitated, then nodded. "I think I'd prefer that to surgery."

"All right, I'll do the small-incision exam first. You'll barely feel a thing." She glanced at her watch. "I need to finish my rounds, so we'll do it tomorrow morning. You need to get some rest. If you need pain meds or something to help you sleep or anything else, just let the night nurse know." She tenderly gripped Lana's forearm. "We'll get this figured out tomorrow. I promise."

CHAPTER 4

Lying prone with her face in a padded donut, Lana's hair was pulled up and tightly away from the rear of her skull. Dr. Perkes had shaved clean a small square over the disk site.

"I'm actually glad we're doing this procedure first," the doctor said, adjusting a tray of surgical instruments on a telescoping stand next to her. "It'll go a long way to making things clearer for both of us."

"I hope so," Lana said, feeling more worried than glad. Her voice was slightly muffled by the cushion, but she could hear just fine.

"Okay. I'm going to daub some Betadine solution to sterilize the area," she said. "It might sting just a bit; mostly it'll just feel cold."

Lana tried to nod.

"Please don't move your head."

"Sorry."

The cool liquid sent a sharp chill down Lana's spine. A muted hiss escaped her lips. Despite the doctor's warning, the sudden sensation startled her.

"Sorry about that," Dr. Perkes said. "Now I'm going to inject some Xylocaine into the area to numb it so you don't feel any pain and to limit bleeding. I'll be as gentle as I can, but you may feel a quick pinch at first."

"Okay."

With her teeth clenched, Lana felt the prick of a needle three different times, then a mild pressure a couple of times after that. The pinpoint flash of pain sent her anxiety to the panic threshold but, luckily, didn't cross it. She hated being so flighty. Her dad had taught her to be strong—physically and emotionally. But the feeling of not being fully aware of any portion of her body scared her deeply. She even hated the numbing of her gums when her dentist used Novocain. Her being *out* of control meant someone else was *in* control. Or some*thing*. That was why she didn't drink or use recreational drugs. And why her migraines bothered her so much—not because the pain was horrible, though it was, but because she was a slave to how much they incapacitated her. That was the *only* reason she was willing to submit to this surgical procedure. This thing in her head, whatever it was, needed to come out. She had no memory of it ever being implanted; therefore, it meant she had no control over it.

She suddenly felt very alone. "I wish Camry were here."

"I'm sure she will be later today, bringing all her internet diagnoses with her."

Lana inwardly chuckled at the doctor's sardonic tone. "She loves learning new facts on the web."

"Facts?" Dr. Perkes huffed. "I can't tell you the number of self-diagnoses I have to refute every single day. The wealth of information on the net is astounding, but laypeople seem to believe everything they read—especially the hokum about health care. I call them cyberchondriacs."

Lana grinned. "So you can't trust anything on the net?"

"Oh, there's lots of good information. The trouble is what most people accept as fact is merely someone's opinion."

"She's just trying to help . . . most of the time."

The doctor sighed. "Well, she is a very dedicated friend, I'll give her that. How long have you two known each other?"

"Only a couple of months. We met when I moved here. She glommed on to me right away, which was fine. I needed a friend."

A couple of minutes passed before Lana felt more prodding on the back of her head.

"Did your parents ever say anything to you about a head injury as a child?"

"No, nothing. My mom died birthing me, and Dad said I was always a healthy kid. Never had any accidents or anything."

"Huh. Did you get your intense blue eyes from your dad or mom?"

"My mother. Dad's eyes were more of a hazel."

The doctor poked at the back of Lana's head. "Okay, you should be numb enough now. You're going to feel some more pressure on the area. Don't be alarmed. There'll be no pain, and I'll let you know what I'm doing every step of the way. Let me know if you get uncomfortable."

"I'm already uncomfortable, but okay," Lana said, unable to mask the shakiness in her voice. "Please just let me know what you see."

"I will."

Lana felt her skin depress but not much else. She heard the doctor picking up and setting down instruments and wished she could see what was happening—but then changed her mind. The sight of blood and her constitution never did get along well. She wasn't squeamish; she simply didn't want to see herself opened up. *Just stay calm.*

"Okay. I'm in. You'll feel some tugging on your scalp, but it's just me pulling the incision open for a better look and . . . excellent. The bleeding's not too bad . . . I need to push the muscles to one side . . . just relax . . . a bit more . . . and there it is. There's some fascia covering the disk . . . I'll just clean it up a bit." More tools rattled against the tray. Lana felt more pressure as the doctor explored the area. "Nice. I can see it clearly now. It's silvery . . . partially embedded. Looks kind of like a nickel." She tapped on it. "Huh. It might be aluminum, maybe even titanium, so it can't be magnetized. The twinge you felt when I tested it with the magnet could have been from some internal composite." Lana felt more tugging at the back of her head. "It's set into your skull pretty securely. I can't tell if it goes through to your brain. I'm now rinsing it off for a better look, and . . . what in the world?"

"What?" Lana asked worriedly.

"Let me adjust this light."

There was a brief pause as Lana felt more prodding and manipulating of the surgical site. Then—

"This makes no sense at all," Dr. Perkes said under her breath.

"What's wrong?"

"There're two words printed on this thing."

"What do they say?"

"I don't know. I don't read Russian."

"Russian?" Lana wasn't sure whether to laugh or cry. "You're kidding, right? Did Camry put you up to this?"

"No. I'm serious."

"How do you know it's Russian?"

"It's written in the Cyrillic alphabet."

Lana frowned deeply. Like the doctor said, that made no sense at all. Russian? No matter how much she tried to rationalize the disk's existence, nothing seemed plausible.

"Hold very still for a minute," Dr. Perkes said. "I'm going to take a picture of this with my phone."

Lana heard the artificial shutter click of a camera.

This whole situation had gone from bad to worse. Why hadn't her dad said anything about this? Did he even know? He'd been a medic for most of his career, and he'd spent some time in the Kazakhstan region, but he hadn't been involved in anything like this. There was no way. A disk with Russian writing on it had been implanted in her skull? When? Why?

The rapid-fire questions racing though Lana's head caused her anxiety to spike. An oppressive weight filled her forehead, and a flash of light crisscrossed behind her eyes. Another migraine was coming. These headaches *had* to be connected to the disk.

"What are you doing now?" Lana asked with impatient dread. Her voice trembled uncontrollably.

"Hold still a moment longer, please. I'm trying to get a clearer image."

She heard another click.

"There," Dr. Perkes said. She held the phone under the table for Lana to see. "Do you recognize this?"

The screen showed *Красная Цикада 19*.

"No. I have no idea what that says."

Dr. Perkes righted herself. "I'm going to run it through Google Translate. And . . . there. Oh, you've got to be kidding me."

"Why—what's it say?" Lana asked, afraid to actually know.

"It translates to *Red Cicada 19*, whatever that means."

"I want it out," Lana cried. "Take it out right now!"

"I can't, Lana. Not without first determining how deep it goes. We have no idea if it's attached to anything inside your skull."

Lana's migraine was rapidly intensifying. She squinted against the pain. "Why is it even in there?" she whimpered, trying not to cry.

"I have no idea," the doctor admitted. "There are several types of cranial implants nowadays. Cochlear implants help the deaf to hear, subdural EEG electrodes help prevent seizures in epileptics, and impulse regulators help people with Parkinson's. But since you have no idea when this was implanted, let alone what it is, I feel uncomfortable messing with it without first getting a better look."

"I don't care what it is. You've already cut me open. Just remove it."

"I still have concerns with—"

"Do the MRI, then. You know it's not a magnetic metal, so it's not going to rip out of my head like Camry said. Do whatever you need to do to convince yourself to remove it as quickly as possible. Please."

"Lana, if there are any wires attached to your brain, an MRI could cause severe damage—"

"I want that stupid thing out!" Lana nearly screamed, pushing aside her short-lived goal to remain calm.

"Okay, Lana," Dr. Perkes said in a pacifying tone. "Try to hold still. Let me first close this site with a couple of stitches. I'll tape on a gauze pad to catch any bleeding, and then I'll schedule you for extraction surgery tomorrow morning."

"Why so late?" Lana cried, unable to withhold her tears. Her migraine was building pressure in her forehead, and she felt acid churning in her gut. "Can't you do it today?"

"The OR is booked until then. I've already checked." Dr. Perkes tenderly rubbed Lana's back. "If there's a cancellation, I'll make sure you're at the front of the line. Until then, I'll look through the medical literature and see if anything like this has come up before."

Lana didn't say another word while she was stitched up. When Dr. Perkes asked a question, she merely grunted a response. She didn't trust herself to speak without bawling.

She again searched her memory for clues to explain this mystery, but the pounding in her head made it difficult to focus. Each beat of her heart threatened to burst through her temples. One thought in particular kept repeating amid the pain: *When was the disk implanted?* She had no memory of it, so it had to have been *before* her earliest memory.

When no memory came, she again reminisced about Lake Julia to distract herself from her anxiety.

Her childhood had generally been a happy one. There were many times she'd wished she had a brother or sister to play with. And she still wished she'd had a chance to know her mother. Lana had had no problem making friends, but keeping them had been difficult because she and her dad had moved around a lot, never staying in the same small city for more than a couple of years.

Dad had had one of those jobs that necessitated a lot of travel—a sales position with a medical-supply company. He'd never had an office; he'd used their home as his hub. But after one or two years, when his clientele was established or the area was saturated, they'd move to a new location so he could build up more business. Working in that way, he'd rarely had to leave Lana alone for long periods. Dad was generally home when she got out of school, and he was able to take time off for her school functions, choir performances, and tae kwon do practices. He was her best friend—her entire world, really—and was involved in every aspect of her life. There was no way he'd allow a strange disk to be implanted in her skull. No way. At no time had either of them left the country, let alone gone to Russia. Perhaps the disk in her skull was simply *made* in Russia. No. Even if it were, why would it say *Red Cicada 19* on it? Was that a brand name?

Lying facedown on the operating table as Dr. Perkes closed her up, Lana watched her tears drip to the floor. If Dad were still alive, he'd know what to do. She closed her eyes as a remorseful sob escaped her chest.

"Are you in pain?" Dr. Perkes asked.

"Another migraine," she said softly through the donut. "That and just feeling sorry for myself."

"I'll give you some meds to tackle the pain. A nice migraine cocktail of sumatriptan, tizanidine, and promethazine."

Not sure what each med did, Lana simply said, "Thanks."

A few minutes later, her muscles relaxed as the medication spread into her system. Thankfully, her migraine didn't fully manifest to incapacitating, and her rising queasiness lessened. Even so, the sedating medicine did little to quell her overall angst.

CHAPTER 5

Rhinelander, Wisconsin, September 1995

The placid lake rippled now and then with a passing breeze or a fish nipping at a bug on the surface. Dad was concentrating on something extra bothersome. He sometimes went into such inward-facing moods. He said that he was a deep thinker, that he liked to figure things out in his head. Lana called it his "brood mood." She'd learned early on not to disturb him at such times.

"You have a sharp mind, and I know you have questions," he'd said after a lengthy silence that day at the lake. "There're a few things I need to tell you. You see, life comes down to a matter of trust."

She smiled. "You tell me things all the time, Dad. And I always trust what you say."

"Thanks, Lightning Bug. But this is extra critical. Do you remember the importance of keeping a secret? It's a big part of trust."

"Sure. It's very important."

He nodded solemnly. "What I need to tell you now is very, very secret, okay? There are things I did in the military, things no one knows about. For security reasons, all the information and records about them were destroyed, so it's like it never happened. Do you understand?"

"I think so."

"Some of those things I . . . well, I broke some rules. But I did them because it was the right thing to do. I did it to protect innocent people."

"I know that, Daddy."

From his coat pocket Dad pulled a necklace Lana had never seen before. It looked handcrafted, which was typical. Dad was handy with just about everything. He rarely asked for help from anyone. He simply thought about a problem from all angles and solved it himself. Quite often, he'd ask Lana to help him resolve a particular challenge or puzzle. She really liked those times.

"Here. You're old enough now to have this," he said, handing her the necklace.

"Thanks, Daddy." She examined it appreciatively. The fine leather strap held a narrow piece of pinkish, mottled stone, roughly two inches long. It'd been sculpted into a straight hexagonal rod with random notches scored into the edges. "It's beautiful. It looks like the stone in your ring."

"You're right, Lightning Bug. It is," he said, holding his marine corps ring next to it.

"What kind of stone is it?"

"You tell me," Dad said, always the teacher.

Lana thought hard. "Is it marble?"

"Close," he said with a soft smile. "It's sometimes called pink marble, but its real name is rhodonite."

"Rhodonite. Rho-don-ite," she repeated, knowing it would help her memorize the name. "When did you get this?"

"A long time ago." His gaze aimlessly returned to the lake, as if his mind had just traveled thousands of miles away. "I got the stone while on an op in the Ural Mountains. I've carried it with me a long time. But it's important that you have it now."

"Why?"

"Because it answers secrets. Don't ever lose it. Do you understand?"

"I think so. It's a special kind of stone, right?"

He again looked at his ring. "Some people say certain minerals have powers attached to them. There's not much scientific proof to that, but sometimes science doesn't know everything."

He paused, and Lana waited patiently while admiring how the brilliant reddish pink of her pendant was veined with random black tendrils. They reminded her of wispy smoke trails in a tropical sunset.

Dad continued in a contemplative tone. "They say rhodonite lays bare emotional wounds and scars of the past for healing, restoration, and reinvigoration. Do you know the meaning of those words?"

"Yeah, I think so."

"They also say rhodonite empowers the holder to reach their full potential and can bring its owner back to center during stressful times. It's used for calming emotional shock and panic and provides grounding when dealing with painful issues."

"Is that what you use it for?"

His smile was strangely affectionate and troubled at the same time. "As a matter of fact, I do, sweetheart. But I want you to have it now. I think you're going to need it soon."

"Why?"

He paused again for a long time, continuing to gaze across the lake. "Sometimes we're faced with decisions that don't seem fair. I did things I'm not proud of." Lana was going to ask what he meant, but he continued softly. "I love it here. I wish we could stay."

"Me too. I have some nice friends on our street. And I love all the times you teach me stuff about the forest and nature. Can we go sailing again before school starts?"

His eyes took on a worrisome sheen. "No, sweetheart. We have to move again. I think they're getting close."

CHAPTER 6

Fort Collins, Colorado, July 2011

"Miss Baker?" a man's voice asked, pulling Lana from her dream. "Excuse me, Miss Baker, I need to ask you some questions. Are you awake, ma'am?"

"I am now," she said, stretching and squinting against the room lights. She had no recollection of having fallen asleep.

Her vision quickly focused on a handsome man in a well-fitting army uniform. He was in his early thirties, was fit, and had a strong jawline and rich brown eyes. The single silver bar on each collar point indicated he was a first lieutenant.

"Sorry to disturb you, ma'am," he said, tucking his hat under an arm.

"That's okay," she said, struggling to sit up. "I was just napping."

The officer quickly set his hat on the bed stand and aligned his upper frame with hers. Placing his head next to hers, he said, "Hold on to my shoulders."

Cloves? Bay rum? Lana could swear she smelled a hint of some manly spice she couldn't identify. She reached up and clasped his shoulders as best she could. Not surprisingly, they felt exceptionally solid. The officer straightened, easily lifting her into a sitting position.

"Thank you, Lieutenant . . . ?"

"Kipling. Lance Kipling."

"Thank you, Lt. Kipling," she said, pushing the button to raise her bed to support her back. "What time is it anyway?"

"Twelve thirty, ma'am."

"Please tell me that's p.m."

"Of course, ma'am. Otherwise it'd be 0:30." His tone indicated his answer was more forthright than condescending. She found his military exactness over-the-top.

Adjusting her hospital gown while trying not to sound overly eager, she asked, "So what can I do for you, Lieutenant?"

"I need to ask you a few questions, if I may."

"Shoot."

"Your father's name was Deacon Baker?"

"Yes. And my mom's was Natalie Berthelsen Baker."

He flashed a curious smile. "What can you tell me about the object in your head, ma'am?"

Lana's brows knit. "How do you know about that?"

"Please just tell me what you know."

"Nothing. I wish I had information to share with you, Lieutenant, but I just learned of its existence myself."

His head tilted to one side. "You mean you didn't know it was there?"

"Nope."

"Has anyone tried to remove it?"

"No. My doctor made an incision to look at it but decided against removing it too hastily."

"An excellent decision. May I see it, please?"

She shook her head. "Dr. Perkes already stitched up the site," she said, gingerly touching the area at the back of her head. "But she probably still has a picture of it on her phone if you need to see it right away."

"I do. I understand it has the words *Krasnaya Tsikada* on it."

"Perhaps," she said with a shrug. "I don't speak Russian, so I don't know. Dr. Perkes says the letters spell out *Red Cicada*."

His eyes narrowed. "May I ask how she knew that?"

"She looked it up on Google Translate when she saw the Russian letters."

"Cyrillic."

"Yeah, those. May I ask how *you* know what it says when you haven't even seen it?"

The lieutenant's questioning gaze faltered. "It's classified, ma'am."

"Huh. Well, it also had the number nineteen after the words, if that means anything."

Lt. Kipling raised his eyebrows but said nothing.

"*Do* you know what it means?"

"No, ma'am. Not yet."

"May I ask why you're interested in it? Is it because it's Russian?"

"Again, it's classified."

She rolled her eyes. "Please don't give me that overused Hollywood answer, Lieutenant. Since it's in *my* skull, I have a right to know."

"All I can tell you is that the military is very concerned about it. For your own safety." His tone was firm but not harsh. Almost apologetic. She sensed his military stiffness was merely a facade, that he was naturally curious while being cautious. When he'd said it was for her own safety, she felt genuine concern from him.

"What branch of the army do you work for?"

"Intelligence. Special investigations. I basically go over cold-case files of unique interest."

"I see," she said, although she really didn't.

Frustration churned in Lana's core, but she kept it down. She sincerely wanted to help the guy. Shc knew the importance of military secrets, and she had no reason to not trust him. In fact, because her dad was a former marine, she had a special place in her heart for all branches of the service. But she still wondered how Kipling had identified the disk when she'd barely learned about it herself. Knowing arguing would get her nowhere, she decided to change tack.

"Kipling. Any relation to the English writer?"

"Not that I know of, Miss Baker."

"Please, call me Lana."

"Yes, ma'am."

Lana huffed playfully. Some people would be irritated by his formal stance, including her. But her current mood was actually pretty good, bordering on happy—although she couldn't explain why. Perhaps it was the medicines the doctor had given her or the restorative nap she'd had. Maybe it had something to do with the officer's good looks and formal manner that bordered on being campy. Or perhaps it was simply because she felt headache-free for the first time in weeks. Months, even.

"Honestly, Lt. Kipling, I know nothing about the disk in my skull. But you're welcome to have it the minute Dr. Perkes removes it."

He cleared his throat. "Dr. Perkes won't be removing it. We have a military surgeon en route now. Once he determines the stability of the unit, we'll be moving you to the 21st Medical Group at Peterson Air Force Base. He'll remove the unit there."

Lana frowned. "Why?"

"I can't say."

"Can't or won't?"

The officer favored her with a gentle smile but no words. As nice as his smile was, she was rapidly tiring of his stubbornness.

"Why do you call the disk a 'unit'?"

"I can't say."

"Fine. Have you discussed this with Dr. Perkes?"

"There's nothing to discuss."

His tiresome manner quickly inflamed her ire. What right did he have to make such decisions? She wasn't a member of the military. He had no authority over her. "Perhaps I should call my lawyer first," Lana mused aloud.

"That would be unwise," Lt. Kipling said, glancing around, giving the room a quick once-over, as if searching for something.

"Why?"

Returning to her bedside, he leaned toward her and whispered, "The fewer people who know about the disk, the better."

"Okay, but I still don't understand why Dr. Perkes can't just remove it and then give it to you."

He glanced around again, then whispered, "Because trying to remove the disk may prove fatal."

"Fatal? As in, it might kill me?" Lana cried. "There's no telling how long this thing's been *in* my head—and you're saying it could have killed me all this time?"

"I said it *may*," Lt. Kipling clarified. "It's not likely to do any harm if left alone. But an attempt to remove it may trigger something. Even so, I wouldn't worry."

"But you just said—" She checked her knee-jerk retort. Lana glared at the young officer, not knowing whether she should laugh or scream. Steeling herself, she said, "Lt. Kipling, you seem to know a lot more about this stupid disk—or this *unit*—than I do. Since I now know it's potentially dangerous, I would appreciate more elucidation than 'it's classified' because, frankly, I *am* worried."

The lieutenant picked up his hat and inched his fingers along the sweatband, studiously avoiding Lana's insistent glare. After a moment of silence, he removed a business card from his breast pocket and set it on her bedside tray. "If anything comes up, please give me a call. Until then, don't tell anyone about this—not even your doctor. Please. It's for your own safety, Lana."

"Shouldn't she know it might kill me?"

"No—since she won't be the one removing it."

Although she was still angry about being kept in the dark, Lana couldn't be mad at the lieutenant's sincerity. He was just doing his job. *Trust him*, she told herself. "Fine. Thank you for your concern, Lt. Kipling."

He donned his hat and gave a nod. "Thank you, Miss Baker. I'll be back soon."

As Lt. Kipling exited the room, Camry entered, nearly colliding with his six-three frame.

"Whoa," Camry said mischievously. "Who planted a tree here?"

"My apologies, ma'am," Lt. Kipling said, touching the rim of his hat.

Camry stepped to one side and ogled the young lieutenant as he walked down the hall. When she turned back, her mouth gaped open and her eyes were the widest Lana had ever seen.

"Oh! My! Good! Glory! He smelled good enough to gobble up. Did you check out that prime specimen of USDA choice American military pride?"

"Lt. Kipling is good-looking," Lana said patiently. "Yes, I noticed."

"Are you blind? He's Lt. McDreamy. He's all that *and* a bag of chips. He's the whole nine yards *plus* a couple of feet. On a scale from one to ten, he's a twelve. Hey, do you think if I told him he has a great body, he'd hold it against me—literally?"

"Geez, Camry. I get it. You're in lust." Lana chuckled.

"Looks like you got your handsome prince after all. So what did Lt. Luscious want with you, anyway? Did he ask you out?"

"Sort of," Lana said with a grimace. "He said the military wants to do the disk removal at a military hospital."

"How come?"

Lana lowered her eyes. "I'm not supposed to say."

Camry sat on the edge of the bed and grabbed Lana's wrist. "Now you *gotta* tell me."

"No, seriously. Lt. Kipling said it's a matter of national security. He said the disk could be . . . extra sensitive."

Camry shook her head and gawked at her friend. "I knew you were exceptional when you first came here, but not *this* exceptional. This is the coolest thing I've ever heard of."

Lana huffed. "I wish I shared your enthusiasm. Frankly, I'm scared to death."

"Oh, I am too. But you gotta admit it *is* cool—well, creepy, but cool, you know?"

Lana fought back tears as she pulled her arm away from her friend's grip. "No, it's not. Honestly, I have no idea how the disk got into my skull. I've been hashing it out in my mind, but there's just no time I can recall when it could've happened. I was sure my dad would have told me about it if he'd known, but I also don't see how it's possible for him not to have been aware of it—which makes me wonder if he *was*."

"Do you think he was?"

"I don't know. Surely he would've told me—especially since it's dangerous."

"What?" Camry cried. "Dangerous how? Is it like a bomb or something?"

"Oops. I shouldn't have said that. Please don't say anything to anyone. I could get into a lot of trouble."

"Hey, we're BFFs, right? Your secrets are my secrets, and vice versa. Remember when I told you about that loser Tinder date I had?"

"No," Lana snapped angrily. Her tolerance for Camry's adolescent tendencies suddenly switched to intolerance. "This isn't some spontaneous fling or one of your stupid guy games. You don't understand. I have a dangerous disk in my skull. It needs to come out. If the military knows about it, who else does?"

Camry looked hurt. "Well, how was I to know?"

"Try listening," Lana grumbled.

Camry stood and put her fists on her hips. "I do listen. And I do care. The very fact that I'm here on my lunch break should prove that. Has anyone else from work stopped by? No. So cut me some slack."

Lana felt bad for offending her coworker, but Camry just didn't grasp the seriousness of the situation. "I'm sorry, Cams. I shouldn't have snapped. But I'm scared. I just want this to be over."

Camry stared hard at her and gave a quick nod. "I'd better get back to work."

"Okay," Lana said. "I'll let you know what I can when Lt. Kipling returns."

Camry drew a quick breath, and her hostility instantly vanished. She pulled a slip of paper from her purse and scribbled on it. Handing it to Lana, she said, "You give that tasty slice of all-American pie my number. If he needs to interrogate me, I'm always available."

Lana rolled her eyes. "If you're that smitten, here," she said, picking up the lieutenant's business card. "This has all his info."

Camry looked like a child on Christmas morning. "You're the best BFF who ever BFF'ed."

Lana grimaced, knowing she would mull over the correctness of that sentence for way too long.

△

An hour later, a hospital employee came in pushing a wheelchair. The man was older—perhaps almost fifty—but he had a warm smile and an easy manner.

"Good morning, Miss Baker," he said lightly. "Are you ready for your X-ray?"

Lana had almost dozed off again, and her head felt a bit foggy. "You mean my MRI? I thought that'd been cancelled."

The man smiled genially. "Your MRI was cancelled. The doctor scheduled second CT." He seemed friendly enough, but his words were clipped, as if he struggled to suppress an accent.

"But I was scheduled for exploratory surgery tomorrow. Why wasn't I told about a second CT?"

"Paperwork mess-up," he said, aligning the wheelchair beside her bed.

"Where's Dr. Perkes?"

"Waiting in X-ray," he said, offering his hand to help her into the wheelchair. "The doctor needs second scan for accuracy."

That made sense. She took his hand and let him guide her into the chair. As he squatted to adjust the foot supports, she read his name badge: Peter Anders.

"Do I detect a slight accent, Peter? Where are you from?"

He gave a look of embarrassment. "My English is not good?"

"Oh no. Your English is fine. I just thought I heard a vowel tone that's not from this area, is all."

"I was born in Europe," he said with a tone of finality, indicating he didn't want to talk about it. Lana understood the preference to keep to himself. But this new scan was unexpected, and she had questions about that.

Anders stood and secured Velcro straps, binding her legs and arms.

"What's that for?" she blurted, immediately hating the lack of control the straps imposed.

"Insurance, so you not fall."

"Seriously?"

"Silly, yes? A hospital regulation."

She forced a smile, figuring the mandate was because she had fainted and had a massive seizure two days ago.

Peter Anders moved her IV bag to a pole on the wheelchair. "If the corridor light is too bright, close your eyes and lower your head. Bright light triggers headaches, yes?"

"Okay, thanks," Lana said, appreciative of his concern. There was an awkward moment of silence as Lana waited for him to continue their conversation, as most orderlies did. When he remained silent, she asked, "So . . . have you worked here long?"

"Not long. I was notified about you only yesterday."

That was a funny way to put it. He wheeled her into the hallway, and she closed her eyes.

"Are you an expert in migraines?" she said.

"Not so much migraines."

"Are you a doctor?"

"A specialist."

Guessing Anders was simply not much into small talk, Lana tried to relax and enjoy the smooth motion of the wheelchair. She focused on memories of Lake Julia, but the images were elusive, fleeting.

They stopped, and she heard the ding of an elevator chime. She felt herself being turned around and backed into the cab. When the doors closed, she opened her eyes. Anders was standing behind her. No one else occupied the space. The silence felt strange; it engendered a feeling of dread in her chest, but she didn't know why. Did the hospital request the second CT scan, or did the military? Dr. Perkes had seemed pretty determined to simply go in and remove the disk. Why the change without letting her know?

Lana glanced up at the floor-indicator lights. Apparently, she'd been on the third floor. She then noticed that Anders had pressed the destination button for the lower parking area.

"Radiology is in the basement?" Lana asked in a nervous chuckle.

"It is shortcut."

Something wasn't right. "I want to talk to Dr. Perkes, please."

"She is in radiology."

Lana struggled against the Velcro tethers. It spooked her that she couldn't move. "I've changed my mind. I want to go back to my room."

"No."

"Why not?" she shot back, her angst rising exponentially.

"We may not get another chance."

"Another chance for what?"

He didn't answer. Lana yanked against her restraints, chafing her wrists. Her chest was now thumping. "Let me out of here," she demanded. "Where are you taking me? What is it you want?" she asked, rapid-fire.

Anders didn't answer. When the elevator came to a soft stop, the readout indicated they were at basement level.

"Let me out, or I'll scream," she threatened.

"I wouldn't."

"Why not?"

"Because then I will slit your throat to silence your scream. I do not wish to hurt you, but I will if necessary."

CHAPTER 7

THE ELEVATOR DOORS OPENED TO a spacious basement parking lot. A number of cars were parked in various slots, but no people could be seen.

"Why are you doing this?" Lana asked in desperation.

"You have information we want," Peter Anders said, pushing her into the lifeless cavern. They headed directly toward an old-model panel van with a vinyl wrap advertising Pampered Paws Pet Grooming.

"What information? And who is 'we'?"

"Is best you do not know."

Somewhere in the vast parking area, the sound of a door shutting echoed toward them.

"Help!" Lana screamed. Her voice ricocheted through the austere space, disappearing around a corner. "Someone help me!"

Anders's strong hand clapped over her mouth. She leaned forward, then quickly back, twisting her head slightly. The fleshy part of one of his fingers slipped between her teeth, and she bit down hard. The man let out a barely contained roar and pushed his free thumb into the pressure point under her ear. Her jaw reflexively opened, and he pulled away, a small chunk of flesh hanging from his digit. Lana spit out a mouthful of blood, wincing at the pain in her jaw.

He punched the side of her head so hard her vision blurred.

"I warned you," he said, wrapping a handkerchief around his bloody finger. He leaned down and growled into her ear. "Cooperate, or I will snap your neck." His voice now had an unmasked inflection—definitely some sort of Eastern European tone.

Lana spit out more blood, realizing she'd also bitten through a portion of her lip. The brutal punch to her head had precipitated a throbbing headache. She had no idea what information this criminal was talking about, but perhaps she could bluff her way into getting some from him. "Kill me and you'll lose anything you hope to get from me."

"Are you really so ignorant? We want the disk you carry. I can remove it just as easily from corpse as live body. Perhaps easier. But my superiors need to know if you have further intelligence, perhaps something learned from your father."

They were after the Red Cicada disk? Well, they could have it, as far as she was concerned. She simply wanted it out of her head. But . . . *why* would they want it? What information did it contain? Was the disk a storage device of sorts? A transmitter?

"If you already know what it contains, why do you still need it?"

"We do not know all. It contains lost secrets."

Lost secrets? Think, Lana. His accent. Russian? Ukrainian? Estonian? The disk's Cyrillic alphabet. Was Peter Anders—if that was even his name—a Russian spy? Did the disk contain Russian secrets? Is that why Lt. Kipling also wanted it?

She clenched her eyes against the pain pulsing in her head. "What information do you think I have? My father didn't even know the disk was in my head." She hated the fact that her voice was so shaky.

Anders slid open the van's side panel door. He grabbed her jaw and yanked her face toward him. "I am going to put you in vehicle, and you will cooperate. That first hit was caress. If you force another, it will not be so gentle. As I said, I do not care if your body is warm or cold. I *will* get disk. Do you understand?"

"Yes. Please don't hit me again," she whimpered, angry that she wasn't stronger.

Anders yanked the IV line from the back of her hand. Lana hissed at the sting. He then unfastened the Velcro on her ankles and wrists and bodily heaved her onto the bare metal floor of the van. He was very strong, in spite of his age. He pushed the wheelchair to one side and slammed the sliding door closed.

Lana heard the click of the door lock. It was stuffy and insufferably hot inside the vehicle. The cargo area had small windows in each of the two back doors, but none of the doors had interior handles or window releases. She could see through the porous decal covering the windows, but not very clearly. She was certain no one could see in. A heavy steel mesh screen separated the cab from the otherwise empty cargo space.

Anders climbed into the cab and rolled down the windows. He removed a large handgun and a metal cylinder from the glove box. As he screwed the cylinder onto the end of the gun, he said, "Remain quiet. I can kill you anytime I feel is necessary. Cooperate, and you may live through this. The call is yours."

"Fine, I get it," Lana grumbled. She did not intend to comply, but at that moment, she didn't have much choice. Her anger battled with her fear. She wanted to be stronger, less frightened. It was easy to mentally build an armament of resolve to outwit her captor, but when put to the test, that resolve crumbled into self-doubt. In spite of her anger, she suspected she'd fail in her determination to fight back. She was definitely not in control of the situation.

Anders put the van in reverse and squealed the tires backing out of the slot. As he came to a stop to put the vehicle into drive, the elevator doors opened, and out stepped Lt. Kipling.

Lana screamed, "Lance! Help! I'm being kidnapped!"

Kipling looked up sharply, trying to pinpoint her voice.

Anders floored the accelerator, smoking the tires as he peeled away. Fishtailing, the rear of the van smashed into the back of a sedan, causing its alarm to trigger.

Lana was thrown against the wall of the van. Scrambling to her knees, she saw Lt. Kipling chasing after the van, but there was no way he could catch them on foot.

Anders careened up the causeway, turning sharply toward the exit and causing Lana to tumble from side to side. The hard metal interior of the cargo area offered no soft landing. She felt new bruises form with each fall. The van rocked violently as Anders turned onto the street. A car horn blared in annoyance. Bursting into bright daylight, Lana put her hands over her face to block the initial glare. Her head throbbed mercilessly.

She managed to sit with her back against the cabin screen and brace her feet wide to keep from tipping over. Slipping her fingers through the thick wire mesh, she held on tightly. She didn't want to show any weakness, but she couldn't stop the tears from streaming in spite of her anger.

Her dad had always encouraged her to be confident and trustworthy. But he'd also taught her to be leery of everyone, not to put complete trust in anyone, regardless of their title or occupation, until she'd had a chance to observe their behavior. The inconsistency had confused her, but since dad was always right about everything, she'd never thought to challenge the instruction. Even into her twenties, she'd regularly sought out his advice.

Remembering her dad's gentle voice and kind eyes caused a sob to burst from her throat. With one hand, she gripped the stone amulet dangling from her neck and willed herself to stop whimpering, but it proved fruitless. The caustic mix of emotions released one gasping sob after another.

"Are you injured?" the kidnapper asked.

"Are you kidding me?" she cried, craning her neck to look at him. "You beat me and throw me in here without a care, then have the gall to ask about my well-being?"

Anders gave a curt nod. "As I said, I do not wish to hurt you. If you cooperate, if you give us the information we seek, you will live. This is a truth, Svetlana."

CHAPTER 8

Lt. Lance Kipling kept running at full speed. He'd distinctly heard Lana's voice coming from the van. He couldn't catch up on foot, but he'd parked near the exit of the garage one level up and knew the sooner he got to his SUV, the sooner he could give chase. It was only luck he'd exited at the same time the van had backed up to the elevator doors. What she was doing in the van wasn't hard to guess. He'd suspected others would be after the disk. This proved it.

In a glance, he memorized the van's license plate. Even though the plate was probably stolen, he'd run it through his DMV connection. He was meticulous that way.

Kipling's Jeep Cherokee had a remote start. The vehicle was already purring when he hopped into the driver's seat. He sped to the exit, screeched to a stop, and flashed his military ID at the man in the kiosk.

"A white Pampered Paws van just left here. Which way did they go?" he demanded of the parking attendant.

The man pointed to the east.

Peeling out, he tapped a notepad function on his smart watch. "Late-model Chevy panel van, perhaps 1990s. Colorado plate EBT-375. White with vinyl wrap. Pampered Paws Pet Grooming. Brief glimpse of abductor: male, around fifty, short gray hair."

Kipling couldn't see the van, so he followed his gut. He stuck to the main road, praying the abductor would be more interested in gaining distance than in evasive maneuvers.

A sustained car horn turned his attention to a side street. He glimpsed a sedan careening into a bus stand while a white panel van with decals sped away. Kipling quickly checked his mirrors, grabbed his emergency brake, and slid his SUV into a sharp U-turn. A chorus of angry horns rose in response. He sped back to the street and turned down it. The driver of the smashed sedan was outside his vehicle, on his cell phone. At a glance, Kipling determined he wasn't seriously injured. No bystanders had been involved.

Kipling slowed at the next intersection and saw the panel van just turning a corner two blocks to the left. Road signs denoted it was the route to Interstate 287. His initial plan was to catch up and intercept, but he reconsidered. Confronting the van directly would put Lana in greater danger. Tailing it would be safer. Besides, the gray-haired abductor wouldn't be watching for an unmarked SUV. If anything, he'd be looking for police cruisers. The man had to know the abduction had been reported; it was paramount that he get to his destination ASAP and hide the vehicle.

His destination. Where was it and how long would it take to get there? Kipling glanced at his fuel gauge. A quarter tank. Not good. He could not lose Lana Baker. She was his only link to something much bigger.

Back in 2005, he had been tasked to review cold-case files on suspected Cold War biological weapons experiments undertaken by the now defunct Soviet Union. Using advanced search engines, he had amassed a huge database of leads, but very few had produced any hard evidence. Many of the old files were all but useless. The Soviets had been very thorough about destroying evidence. But one enigmatic lead had caught Kipling's eye. It was a project named Red Cicada—a high-priority, ultra-top-secret venture. But no one seemed to know what it actually involved. Even so, disturbing trigger words were included in some of the old reports and encrypted communiqués—words like *pandemic virulence*, *viral manipulation*, and *global impact.*

Running basic internet scans on *Red Cicada* brought back nothing but facts and images of a hideous-looking insect. As a child in New England, Kipling had witnessed the massive cicada swarm that hatched every seventeen years. The bugs were everywhere, got in everything. And their incessant trilling was deafening. The event still gave him nightmares. But there was no clue as to why Red Cicada was used as a name for a secret Russian project. When he added filters to eliminate references such as *insect*, *red-eyed*, *red-winged*, or any other permutation that led to cicada entomology, his searches had come up blank.

He was about to put the case back into cold storage, but a gut feeling had told him this decades-old project was inherently insidious and still viable. He couldn't convince himself to shelve it like so many others had. So he'd created a top-level tracking program that looked for internet hits on word combinations of *red cicada* and *biological warfare*, *chemical warfare*, *viral manipulation*, and so forth and launched it in several languages on the World Wide Web.

After a few days of searching, the names Deacon Baker and Aaron Goodwell had come up a number of times. Running the names to the army's Cray supercomputers in Aberdeen, Maryland, had brought some success.

Sgt. Aaron Goodwell had been in a unit of marine special forces involved with a UN investigation of Soviet nuclear proliferation experiments shortly after the collapse of the Wall in 1989. The unit's reports were available to anyone with a top-secret-level clearance, which Kipling had. The reports were thorough, and one of them had mentioned Red Cicada, but it had listed only the name. Nothing more. Goodwell had an excellent service record, had retired from the service in 1995, and had used his GI Bill to earn a medical degree from the University of Wisconsin. But the man had turned out to be a brick wall to any discussion of his activities in the corps. His involvement was highly classified, and as far as he was concerned, it would remain that way forever.

Sgt. Deacon Baker had joined the medical corps of the marines, excelled at his training, and quickly attained the rank of corporal. Because of his high marks in deductive reasoning and problem-solving, he had been transferred to an investigative unit of special forces in 1989 and was promoted to staff sergeant. He and Goodwell had partnered in several investigations, but again, none that specifically sought out the name Red Cicada.

Strangely, Baker had left the corps in 1991, citing personal medical reasons, though nothing specific was listed. Kipling had been unable to follow the man's whereabouts because the former special forces sergeant had moved frequently without notice and used mostly burner phones. No cancellation of services, no closure of rental contracts, no forwarding mailing addresses. Therefore, he'd been unable to interview Baker about his service. The only hit of note was that in 1994 Deacon Baker had suddenly shown up on a medical registry as having a daughter. He was listed as *father* on a nine-year-old female's visit to an InstaCare facility in rural Kentucky. But that hit had proved a dead end. No matter where Kipling searched, there was no record of an adoption linked to Baker's name, and no record of any birth that he was tied to nine years earlier. Even more mysterious, there was no record of the young girl ever being born. The child's name was listed as Lana Baker. Finding more on the mystery daughter had proved a bust. There were hundreds of Lana Bakers in national registries, but none were related to Deacon Baker.

So as not to waste time on what was ostensibly turning up nothing, Kipling had put all Goodwell and Baker data in a file and moved on to another project.

Then, two days ago, several internet traps had triggered at once. A twenty-nine-year-old woman was admitted to a Colorado hospital with some kind of disk under her scalp. The words *Red Cicada* were printed on it with Cyrillic letters. And her name happened to be Lana Baker. Kipling had immediately reopened the file. If his calculations were correct, the young Lana Baker in Kentucky could be the same Lana Baker in Colorado. He quickly drove to Poudre Hospital in Fort Collins, Colorado, to check it out.

His brief interview with Lana Baker had confirmed his suspicions. She was Deacon Baker's mystery child. Then seeing Lana whisked away against her will had confirmed another suspicion. Someone else knew about the Red Cicada project.

So who were the abductors? Russian? Eastern European? Another branch of American military, CIA, or NSA? It didn't matter. There were much bigger players at work here. If not entire governments, then clandestine forces that did not want past secrets revealed.

Was the gray-haired driver of the van a pawn or a major player? Did *he* know what the disk contained? Regardless, Kipling had to assume the abductor wouldn't hesitate to do whatever was necessary to obtain the disk.

And he knew if he didn't catch them in time, Lana Baker was about to die.

CHAPTER 9

The panel van continued to accelerate and brake violently. It swayed dangerously back and forth, almost to the point of tipping. The moves were often followed by the sounds of skidding tires and blaring horns. Anders merged onto a freeway heading south. They traveled for what felt like a half hour. The interior of the van was sweltering. The outside temperature had to be over ninety. Sweat saturated Lana's thin hospital gown. She was self-conscious about being so scantily dressed, but she could do little about it. Yet what she craved most—besides her release—was some fresh air and water. She suspected requesting either would lead to demands for information she didn't have. But her dad had never told her anything about the stupid disk or—

Lana drew a sharp breath. It suddenly occurred to her that admitting she knew nothing might not be such a good idea. If Anders was sure she could add nothing to what was on the disk, then why not just kill her? She needed to play along—and do so convincingly—in order to stay alive. Plus, it may give her a chance to get information from him—particularly why he'd called her Svetlana.

She struggled to her knees. Anders had his window down, and the bit of breeze coming in felt life-giving.

"Doesn't this thing have AC?" she asked.

"Yes, but does not work." He glanced at her via the rearview mirror. "Are you not comfortable?"

"Hardly. It's like a blast furnace back here."

"We will be to rendezvous point soon."

"Great. So is your name really Peter Anders?"

"No. This is a falsehood."

"Ivan, then? Boris?"

He chuckled without humor. "My name is Petrov. But Peter sounds more American, does it not?"

"And my name is Svetlana?"

"This is a truth. It is the name your mother gave. You do not remember?"

"No. None of what's happening makes any sense."

"It will soon enough. Try not to worry."

"Fat chance."

Lana sat back down and strained to bring up any memory that would corroborate Petrov's story. Her dad had never once called her Svetlana—even in a joking manner. She'd been Lana, Lightning Bug, Lana-bug sometimes, or any number of other endearments, but never anything Russian-sounding. Dad had never said anything that made her suspect she had any name other than Lana. But he *had* said things that still mystified her to this day.

And now, why would Petrov insist her name was Svetlana? Was he mistaking her for someone else? Did he kidnap the wrong person? No. It was all about the disk. It didn't matter what her name was. Or did it?

Svetlana. It was a decidedly Slavic name. And yet her parents weren't from that area, which meant neither was she. It was ridiculous to think otherwise. Facts were facts. Lana was born in Atlanta, Georgia, to Deacon and Natalie Baker. Mom had died immediately after childbirth. Dad had raised Lana while moving from town to town but always within the forty-eight contiguous states. After Dad died eleven months ago, she had continued to relocate, going from one job to the next like she'd been taught. But never once had she been out of the United States—let alone to Russia. Those were facts.

Lana massaged her temples and wished she were at Lake Julia, sitting next to her dad. She gripped the rhodonite pendant and tried to clear her mind, gaining resonance from the stone. But her peace was short-lived. Something else Petrov had said continued to plague her mind.

She struggled to her knees again. "So you don't know everything that's on the disk?"

"We know mostly. It was a long time ago. There is lost information we need."

"Aren't you worried about it being dangerous when removed? It's filled with poison or something, isn't it?"

Petrov scowled at her in the mirror, then burst out laughing. "This is a joke, no? Such nonsense."

Not a deadly device? Was he telling the truth, or had Lt. Kipling lied? But why would Lance do that? Of the two of them, she certainly should believe her own countryman over this Russian kidnapper.

"If it's such crucial information, why aren't there any backup sources?"

"Our government collapse was very fast. Many records were destroyed."

"So that makes me pretty important, huh? Especially if *I* already know what's on it."

He again glanced back at her, then shook his head. "I have said too much."

"But why now? I mean, why are your people all of a sudden interested in it?"

Petrov didn't answer for a few minutes. He seemed more concerned about the traffic behind them. Then he continued, as if making light conversation. "You have been difficult to find, Svetlana. Your father was expert keeping you from us. That must create a difficult childhood for you, yes? He did well hiding what you carry inside."

Lana frowned. "Wait—what are you saying? That my father *knew* about the disk in my head?"

Petrov nodded. "Of course. Did you not wonder why you changed locations so often?"

"It was for his job. We had to move every one or two years to establish new sales territory."

"This was his . . . *deception*, yes?"

It was one thing to accuse Lt. Kipling of lying to her. But to claim Dad had intentionally deceived her was laughable. That was so unlikely it was insulting.

And yet, what was the likelihood she had a Russian data unit in her head? The disk was an undeniable fact. Lana scoured her memory. The vignette of the day Dad had given her the pendant prevailed, as it always did. He'd said some very strange things that day. But he'd been in one of his brood moods, so at the time, it hadn't seemed that unusual.

Sometimes we're faced with decisions that don't seem fair. I did things I'm not proud of.

What decisions had he meant? He'd known about the disk but had decided not to tell her about it? Surely something that bizarre would warrant an explanation. But perhaps he'd felt keeping it—and her—a secret was the safest route to take.

We have to move again. I think they're getting close.

Who were "they"?

"I always wondered why we moved around so much," she said, mostly to herself.

"Come now, Svetlana. This must be a deception. Your father was very artful. A good agent. And after his timely death, you have continued this training, yes? Moving often, not keeping paper records? Therefore, you *must* know."

It was a logical supposition but not at all true. Even so, Lana didn't know exactly why she'd continued to move from one city to another. She didn't really need to. Perhaps it was simply a way to keep the memory of her father alive. His death had occurred suddenly, so unexpectedly. It had created a hole in her core that no self-help book or casual friendship could fill. She didn't dare go to a mental health counselor. They were doctors, and Dad had said doctors were for life-threatening emergencies only. She'd been raised believing most vicissitudes and challenges in life could and should be handled alone. They built character, skills, and endurance. What didn't kill her made her stronger—but only if she used the event as a stepping-stone instead of a stumbling block. So immediately after Dad's burial, she'd moved from Terre Haute, Indiana, to Gilbert, Arizona. But the Grand Canyon State was too hot for her liking, so she'd taken the auditing job in Fort Collins, Colorado.

"How long have you been trying to find me?" she asked.

"A long time. Ever since you were child. We never stop the search for you because the information you hold is still critical. We follow one lead, then another, then another. It was just two days past you appeared on our network."

"What network? Who's 'we'? Are you KGB?"

"Again, I have said too much. You will find out soon enough. We were very excited to finally find number nineteen."

"Why am I number nincteen?"

Petrov didn't answer.

Was the number in reference to the nineteen printed on the disk? Did that mean there were eighteen others before her? And if so, how many came afterward? So many questions whirled through Lana's mind that she had to grasp the screen with both hands again to stay upright. This all sounded so far-fetched.

She shook her head, trying to focus. "So what are you, a spy?"

"I told you my specialty is relations."

"No, actually, you didn't," she said. "But if you're going to work in English-speaking relations, you need to work on your grammar."

"Is no good?" he asked, intentionally amplifying his accent.

"You got an adjective wrong. You said my father's '*timely* death.' You should say his 'untimely' death."

"Ah, so it was, but not in the way you mean. Each time we found him, he disappeared, yet his deceptions proved you were still alive, even though he denied such at the end."

Lana felt her lungs empty. "What do you mean 'at the end'? He was killed in a traffic accident."

Petrov chuckled deeply. "And this is *our* deception."

"What deception? He blew a tire coming back late at night from a sales meeting. His car swerved off a bridge."

"Yes, this is how it appeared. But he was already dead when his car fell from bridge. I should know. I helped kill him."

Lana's stomach lurched and knotted. She slumped to the floor of the van and buried her face in her hands. Petrov's declaration crippled her. She'd believed for the past eleven months that her father had died in an accident. The police investigation had been conclusive. Yet that had always bothered Lana. Dad was meticulous in the care of his Nissan. And now to learn Petrov had set it up to *look* like an accident . . .

"Why?" she asked in little more than a whisper.

"Please repeat?" Petrov said.

She turned toward him and yelled, "Why did you kill my father?"

He shrugged. "He would not cooperate."

"What does that mean?"

Petrov didn't answer. He glanced anxiously at each side-view mirror, then accelerated. Lana crawled to the rear windows and saw several sets of flashing lights about a mile back. Good. Lt. Kipling must have reported the van's plates and description.

Petrov called someone on his cell phone and spoke curtly in Russian. Driving with one hand, he suddenly swerved into the far-right lane, causing Lana to tumble and gash her knee on a flange of metal. A chorus of angry horn blasts followed. A moment later, Petrov swerved again, almost tipping the van, taking an exit at the last second.

Moving back to the wire screen, Lana again threaded her fingers through the grate. Her knee throbbed sharply. She felt wetness trickling down her leg—probably blood.

"Stop driving like a madman! The police already know what your van looks like. Your Pet Grooming decal doesn't exactly blend in with the crowd. You can't get away."

In response, Petrov turned abruptly again, straining Lana's grip on the divider. "Geez, take it easy. I cut my knee on that last insane maneuver."

"Then, sit down and shut up."

She stayed put but continually glanced out the rear window to see if police were getting closer. Although the van's speed had decreased, it continued to skid around corners and make sudden starts and stops.

"Where are we going?" she demanded.

"I said shut up!" Petrov slammed his palm against the screen, smashing her fingers.

She cried out and pulled away, crumpling to the floor. Several swerves, accelerations, and brakings later they skidded to a crawl in front of a large nondescript warehouse. A retractable door opened, and they rolled inside. The interior was dimly lit, seemingly devoid of life. The building was sparsely filled with boxes and machinery. The rest of the generous space was too dark to see much else. Musty light and shadows prevailed. Petrov parked the vehicle and hopped out.

"Wait!" Lana shouted as the door slammed shut.

Through the windshield, she watched a large man emerge from the darkness and begin a heated discussion with Petrov. She couldn't hear what the men said, but both were noticeably upset. Petrov pointed repeatedly at the van, clearly discussing Lana. The other man kept glancing at his watch.

Lana heard sirens in the distance. The second man pulled a switchblade from his coat pocket and clicked it open. The blade picked up a ray of dingy sunlight that glinted with evil intent. He took a step toward the van, but Petrov clasped his shoulder, stopping him. Another argument ensued. After a few harsh gesticulations, Petrov stared at the van and slowly nodded. The look on his face was a strange mix of concern and resignation.

Lana quickly moved to the rear of the van. She again took in her surroundings, desperately searching for a weapon yet knowing her search was in vain. She slumped to the floor and drew her knees to her chest, instinctively making herself as inconspicuous as possible. Not that it would help.

The side panel opened. The large man placed one foot on the doorframe and leaned in. Only then did Lana notice half his face was hideously marbled with burn scars. The ear on that side was missing.

"Come," he ordered, his Russian accent heavy with malice.

Lana didn't move. She couldn't. Terror paralyzed her muscles, making it hard to breathe. Whatever this man wanted wasn't good.

"Come," he repeated harshly. "Now."

She shook her head, not trusting her voice to articulate a no.

The man cursed in Russian and stepped into the cargo hold. Lana tried kicking at him, but he deflected her attempts and yanked her to her knees. Pressing the switchblade against her throat, he said, "You like to die now?"

"No," she squeaked.

"Good."

He pushed her out of the van, but her lacerated knee would not support her weight, and she buckled to the ground. Blood now covered her leg.

Outside the van, the sirens were much louder.

"You're going to get caught," she said to Petrov.

He shrugged. "I think maybe not." He nodded toward a pair of motorbikes near a grime-caked back window.

The scarred man hopped out of the van and pushed his foot into the center of her back, pressing her to the ground. When she struggled to free herself, he straddled her and pinned one side of her face against the filthy cement floor. Showing her the switchblade up close, he said, "This will hurt only little bit."

"Wait. Wait. I'll tell you what you want to know," Lana cried, dust puffing away from her mouth as she spoke.

The sirens reached a high volume and seemed to pause. Everyone looked toward the sound. Then their tone changed as they faded into the distance. Turning his head to follow the decreasing noise, Petrov said something in Russian. His partner answered back angrily.

"What did you say?" Lana asked Petrov, hoping to delay the inevitable.

"I said they have not followed, so we do not have to hurt you."

"And what did he say?"

"He disagreed."

Lana felt the sharp bite of the blade pierce the back of her head. She sucked in a hiss between her teeth.

Just then the utility door beside the large service entrance burst open. The backlighting revealed a man in a military uniform entering in a crouch, his gun held at arm's length in front of him. *"Ne dvigaytes!"* he shouted.

The next set of events registered as a rapid blur. The switchblade-wielder stood and threw his knife at the newcomer. At the same time, Petrov pulled his gun from where it was tucked at the small of his back and fired. As if anticipating the attacks, the soldier rolled to one side, narrowly avoiding both blade and bullet. He quickly came up on one knee and fired back. Petrov's shoulder jerked back, spinning him to the floor. His gun skidded away.

The scarred man grabbed a large wrench from a table and hurled it at Lt. Kipling, then turned and ran toward the motorcycles. The man in uniform fired again but missed the escaper. A motorcycle roared to life. The soldier jumped to his feet and took aim, but the scarred man raced away into a darkened section of the warehouse before the lieutenant could fire a clean shot. The engine's whine lasted only a minute before it faded abruptly. Evidently, there was a back exit. The soldier then ran to Lana and knelt at her side.

"Lt. Kipling?" she gasped.

"Sorry I took so long."

She'd never been happier to see anyone in her life. "How'd you find me?"

"I was following at a distance but missed the last turn. Are you hurt?"

"Mostly my knee."

"Your head's bleeding pretty bad."

Sitting up, Lana felt the back of her skull and brought back into view her fingers covered with blood. The Russian had cut deeper than she'd thought and reopened the unhealed surgical site.

Petrov groaned and sat up, holding his shoulder. With gun in hand, Kipling retrieved the Russian's gun and said something to him in Russian. Petrov didn't answer. The lieutenant then searched the area around them and found a partial roll of duct tape. He bound Petrov's ankles and wrists together, all the while speaking angrily in the man's language. Finding no other weapon on the Russian, Lt. Kipling stood and glared at his captive. He growled something Lana assumed was a command to hold still.

"I speak English," Petrov grumbled.

"Good. Then, when I say sit there and don't move or I'll shoot you, you understand."

Petrov scowled. "Yes."

The lieutenant again knelt beside Lana and pulled a handkerchief from his pocket. "Hold this against the back of your head as tight as you can." He then removed his tie and wrapped it around Lana's bleeding knee. She hissed but didn't flinch.

"You know how to use one of these?" he asked, holding out the Russian's gun.

"My dad took me shooting all the time," she said, accepting the weapon. She indicated Petrov with a nod. "Do I have to wait for him to make a move, or can I just shoot him now?"

Kipling smiled. "I think we should wait for now."

He holstered his sidearm and pulled out his cell phone. Dialing 911, he detailed the location of the warehouse and the specifics of what had transpired and ordered two ambulances.

When he disconnected, Lana asked, "If you missed a turn, how did you know to come here?"

He tugged at the hospital ID band she wore. "This has a tracker."

"Really? Isn't that a privacy violation of some kind?" she asked, only half joking.

"It was per my request. Just in case."

Lana frowned. "You knew something like this could happen?"

He shrugged. "A contingency plan. When dealing with these guys," he said, tipping his head toward the Russian, "you need to cover all bases."

Her frown deepened. "What bases? You're not making much sense, Lieutenant. I have no idea who 'these guys' are, other than they speak Russian and they want the disk as much as you do. Tell me what's going on here, and don't sugarcoat anything. I *need* to know."

Kipling held eye contact with her for a long time before he let out a lengthy breath and averted his eyes. "I was kind of hoping you could tell me."

Δ

"Me tell you?" Lana shrieked, hurling eye-daggers at Kipling. "For the last time, Lieutenant, I know nothing about this mess!"

Kipling wanted to believe her. Her sincerity was evident; her tone and body language indicated she was telling the truth. But it was difficult to accept. Was Lana truly clueless regarding her predicament? If so, he wondered how her father could've maintained such a complex deception for so long. More importantly, *why* would he do so? Kipling was sure Deacon Baker would have told her . . . something. And yet the genuine confusion in her eyes—in her entire being—suggested otherwise. Perhaps she didn't know that she knew. Perhaps what she thought was ordinary was actually a clue to her past.

"If you say so." He offered his hand to help her stand. "We can discuss options later. Let's get you cleaned up and stabilized first."

Pushing his hand away, her eye-daggers turned to ballistic missiles. "No! I'm not going to discuss options later because there's nothing to discuss. This is *my* life. The disk is in *my* head. Therefore, it's *my* decision. Apparently, everybody knows about this stupid implant except me. So you, Lt. Kipling, are going to tell me what's going on right now, or I will refuse any treatment and just walk away."

Kipling remained silent. Mostly, he didn't want to say anything in front of the Russian. The man had admitted he understood English, so Kipling had to be careful what he revealed. Even so, he had to tell Lana something. Even if it was a mere sampling of the truth.

"Lana, I understand how you feel," he said softly. "But I—*we*—have to be careful about what's said in public."

The sound of sirens grew louder. If Kipling were going to get anything out of the foreigner, he'd have to act quickly.

"Let me make certain first," he said to Lana, nodding toward the Russian.

With narrowed eyes, she whispered, "He says his name is Petrov Anders."

Kipling moved to the foreign operative and spoke to him in Russian. "What is your name, comrade?"

The man glared at him silently. Kipling knelt, then suddenly punched him in his wounded shoulder, eliciting a howl of pain.

"Your name," he repeated.

"Petrov."

"Petrov what?"

"Petrov Yurievich Vordechevski."

Lt. Kipling slugged his shoulder again. "My associate says otherwise."

Hissing, Petrov said, "Svetlana is not so bright."

Kipling punched the Russian's shoulder a third time, causing him to curse in pain, then asked, "What is the name of the man who ran away?"

"Tarus. But I do not know his last name."

When Kipling threatened to slug him once more, Petrov held up his bound hands and whimpered something unintelligible. When Kipling leaned closer, Petrov spat in his face. Without hesitation Kipling punched the Russian squarely on the jaw, and he folded to the floor without further sound.

Kipling shook out his fist and wiped his face with his sleeve. Turning to Lana, he said, "You didn't see that."

"You kidding? I wish I'd been the one to do it."

Kipling searched the man and found a wallet with a couple hundred in twenties and a New York driver's license. Unless the license was fake, Petrov's last name really was Vordechevski. As he returned to Lana, the sirens cut out directly in front of the warehouse. From the sound, he counted three separate vehicles.

"Lana, listen," he said quickly. "At this point, I'm not sure who to trust completely. Suffice it to say you're in imminent danger. The disk in your head is Russian-made. I don't know when it was implanted, but I have a theory. I need your help to put all the clues together. Please, trust me."

"How can I when you've already lied to me?" she said in a sour tone.

He frowned. "When have I lied to you?"

"You said the disk was dangerous. Petrov laughed when I mentioned it," she said, nodding at the unconscious foreigner.

"Lana," he began just before the warehouse door burst open. A policeman entered with his gun drawn. Kipling raised both hands. "Officer, I'm

Lt. Lance Kipling, US Army Intelligence. I have an unconscious suspect and this civilian in need of medical attention. Another suspect escaped roughly four minutes ago on a motorbike similar to the one against the far wall."

The officer instantly took in the scene and said, "Ma'am, drop your weapon."

Only then did Kipling remember he'd given a handgun to Lana.

She gently laid the gun on the floor and slid it toward the officer.

The policeman approached cautiously as Kipling continued to explain the situation. "This is Lana Baker. She's under my care as a key witness in a matter of national security. She was kidnapped from Poudre Valley Hospital this morning by this man," he said, nodding at Petrov. "His name is Petrov Vordechevski. I believe he and his associate are foreign operatives. The one who got away is in his forties, easily six four, two hundred forty pounds, and distinguishable by severe burn scars on the full left side of his face. He goes by Tarus."

"He's also missing an ear on the same side," Lana added.

Kipling continued. "I have identification in my wallet if you'll allow me to get it."

The lawman nodded, and Kipling slowly removed his wallet and ID. After a brief examination, the officer handed back the ID, holstered his gun, and called the okay for the medical personnel to enter the building. One pair of EMTs saw to Petrov while a second pair treated Lana's wounds.

Upon waking, Petrov was very uncooperative.

"Do you have any more information on this guy?" the police officer asked.

"He's got a New York driver's license but nothing else," Kipling said. "I haven't had a chance to interrogate him, but he's definitely Russian."

"Russian?" the officer replied, greatly surprised.

"Yes. You should get the CIA here as soon as possible."

The officer smirked and pulled out his cell phone. "I think we got this. Since his crime is on Colorado soil, we'll book him here on assault and attempted murder. If we can't get anything out of him, we may call in help."

Kipling thought the officer's old-school reticence for involving government agencies unfounded. What used to be intense rivalry between branches of law enforcement was now mostly a cliché attitude seen only in movies and on TV.

As the policeman stepped away to talk on his phone, Kipling asked the EMTs if he could speak to Lana privately for a moment. He then whispered to her, "Don't say anything about the disk. I'm going to check out the motorcycle, see if I can find any clues."

She nodded, and the emergency personnel returned to their ministrations.

Kipling found nothing telling on the remaining motorbike. There might be fingerprints, but he currently didn't have the equipment to collect them.

He couldn't believe the Russians had zeroed in on Lana so quickly. *He* had barely just connected her with Deacon Baker. Since the Russians had also, it meant project Red Cicada was definitely still active. How could Lana not know that?

"You're not strapping me down to anything," Lana yelled at the EMTs trying to help her.

Returning, Kipling asked, "You guys about done?"

"Just finished," the one facing off with Lana said. He'd wrapped her head and knee with bright-yellow bandages. "Her head wounds require extra precaution. I think she'll be fine, but we need to immobilize her neck and spine on a backboard before we transport her. It's a standard precaution."

"I'm fine," Lana grumbled.

"I'm sure you are," Kipling said. "Gentlemen, I can take her back. I'll assume full responsibility for her condition."

"Can't do it, sir. We're *required* to immobilize her and transport her to UCH Emergency. We've already called it in."

"She was at Poudre Valley before these guys abducted her," he explained, gesturing at Petrov. "She's scheduled for surgery at Peterson Air Force Base. If she's not going to Poudre, she should go directly to Peterson."

"Not our call," the EMT said. "We're dispatched out of UCH Emergency. It's state procedure. Peterson can transfer her afterward if they want. I'll call my superior if you'd like, but he'll tell you the same thing."

"Hello?" Lana said from the floor. "I'm right here, and I do speak English. Don't I get a say in this?"

"I'm afraid not," Kipling said, indicating with his eyes for Lana to go along with his reasoning. "You are a national security risk at this point. Foreign factions clearly know your whereabouts, and—"

"National security risk?" Lana cried. "Me? Why? What have I done? I didn't *ask* to have this stupid thing put in my head. I don't have a clue who these guys are or why they want it. Frankly, I don't care who gets it. I just want it out."

The EMTs stared questioningly at each other.

"That's what we're trying to do, Lana," Kipling said, his tone imploring her to keep silent.

"By labeling me a security risk?"

Kipling looked at the EMTs and the Russian. The police officer had returned and was also listening in. All eyes were fixed on him, awaiting his reply.

"We'll talk about it later," he said evenly to Lana. "Trust me on this. The less said, the better."

"What is she talking about?" the policeman asked.

"It actually *is* a national security matter," Kipling said, putting as much authority in his demeanor as he could. "She could be a threat to the country."

"Uh-huh," the officer mumbled, unconvinced.

"What about patients' rights?" Lana angrily asked the EMT. "I'm awake and fully lucid and not in critical need. Don't I have a right to deny any treatment?"

"No, you don't," the policeman said. "Under these circumstances, you have to receive emergency treatment."

"What circumstances? *I* was abducted by Petrov—not the other way around."

"If you *are* a threat to the country, as the lieutenant here says, then you are to this community too," the officer said. "Therefore, we can insist on treatment."

"Which is why she has to go to Peterson or at least back to Poudre Hospital," Kipling said with more force, "where there's already sufficient security in place."

"Sufficient enough for her to be abducted by a Russian spy?" the officer said in a monotone dripping with irony.

Kipling fought to choke down his caustic retort. Normally, his trust of law enforcement and medical personnel was ironclad. But recent events had cankered that trust. He couldn't believe Lana had mentioned the disk after he'd warned her not to. He needed to get her away from all outside influences, regardless of their purpose or rank.

"I never said he's a spy," Kipling said. "Even so, I have an obligation on a national level—which supersedes your local mandates."

The officer thought for a moment. "Okay, here's what's going to happen," he said with finality. "Miss Baker will be transported to UCH Emergency. I'll leave it to these gentlemen whether or not she's immobilized on a backboard. Lieutenant, you can follow them there and keep tabs on her the whole time." He then smirked again and added, "I'll follow behind you to make sure no one sneaks up from behind."

"Maybe I didn't make myself clear," Kipling said, his temper at a boiling point. "This a military matter of national—perhaps even *international*—security. It's not a simple traffic violation in Small Town, Colorado."

"Hey! Stop talking about me like I'm a criminal," Lana demanded. She thrust a finger at Petrov. "He's the bad guy."

Kipling waited for the officer's response.

"My apologies, ma'am," the officer replied.

A silent standoff followed, each person glaring at the next. The air was heavy with tension. Petrov chuckled and muttered in his language.

"What'd he say?" the policeman asked.

Lance clenched his jaw a few times, fighting back anger. "He said we're pathetic, a joke."

The officer turned to the foreigner and scoffed. "Buddy, I'm not the one taped up on the floor with a bullet in my shoulder."

Swallowing his frustration, Kipling again knelt beside Lana. "Let's just go along for now. I won't let you out of my sight. I promise."

Still clearly livid, Lana grumbled an okay and lay on the backboard. "No head restraints," she growled at the EMTs.

"Sorry, miss. Safety standards and resources requires it."

She huffed and folded her arms defiantly.

"Lana," Kipling said, squeezing her arm. "It's a short drive. I'll check out the ambulance before you get in. And I'll be right behind you the whole way."

She scowled at the men surrounding her with indignant scorn—including Kipling. In a tone brimming with acid, she said, "Fine."

"Thank you, Ms. Baker," the EMT said. "Now, I need to remove your necklace—"

"Not a chance," Lana snapped, batting his hand away. "This stays on me, or I don't go anywhere."

The EMT looked up at Kipling, his eyes begging for help.

"Lana," Kipling began.

"No."

"Lana, please."

"No, Lieutenant. And that's final."

Kipling exhaled slowly and nodded. "Let her keep it on, boys. It's a short ride, and she's not showing any signs of respiratory trauma, right?"

The second EMT said, "They may insist on removing it at the hospital."

"Let 'em try," Lana grumbled.

Kipling sighed. "We'll cross that bridge when we get to it."

The EMTs shrugged and loaded her into an ambulance.

CHAPTER 10

To say Lana was fuming was a gross understatement, and yet her anger barely reached the level of her anxiety. The longer this insanity continued, the more threatening the craziness became. She just wanted it to be over, wanted to return to her unremarkable, average life. Although . . . was her life average? As a youth, it hadn't taken her long to recognize that they moved around more often than anyone else she knew. It had made developing friendships difficult. As a teenager, she'd opted to remain a loner rather than make new friends. She knew any friendship she fostered would be cut short. Moving to another town was as inevitable as it was unpredictable. Their departures were always abrupt and always without warning. That definitely was not average.

Now she lay strapped to a stiff plastic stretcher, her head braced securely between two foam blocks. The immobility piqued her anxiety. She closed her eyes and tried to think of Wisconsin. Lake Julia. But the comforting image grappled to form in her mind; the road noise and static crackle of radio traffic sullied the picture. The foam blocks did little to soften the sharp sounds or the relentless pounding in her skull. At least it hadn't progressed to a migraine. Yet.

"We're almost there," the EMT next to her said.

"And the lieutenant?" she asked.

"Right behind us, as promised."

Lance Kipling gave the impression he was sincerely concerned about her health and safety. But his involvement in this mess was about as consistent as an ice flow in July. No telling when his story would shift, where cracks in his narrative would form, or even if he'd cave, his personal involvement turning completely over. The whole fatal-disk fallacy still irked her.

She wanted to believe him. He *had* rescued her, after all. Risked his life for her. He knew more than he was saying, but his reasons for not telling all made sense. And he did promise to explain everything. But had he said that solely for her benefit, or was he simply interested in obtaining the disk for his own gain?

Δ

The UCHealth Emergency department seemed awfully busy—but then, really, how would Lana know? The first time she'd ever been to an ED was three days ago. It could be they were just being thorough. It could be the aftermath of a college rave. It could be anything.

The hospital staff checked her over from head to toe. Her bumps, bruises, and scrapes were nursed with expert care. They gave her a quick sponge bath, a new hospital gown, and a pair of flip-flops. The laceration on her leg required four stitches and a tetanus shot. She'd never had a vaccine as an adult, and the pain it caused in her shoulder made her vow never to get another. Because of the reopened incision on the back of her head, the ED doctor wanted to do a CT scan. Lana flatly refused. To her delight, Lt. Kipling agreed with her, insisting that no X-rays or scans take place.

"CT scans were previously done at Poudre Hospital three days ago," the lieutenant explained to the physician. "If you'd like to see the films, I'm sure they'd comply. For now, I need to get Ms. Baker under more protective care than I can offer here."

Gratefully, the doctor, a former air force officer, did not argue the point. When Lana refused a painkiller, he gave her a mild muscle relaxant and an anti-nausea medication for her headache. She was allowed to rest in a recovery area made private by nylon partitions that reminded her of shower curtains. Drifting in and out of wooziness, she was grateful for the privacy, no matter how scant. But her rest was short-lived when Lt. Kipling parted the curtain.

"Lana? You awake?"

"Sort of," she mumbled.

"I have Detective Ortiz here from the Fort Collins police force. He needs to ask you a few questions. I told him to keep it short."

"Fine."

Kipling stepped in, followed by a Hispanic man in blue jeans and a plaid button-down. A white tee showed through where the buttons strained to keep closed across his midsection.

"Ms. Baker," Ortiz began, pulling a pen and a small notepad from his shirt pocket. "Thank you for taking the time."

"It's not like I'm going anywhere soon," she replied.

"You're not wrong."

What is that supposed to mean? she wondered.

"The lieutenant here told me you were admitted to Poudre Valley Hospital three days ago because of seizures resulting from a severe migraine. Is that correct?"

"Wish it weren't."

"Anything else you care to add about what happened?"

She glanced at Kipling, who gave an almost imperceptible shake of his head.

"They just gave me some drugs. That's about it."

"Huh. And you were there three days?"

"Only two and a half."

"That seems an awfully long time for a headache."

"A migraine. You ever had one, Detective?"

"Can't say I have."

"Then, you wouldn't understand."

Without skipping a beat, he asked, "What can you tell me about the abduction?"

She drew a breath steeped in long-suffering and dulled by brain fog. "I was scheduled for a minor surgery the next morning. The orderly who came for me turned out to be a Russian who claimed his name is Petrov Anders. He strapped me into a wheelchair and took me to the basement parking lot and tossed me into his van before I really knew what was happening. Lt. Kipling witnessed the van pulling away. Petrov took me to a seedy warehouse a few miles away. I don't know the address, but the lieutenant does. All I know is that Lt. Kipling came in just before they were about to kill me."

Ortiz tipped his head to one side. "You said the hospital staff . . ." He flipped back a page in his tiny notebook. "Just gave you some drugs."

"Yeah."

"So what was this scheduled surgery?"

Kipling cleared his throat. "That's irrelevant, Detective. You should focus on the abduction."

"Should I?" he asked, not looking up.

"Yes. I am investigating the national security implications of this case," Kipling explained in an even tone. "The Fort Collins police should only be concerned with the traffic violations in relation to the abduction."

"Should we?"

"Yes."

Ortiz scribbled something in his booklet. "Ms. Baker, what time was your surgery scheduled for?"

"Why do you need to know that?" Kipling asked harshly.

"It gives me a perspective on the time Ms. Baker was taken from the hospital."

"Then, how about you just ask that?"

Ortiz looked up. "How about you let me do my job my way and you do yours your way?"

"Boys," Lana cut in. "We're all on the same team here."

Ortiz turned back to Lana. "Ms. Baker, I can only help if I'm given all the facts, not partial truths. I'm not saying you lied to me, but it wasn't full disclosure either. Did the surgery have something to do with your head wound?"

Kipling, scowling at the screen of his cell phone, stepped forward and inserted himself between the detective and Lana. "Okay. We're done here." He pocketed his phone and handed Ortiz a business card. "This is my liaison at the CIA office in Denver. I've already notified him of the situation, but if you'd like to verify my role in this, give him a call. Until then, this patient is under military custody."

"Military custody, huh?" The detective looked closely at the card.

"Yes. Call my superior if you'd like."

Ortiz closed his notepad and turned to Lana. "Pleasure to meet you, ma'am. Thank you for your time."

When Detective Ortiz left, Kipling said, "My superior just texted me. I've got to make a secure phone call to make sure this doesn't get more out of hand. I'll be right back."

As he stepped through the curtains, a young nurse entered to attend to Lana—but not before casting a lingering gaze on the departing army officer.

"My, you're living quite the fairy tale, aren't you?" she said, checking Lana's stats.

Unsure she'd heard the nurse correctly, Lana said, "Excuse me?"

"A handsome young lieutenant rescuing you from a dangerous foreign kidnapper." She nearly swooned. "Some women have all the luck."

"Luck?" Lana scowled at her bandages and her deplorable state of dress.

"Yes. So what are you—his girlfriend? Fiancée?"

"I'm his prime suspect."

She blinked. "Prime suspect?" Her tone hovered between humor and disbelief. "What did you do?"

"I'm under investigation for something I didn't even know about—not anything I did." The implications from the nurse's timbre irritated her. "Apparently, the bad guys also know about it. That's why I got kidn—wait. How did you know the kidnapper was a foreigner?"

"The ambulance following yours brought in a GSW. He's surrounded by cops in the far bay."

"GSW?"

"Gunshot wound. The guy doesn't speak a lick of English, but the EMTs told me what happened."

"He actually speaks very good English. If his name is Petrov, he's the man who kidnapped me. There was a second bad guy who got away."

"Holy cow. You're lucky the lieutenant was able to find you."

"He only did because of this tracker," she said, tugging at her Poudre Hospital wrist ID.

The nurse held up Lana's arm and examined the thin plastic band. "This is a standard admissions ID. It's exactly like the one we put on your other wrist." She held Lana's two wrist IDs side by side. "See? The printing's identical. They're even the same shade of green. The only difference is the PVH band is secured with a black plastic rivet. Ours has a white rivet."

"Are you saying this isn't a tracking device?" Lana asked.

"Don't be silly. It's just a piece of plastic."

"Then, how *did* Lt. Kipling find me?" she asked, almost to herself.

The nurse shrugged. "He must have followed you from the start. Or he knew where they were taking you to begin with. Either way—"

She stopped abruptly as the lieutenant slid open the curtain and pushed in a wheelchair.

"I signed you out so we can—" He too abruptly stopped when he saw Lana wasn't alone. "Oh. Hi."

"Hi yourself," the nurse said, pulling her shoulders back and coyly biting a corner of her lower lip. "My name is Amber."

Lana rolled her eyes.

"Amber, could I have a moment alone with Ms. Baker?" he asked.

The flirty nurse flashed a wide smile. "Sure. Call me if you need anything." She paused before closing the curtain and gave him a blatant come-see-me look.

Lana didn't know whether to laugh or gag or snap at Kipling for lying about her ID band. "You need to answer a few questions," she said harshly.

"Later. We need to get you out of here. I signed a release form authorizing me to take you back to Poudre Valley Hospital."

"Really? Not Peterson?"

Kipling said nothing as he helped Lana into the wheelchair and pushed her to the main exit. Outside the hospital, the lieutenant opened the passenger door to his Cherokee and helped her inside, even though she insisted she didn't need the help. Her knee was sore and her head still pulsed, but the meds in her system kept things to a dull roar.

He buckled in and started the car.

Turning, Lana said, "Seriously. I need to ask you some—"

"Not yet," he interrupted. Although it was near sunset and cooler out, he turned on the air conditioner and cranked the fan to high. He also turned on the radio and rolled down the windows. When he leaned over to speak, his voice was barely audible with all the background noise. "There's a chance my car is bugged. I need to check it out before we discuss anything."

Her frown deepened. "Really?"

"Yes. I'm taking you off-grid until I get a better handle on who all knows about this."

"Are you allowed to do that?"

"I pretty much make my own schedule."

"Okay, but why off-grid?"

"It's a given that if my people know where I am, there's a chance the bad guys will know too. Which means they'll know where you are."

"And you think the bad guys are still after me," she intuited.

He nodded. "I think it's best if we go dark."

CHAPTER 11

They stopped for gas, then drove for a half hour, heading north along Highway 287. It took only a few minutes before they were in a rugged, alpine-like setting nearly devoid of life. The sun had dipped behind the Rockies and painted the sky a gorgeous orange-pink. But the tranquil setting did little to soothe Lana's whirlwind emotions.

Most vehicles they passed had their headlights on, probably more to avoid the ubiquitous antelope than to illuminate the road. Kipling had rolled up the windows and turned down the noisy climate-control fan. The music he'd chosen was contemporary country—or perhaps it was the only station he could get out in the middle of nowhere.

"Never figured you for a country-music lover," she quipped.

"You didn't, huh?" It was more of a comment than a question. The man looked seriously deep in thought.

Lana had a million questions for him, but she wasn't sure where to start. More than anything, she wanted to ask about his last comments: *There's a chance my car is bugged and it's best if we go dark.* It wasn't so much what he'd said as how he'd said it. If he was nervous about the situation, she was scared to death.

Pointing to her ear, she asked, "Are we still . . . being cautious?"

He nodded. "Out here we're probably safer, but yeah, it's for the best."

She lowered her voice. "So why do you think your car is bugged?"

He turned up the music a bit. "My supervisor texted and asked why I was at UCHealth instead of Peterson Air Force Base."

"So?"

"So how did he know where I was? My phone's GPS app was off. Same with my car's GPS. In my line of work, it's best if I remain undetectable.

The bad guys are pretty tech-savvy, and I'd rather they not know where I am 24-7."

"So you don't trust your own people either?"

He took a moment, as if organizing his thoughts. "I thought I was the only one assigned to your case—actually, your father's case. But the more I look into it, the more I think otherwise. I believe other agents are involved. We're all on the same team, but I'm wondering if we have the same objective. This may get a lot worse before it's over."

His tone frightened her. How could it get any worse? In a matter of hours, her life had been turned completely upside down. Now she was on the run from people wanting to kill her for information she didn't even know she had, with a guy she knew next to nothing about.

After an eon of silence, with nothing in the background but songs about the numbing virtues of beer, Lana was stir-crazy. She turned down the music. "You know, I could really use a shower and some real clothes," she said, tugging at her hospital gown.

Kipling's eyes registered surprise, as if just now realizing how little she had on. "Oh. Sorry. Yes, of course." But he kept driving north, seemingly ignoring her suggestion.

"Um, my place is back thataway," she said, jabbing her thumb over her shoulder.

"I realize that." He turned up the radio again—some twangy tune about regret. "We can't go back to your apartment. The place may be under surveillance. Perhaps even booby-trapped."

"What about all my stuff?"

"It's just stuff. You can get more."

She let fly a derisive snort. "Since you know so much about me, you'll know my bank account barely clears three figures. I pretty much live check to check, and I don't have enough credit to go on a wild shopping spree."

"You just need the basics. I can cover that. Laramie is a few miles ahead. We can grab you some clothes there."

"What about my personal things? You know, memorabilia, pictures . . . stuff I can't replace?"

The lieutenant didn't reply. He looked caught up in some angry thought, his brow furrowed, his eyes intense.

"Please, Lance," she said, deciding to use his first name in hopes of getting him to open up. "It means the world to me."

He glanced at her with a critical scowl. "You really have no idea how much danger you're in, do you?" Again, his comment was more accusatory than questioning. "Unbelievable."

His flip-flop nature was deeply irritating. Lana's fatigue and anxiety were such that even an innocent sideways look from him would have set her off. Her head still pounded just below the level of a migraine. She'd had enough.

"I don't, huh?" she growled, her tone dripping with ire. "Let's see: I've been subjected to medical tests and X-rays against my will; I've been questioned as if I were a criminal; I've been kidnapped by foreign agents and beaten, cut, scraped, stabbed in the back of the head, threatened with my life; and now I'm being abducted again, this time by the guy who is supposed to be on my side. And all this with a pounding headache that can cross into a migraine at any moment. Yeah, I have *no* idea."

"I *am* on your side," he said defensively.

She huffed and tightly folded her arms. What had happened to her safe little world? She knew life was full of vagaries, many decidedly unfair, some downright cruel. But the last thirty-some-odd hours had been absolutely insane. She needed full disclosure, not *half-truths, half answers*. She needed more than assurance from Lance; she needed confirmation. And she needed a friend.

The radio now blared a tune about an unfaithful husband the singer was still in love with. She was tempted to turn off the music but decided to trust what Lance had said about possible eavesdroppers. Even so, her sanity demanded information. If the bad guys already knew so much about her, they probably knew an equal amount about the lieutenant, just as he'd said. But *she* didn't. In fact, she knew basically nothing about the man driving her to somewhere "off-grid." She was tired of being the last to know. It put her at yet another disadvantage.

"Look, I know we can't discuss anything critical to national security, but I'd like to ask a few questions about other things, if that's okay."

Lance regarded her with steely consideration before returning his eyes to the road. "I'll tell you what I'm allowed to."

She took a steadying breath. "Tell me about Lt. Lance Kipling."

He scoffed. "Lana, this isn't really the time or place for—"

"Stop! Either I get some answers, or you don't get anything from me," she snapped, folding her arms even tighter. "I hate, hate, hate being kept in the dark about everything."

He fumed for a half mile, then said, "I was born in Glasgow."

"Scotland?" she asked with a grin.

"Delaware. It's about forty miles north of Dover, a hundred miles east of DC. I pretty much grew up there and attended Glasgow High."

"Were you a jock or a nerd?"

"Neither, really. Or maybe a little of both. Glasgow High was full of contention, bitterness, even hatred. Testosterone-charged teenagers, you know? PE was the worst. Contact sports took on a whole new meaning. So, to avoid fights in gym class, I joined the Army JROTC program, where we were taught unity, not rivalry. I really liked the discipline and principles they drilled into us."

"Enough for you to join up right out of high school?"

"Yes. JROTC helped pay for college and put me through OTS."

"OTS?"

"Officer Training School. I graduated with honors."

"And college? What did you study there—military history? Politics?"

"Microbiology."

That made her laugh. It was the last thing she would have guessed. "Seriously? Why?"

He shrugged. "It fascinates me."

"Yeah, but . . . you're in the army. Special investigations or something like that. Why—" Lana stopped short as fresh understanding flooded her brain. "Biological warfare? Is that what you do?"

"I can't comment."

She turned the music up. "If it *is* biological weapons, then why, for the love of Mike, are you investigating me? Is that what's on the disk?"

He leveled a cautionary gaze her way. "I really don't know at this point."

"Is that why the Russians are after it? Petrov said they wanted the information on it—but it sounded like he didn't know what that information was either. If no one knows for sure, why are so many people after it?"

"It's . . . complicated."

Another blockade.

"Great," she mumbled, feeling exactly the opposite. "I'm stuck in the middle of a mystery that you guys don't have a clue how to solve. If you'd just give me a chance, perhaps I could help you figure it out before they do."

"Perhaps," he said, turning up the music even more, indicating he was done with the conversation.

△

The somber sky had turned a deep shade of indigo by the time they pulled off the exit to Laramie. Stars were now visible, with Venus showing brightly just above the horizon. They connected with I-80 and followed it a few miles to a Walmart. In the parking lot, Lance stepped out of his Cherokee and opened the rear passenger area. Lana got out of the car too and watched as he pulled a fob that raised the seat cushion to reveal a storage space underneath. A small metal lockbox sat nestled among flares, a flashlight, a laptop computer, boxes of ammo, and several burner phones. He dialed a code on the combination lock and opened the box. Inside were a variety of papers, passports, and a stack of one-hundred-dollar bills bound with an elastic band.

"Gives a whole new meaning to a fully loaded vehicle," Lana quipped.

Lance peeled off three hundreds and handed them to her. "Get what you need. We shouldn't be seen together. Everyone knows we left the hospital together, so they'll be looking for two people."

"They also know how I'm dressed," she said, tugging at her hospital gown. "Don't you think this is kind of obvious?"

He grinned. "It's Walmart. You'll fit right in." He then reached into the cargo hold and pulled out an army windbreaker and ball cap. "Slip these on. It'll help. But change your clothes ASAP."

"What are you going to do?" she asked, accepting the light jacket and hat.

"I'll enter from the other door and will be watching your back the whole time," he said, removing his tie and collar pins. "Go in and get what you need, but don't be too rushed. And don't look around too frequently. It makes you look guilty. Get stuff you'd normally get on a weeknight. Try to blend in."

"I'll see what I can do," she said, irritated that he felt the need to spell everything out.

"Wait. Before you go, chew this," he said, handing her a stick of gum.

"Gum? Why? Is it my breath?" She popped it into her mouth and chewed.

"Not at all," he said, chewing a stick himself. He then pulled a pair of scissors from the seat compartment. "Let me see your wrists."

With a raised eyebrow, Lana complied.

He snipped the hospital ID band off each wrist, then pulled the gum from his mouth and squished it onto one band. He held out his hand to Lana. "Gum."

She removed the masticated wad from her mouth, and Lance squished it onto the second wristband. He glanced around, then stepped to the car next to them and secured one band inside the wheel well. He then moved to a truck a few spaces down and secured the second band the same way.

Lana wanted to ask about the action, but Lance was already heading toward the store. She appraised the few inches of hospital gown extending below the windbreaker. Good thing the hospital attire also included flip-flops. Her legs glowed white in the parking-lot lights. She really needed to get some sun. She removed the wrap around her head and donned the ball cap. Then, with a heavy sigh, she followed several yards behind Lance into the store.

CHAPTER 12

Lana picked out a complete ensemble, choosing to go with a contemporary Western style some people were wearing instead of the spandex and crop tops most of the local college girls sported. She wanted to blend in as much as possible without looking ridiculous.

Her mind would not stop thinking about the switch in Lance Kipling's conduct. He'd gone from military correctness to breaking procedures to forcing her to go off-grid. But why? What was his endgame?

After changing into a new outfit, Lana pushed a cart around the large box store, trying to appear as if casually shopping. Lance had said not to look too rushed and not glance over her shoulder too much. But since she realized anyone could be a bad guy, it was easier said than done.

She felt much better in clothes that were significantly more modest than the thin hospital gown—but she still needed a shower. She loaded her cart with extra clothing, shoes, and some personal items. She also got a six-pack of bottled water, a box of granola bars, a bottle of ibuprofen, and a family-sized package of Double Stuf Oreos.

Even traversing the entire store twice, she never caught a glimpse of Lance. She thought his tall frame and military shirt and slacks would stand out. But she couldn't find him anywhere—and that infuriated her. They needed to talk. They needed to clear the air and get on the same page. No more secrets. He was determined to keep her off-grid until he could figure things out, but how was he going to accomplish that? Where was he going to start looking? As much as *he* wanted to figure things out, *she* wanted it even more. As such, she resolved to be part of the planning.

With her jaw set, Lana wheeled the cart to the checkout.

"Good evenin', hon," the matronly cashier said. "How ya doin' tonight? You here for school?" Her name badge read *Patty*.

"School?"

"Of course. University of Wyoming? That's what most kids your age are here for."

"I, um . . . I already have a degree," Lana said, confused by the woman's dialogue. She didn't think she looked *that* young.

"Oh, grad school, then? Are you in the nursing program or the pharmacy school? I hear they're top-notch."

Lana opened her mouth to explain, but the cashier cut her off.

"No, wait. You got into the law school, didn't you! Land's sake. I knew it. I just knew it. I have a sense for these things, hon. You got that determined look in those gorgeous blue eyes. I'm right, aren't I?"

Lana gave a fleeting smile. "Guilty as charged."

The woman laughed heartily. "Lands, how I envy you. We need more women like you in this society. Men have screwed it all up. We need us a female perspective. When the world comes crashing down and the dust settles, it's the womenfolk who'll have the know-how to put it back together right. I say good for you, sweetie." She pressed a button on the register pad. "Your total's a hundred ninety-two 'n' sixty-three cents. That's a bundle of change, but you sure got some nice duds here. Course, anything'd look good on a figure like yours. And those blue eyes! Lands' sake!"

"I'm really not all that into fashion," Lana said, handing her two hundred-dollar bills.

"I knew it! You got something about you, like I said. You know what you want, and you just put your head down and go for it until you got it. You're a young woman who's got her life figured out down to the last second. Ain't that right?"

She smiled at the overly friendly woman, wondering if she was this uncensored with all her customers. "Not really," Lana ruefully admitted, "but I'm trying."

"And succeeding," the cashier said before counting her change back. "I wish you all the luck in the world, honey. But I bet you don't need it. You're the kind of gal who makes her own luck, ain't cha?"

Self-incrimination slackened Lana's countenance. "You'd be surprised. But thanks for the encouragement."

"Hope to see ya again, dear."

Pushing her cart from the checkout area, Lana again searched for Lance but couldn't see him. If he was still covertly watching her, he was doing a great job. Dad had taught her how to recognize when someone was stalking her or feigning interest. People weren't as sneaky as many thought they were. Unless they'd had expert training.

Deciding she looked more suspicious just standing around, Lana exited the store. The parking lot was full of evening shoppers. She moved to a wire bench near the entrance and sat.

The brief encounter with the genial cashier played in her mind. The woman had mistaken Lana's resolute expression as ironclad confidence. The topsy-turvy past few days made her feel anything but confident. And yet, the cashier's parting words rang in her mind. *You're the kind of gal who makes her own luck.* Was she?

Dad had tried to instill in her unbreachable self-confidence. He hadn't sugarcoated anything. He'd always spoken the truth and allowed her to stumble and make mistakes. But he'd always been there to help her stand back up. He wasn't a helicopter parent, always hovering about, doing everything to guarantee Lana would never be hurt or disappointed. He'd been there, watching, protecting against catastrophe, but he'd allowed her to experience her share of disappointment and failure. Dad had been more of a safety net, and Lana had proudly earned bumps, bruises, and even a scar or two—both physical and emotional. She was confident he'd never have let a complete tragedy strike.

Until he died.

She shook her head. Until he was *murdered*. Petrov had gleefully admitted his people were the ones who'd killed her father. She was determined to get even. She needed to solve the mystery surrounding the disk in her head. More than anything else, she wanted to get the men who had taken her father from her. And her best bet for doing so was Lt. Lance Kipling.

She stood from the bench and scanned the harshly lit parking lot. Lance was still nowhere in sight. The man was a mystery himself. What was in the file he had on her father? He never did confirm why he was investigating him. Was her dad connected with bioterrorism?

Ha! Not likely.

She grew tired of waiting. Too many things needed to be done. And rather than trusting her future solely to the lieutenant, Lana vowed to take the cashier's suggestion to heart. Starting right now, she would make her own luck.

CHAPTER 13

LANCE LEANED AGAINST HIS CHEROKEE, acting casual. He was now dressed in jeans, a short-sleeve Western shirt, and a ball cap that matched the one Lana wore. Knowing his uniform was even more glaring than Lana's hospital gown and slippers, he'd made the change. He was checking out a weather app when Lana walked up.

"Where'd you get the duds?" she asked.

"Same place you did," he said, nodding toward the box store.

She appraised him with a not-so-subtle grin. "It really works for you."

"Thanks."

"Did you see anyone watching me in there? Because I didn't see you anywhere."

"Good," he said as he helped Lana load her purchases into the cargo area. "There were plenty of people staring at you. One girl even tried taking a picture while you were still in the hospital gown, but you moved too fast, just like you were supposed to. No one tailed you though. Like I said, not only is this a Walmart, Laramie is a college t—" He stopped and held up the Oreos with a questioning expression.

She smiled and shrugged. "Everyone has their addictions."

"Anyway," he continued. "This is a college town. University kids are generally a shameless bunch who don't care how they dress when shopping." He shut the cargo door. "Did you get what you needed?"

"Clothing-wise, yes. But I still need a shower." She glanced at the car that was still next to them. "Aren't you concerned about the bad guys going after the poor saps whose cars you stuck the trackers to?"

"No. They'll probably fall off after a couple of miles. And even if they stay on, they're attached to cars, not you. The bad guys will figure it out real quick."

After buckling in, she turned to him. "Lance, I really appreciate what you're doing for me. I don't know why you're risking and sacrificing so much for a stranger, but I recognize the consequences it may have on your career. You've already saved my life at least once, so I owe you that."

"You don't owe me a—"

"Please, let me finish," she cut across, silencing him.

"Hang on," he said, starting the SUV and turning on the radio. "Okay."

She took a steadying breath. "So here's what's going to happen. We both know the bad guys know who I am. We know they want the disk in my head because of the information it contains. I honestly don't know what that information is, but I suspect you do—at least partially." She held up her palm to stop his objections. "Like you, I just don't know who to trust anymore. Even you have done some shady things—lying about improper disk removal being fatal, putting a tracker on me without my knowledge, telling me half-truths." She again stopped him from commenting. "Why else would you stick both hospital bands to separate vehicles? You want to confuse the people following me. Yes, you have national security reasons. I understand your motives, though I still don't appreciate your tactics. But that's water under the bridge. Right now, you're the only person who seems to be on my side. I need to know I can trust you, Lance. No more games, no more lies."

He took his eyes from the parking lot and looked at her with a steady gaze. "Agreed. And I'm sorry for any previous deceptions."

"Again, water under the bridge. Let's move forward. You're right that I have no idea who we're dealing with, but I assume they're the worst of the worst. *However*, the stuff I want to get from my apartment may have some bearing on what's happening—including my dad's old memorabilia. Some knickknacks and a stack of papers. I have a feeling the information you've gathered on my father may be substantiated by what's there. Dad was all about keeping secrets. Nothing top secret, of course, but perhaps an item or two may clue you into something. I've never looked closely at them because, well, frankly, his passing is still rather painful. Even more so now that Petrov admitted to killing him."

Lance looked over sharply. "When did he do that?"

"In the van." She quickly rehearsed the conversation. "He said Dad was dead even before his car left the bridge."

"I'm so sorry. I'll have to look into that. I saw the death notice come through the wire. I also saw the investigation report confirming it was an accident." He shrugged. "I didn't know what else I could accomplish by going there."

"I figured as much. Anyway, I need to get my things from my apartment. Let's go back, sneak in to grab some things, and get out. I'll be quick." She pointed at the dash clock. "By the time we get there, it'll be after midnight. Nobody will see us. Fort Collins isn't exactly known for its nightlife, so we can do it covert-like, the way you guys do things."

He shook his head. "You watch way too many spy movies. Don't always swallow what Hollywood feeds you." But he considered her petition, impressed by her determination. He nodded. "You do exactly as I say. No talking. No noise. If I hold up my fist like this," he said, demonstrating the sign, "you freeze. If I do this," he said, thrusting his palm flat toward the ground, "you drop. And this," he said, jabbing his thumb over his shoulder, "you run. Agreed?"

"Yes."

He nodded again. "Okay, then."

Δ

Fourteen minutes after midnight, Lana unbuckled her seat belt as Lance parked his SUV two blocks from Lana's apartment complex. Contrary to what she had told him, there were quite a few apartment lights on, with people visible through their living-room windows. In the summertime, college towns seldom settled in until the wee hours of dawn.

As they set off, Lana took Lance's hand in hers. "Since we're wearing matching hats, it'll look less conspicuous if we act like a couple," she explained. "The bad guys will be looking for two separate people instead of a couple."

"You catch on quick."

"Not all spy movies are filled with clichés."

He reached over and playfully pulled the brim of her cap down. She laughed as she righted it. They walked casually, talking about college classes, movies, and the coolness and fragrances of the evening air. Lance contributed to the conversation but kept an eye out for lurkers. They paused at a bus-stop billboard in front of her apartment complex and pretended to read some advertisements.

"You see anything we should be worried about?" Lana asked.

"Not so far."

"How do you want to do this?"

"Can we access your place from the back?"

"I think so. I'm on the second floor, but I have a balcony."

He pointed at one of the fliers as if he were referencing it. "Let's stroll around the block and come in from the back. If your downstairs neighbor has a deck chair or table, we can use that."

She also pointed at the flier. "There's a metal trellis on the back wall. I've seen some college boys climbing it when they thought no one was looking."

They took another eight minutes to walk around the block. The apartment complex consisted of several buildings surrounding a green space. A clubhouse and pool sat at the far end of the space, away from Lana's unit. Good thing too. The pool was filled with late-night frolickers.

"Should we be worried about them?" Lana asked.

"No. It actually helps our cover."

They walked along the green space, staying within the shadows as much as possible. When they reached Lana's apartment, Lance examined the trellis. Fortunately, it was not well lit. "Let's go one at a time while the other is lookout. I'll go first."

"There's a key behind a tin gecko hanging on the wall."

Lance gave her a quirky smile.

"My dad taught me to always be prepared. The keypad for the alarm is directly across the living room next to the front door. The code is 0229."

"Your dad's birthday."

Lana smiled. "On a leap year. You *have* done your research."

"The bad guys have too. Let me go in and case the apartment before you come up."

She nodded.

Lance clambered up the trellis without a problem and stepped onto her balcony. She heard the scraping of tin against the stucco wall and then the sliding of her balcony's glass door. Lana settled into a deep shadow and took in the surrounding area. Soft music and laughter filtered from the pool area. An older gentleman walked his small dog on the green space until the animal found a spot worthy to receive its feces. Fortunately, the man was cultured enough to have a plastic baggy with which to carry away his pet's little deposit.

"Clear," a whispered voice came from above.

When man and dog went back inside, Lana scrambled up the trellis and onto her balcony.

"You do that like you've done it before," Lance whispered.

"It's my ninja training."

"Right . . ." He gave the green space one last scan. "Let's go. The place is empty, but I didn't have time to check for bugs. Go in, get what you need, and then we'll exit this way. No talking. Try not to make any noise."

"Affirmative," she said, stepping inside.

CHAPTER 14

Lana went to her bedroom, where she grabbed a medium-sized carry-on from her closet, and Lance followed. He held up his fist, and she froze as he examined the luggage very closely, checking for bugs or trackers, she guessed. She appreciated his thoroughness, but nothing in the apartment appeared out of place. If her quarters had been searched, she'd find something awry. But she saw nothing. As soon as Lance gave the go-ahead, she filled the carry-on with underwear, socks, toiletries, and a few items of clothing. When she placed a few pictures atop her clothes, Lance took each photo from its frame, then collectively slid the photos inside a pouch in the luggage lid. She doubted the frames had been bugged, but she'd decided to trust that he knew what he was doing. He removed a plastic trash liner from his pocket and put the frames inside.

Lana reached under her bed and removed an aluminum lockbox from one of the drawers hidden by the mattress skirt. The container was slightly bigger than a standard shoebox and was secured with a combination lock. She handed the box to Lance. When he determined it was secure, he handed it back, and she nestled it inside her carry-on.

She then went to the bathroom to grab her favorite hairbrush—a natural-bristle tortoiseshell brush a friend had given her in high school. A small night-light allowed her to find the brush quickly, along with her favorite skin lotion and lip balm. Catching a quick look in the mirror actually made her flinch. Her eyes were sunken and zombielike. Her skin looked dull and saggy. She sighed heavily. A flying broom would be the perfect accessory to her current visage. She exited the bathroom, walked back to her bedroom, set the items in her luggage, and zipped it closed. She nodded toward the doorway, indicating she was ready to go.

Lance stood staring up at a small box in the junction between two walls and the ceiling. The box had a single glass circle in the middle and a pinpoint red light glowing in one corner. He indicated it with his eyes.

"It's a motion sensor. It shuts off when the alarm is shut off," she whispered.

"Has it always looked like that?"

She frowned at it. "I guess so. Why?"

"Because that's a camera, not a motion sensor. And the light indicates it's transmitting." He leapt to the camera and ripped it off the wall. "We need to leave."

"What about my stuff?"

"I'll take the lockbox. Leave the rest. We need to go now!"

He quickly cased the living room, then sprinted to the balcony door. Just as he got there, they both heard the scraping of a key inserting into the front door lock. Stepping onto the balcony, he pointed behind Lana and thrust his palm flat toward the floor.

He wants me to hide, she realized in a panic. *But where?*

The front door burst open, and a man dressed in dark clothing leapt in. He carried a flashlight muted by a red lens and a handgun similar to what Petrov had carried. He swept the area with his light. Lance had left the balcony door partway open. As the man dashed to the balcony, Lana eased back into the darkness of her bedroom.

Δ

Tarus quickly assessed the living room and kitchen, then strode to the balcony and looked down. No one was directly below the terrace. There was a man a few yards away softly calling for his dog. The man stooped and stayed in the shadows. Tarus couldn't tell if it was the lieutenant, but the man's clothing seemed to differ from what he'd seen on the camera.

Stepping back inside, he darted to the bedroom and shoved the door fully open. He swept the area with his flashlight and gun. There were random clothes and a small suitcase on the bed, but otherwise, the room appeared vacant. Entering cautiously, he checked behind the door, then searched the bathroom and closet for the lieutenant and Svetlana. Nothing. They had disappeared. *Impossible.* He cursed. He had just seen both of them minutes before on the camera. He checked the closet a second time, looking for a secret cubbyhole or attic access but found neither. Noticing the queen-size bed sat high off the floor, he knelt and quickly lifted the mattress skirt. The red glow of his flashlight revealed a facing of wooden drawers running the length of the bed. But the drawers were too small for anyone to crawl inside. Moving to the opposite side, he found an identical set of drawers. He slammed his fist on the bed and yelled another curse.

Δ

Lana lay squished between the backs of the two storage units used to prop up her bed. If the intruder had looked under the bed from its foot, he would have seen her. She'd almost let out a scream when he hit the top of the bed and yelled in Russian. His tone sounded just like that of Tarus, the scarred man from the warehouse.

Lana was too frightened to move, too terrified to even breathe. Lance had been right; they had already bugged her apartment. How was that even possible? Listening to the intruder's coarse inhalations after each round of swearing, Lana prayed her trembling limbs would not betray her hiding place. He sounded animalistic, like a large predator angry at having lost its quarry.

At length the man grumbled in broken English, "I will find you, Svetlana. And I will kill you."

Then, watching the red glow of his flashlight finally leave the bedroom, she released a sour, tremulous breath as silently as possible. She heard him rummaging through kitchen cupboards, all the while grumbling and cursing. After a few minutes, she heard the front door slam closed.

She dared not move, dreading the possibility that the man had merely opened and shut the front door as a ruse to flush her out. She closed her eyes and tried to force mental images of sailing on Lake Julia with her dad, but her level of angst thwarted all efforts to form the cathartic memories. After what seemed an eternity, Lana heard Lance whisper urgently, "Lana? Are you in here?"

Peeking out from under the mattress skirt, she saw his shoes standing in the bedroom doorway. She was surprised she hadn't heard him enter.

"Under here," she whispered back.

The feet moved to the bed, and the valance was lifted. "Are you okay?"

"Fine. Just cramped up." She extended her hands out from under the bed. "Pull me out."

He grabbed her wrists and slid her from her hiding place. He then used his flashlight to illuminate the narrow cavity under the bed. "How'd you even get in there?" he asked with a bit of mirth.

"You'd be surprised what you can do when you're desperate. Did you get a look at the guy?"

"Briefly. I'm pretty sure it was Tarus."

"Me too. Do you think it's safe to leave?"

"It's safer than staying here. No telling if there are other hidden cameras. Come on. Let's get out of here."

Lana quickly gathered her items and accompanied Lance to the balcony.

"I'll go first," he whispered. "Drop the luggage to me, and then come down."

She nodded. The transition went smoothly.

At the street, Lance told her to wait in a darkened area while he retrieved his vehicle. He sauntered off as if nothing were wrong with the world, undoubtedly to avoid attracting too much attention, but he'd certainly get more than a few double takes from any female who saw him. Even in the subdued light of the neighborhood, Lana could tell his jeans fit very well.

She snorted and shook her head. What was wrong with her? She couldn't believe that thought had even entered her mind—especially considering what she'd just been through. Perhaps it was a case of being extra vulnerable right then. Even so, this was a man she barely knew and still barely trusted. Sure, he was good-looking and had an amazing warm smile. But considering how *she* looked and felt, she thought it best to push such feelings aside. She needed some serious refreshing time. She was exhausted and sore from head to toe. Why in the world would she have amorous thoughts right now? Her mind was not functioning clearly.

It took about ten minutes for Lance to return with the Cherokee. She climbed in, and they drove off at a casual pace.

After a few minutes of silence, she said, "Well? How do you think it went?"

Lance checked his rearview mirror. "I think we got lucky."

"Are we being followed?"

"Not that I can tell." He tapped his ear and shook his head.

Lana wanted to scream. She wanted to cry. She wanted to hug Lance for rescuing her yet again, and she wanted to hit him for still keeping secrets from her. Mostly, she wanted this nightmare to be over.

When every song on the radio began to sound the same, Lana turned in her seat to wrest the lockbox from her suitcase on the back seat. She needed a distraction. Setting the box on her lap, she dialed in the combination and opened it. There was just enough ambient light from the dashboard and moon for her to see inside. Regardless, she knew exactly what it contained. The last time she'd opened the box was to add a copy of Dad's death certificate. She'd had no desire to open it since, nor did she really want to now, but the quietude was killing her.

In one corner of the lockbox sat a Rubik's Cube. Even in the subdued light, she could see that the sides were all mixed up.

"That's a mess," Lance said, casting a glance at the toy.

"Yeah. I've never figured out how to solve these things. I've tried following cheat sheets online, but I still get lost."

"How come it isn't colored like the normal ones?"

"My dad made it. He loved puzzles." She fiddled with it for a moment. "Dad used to align this thing very quickly, but he always scrambled it immediately afterward. He never taught me how to solve it."

"Let me see."

Lana placed the cube in Lance's open hand. He gave it a cursory exam. "This appears to be a military insignia," he said, tapping one side with his index finger. "These letters unscramble to spell *semper fi*."

"'Always faithful,'" she said. "The marine corps motto."

"Short for *semper fidelis*. True marines live by that motto." He handed it back. "Many take the pledge. Most are loyal, but a few disrespect it."

"My dad had nothing but pride for the corps."

"So I've heard."

She set the cube in the box and closed the lid. "Good thing you're the real deal too, right?"

"Hoorah."

CHAPTER 15

THE SCAR-FACED MAN MADE IT back to his temporary safe house on the south side of Fort Collins without detection. He was furious and let fly a nonstop string of curse words to the Spartan room. He'd been so close to obtaining the disk! Timothy, an American IT specialist recruited by Petrov, had assured him that the miniature cameras he'd swapped out for Svetlana's two motion sensors would go unnoticed. When movement triggered them, an alarm had sounded on Tarus's phone and the cameras had begun transmitting live images from her apartment. Svetlana and the lieutenant had entered through the balcony window and were gathering materials from her room. The lighting was low, so it was hard to tell what was gathered, but Tarus was convinced it had something to do with project Red Cicada. He had the location of her apartment on his GPS, and he'd immediately set out. As he'd parked in front of the complex, his phone had shown the lieutenant reaching for the camera just before it had cut out. It hadn't been as concealed as Petrov's man had claimed.

Tarus had never had much faith in old Petrov. He'd never quite trusted his commitment to the motherland. Even in the warehouse—when they'd had Svetlana in their hands!—Petrov had tried to convince Tarus to spare her life.

He cursed again and rammed his fist into his bathroom mirror, shattering it. Looking at his bleeding hand with morbid appreciation, he smiled to the extent his scars would allow. Petrov was soft. He'd spent too much time in the United States and had been poisoned by their media and a government too eager to please their masses. Sure, the woman was pretty. She may even have had valuable information that would be worth lots of money. But she was expendable. The real money—the real power—was hidden under a few millimeters of flesh and muscle. A sharp knife was all that was needed to secure

Tarus's fortune. His superior's too. But Comrade Petrov had no backbone. He had no passion for the cause. The Red Empire would rise again, but only after the rest of the world was brought to its knees.

The world! It was almost at his fingertips, and he'd just seen it vanish for the second time in a day. But neither time was his fault. He was fettered by the incompetent agents he worked with. None of them were prepared to do what had to be done. Not to the extent he was willing to go.

"Petrov is a fool!" Tarus bellowed at his reflection in the remaining shards of glass. "You, Tarus, will succeed in spite of Petrov's incompetence."

He turned away and angrily paced the small apartment.

It was Petrov's indecision, his stalling, that had allowed the American lieutenant to surprise them and get off a couple of lucky shots. The first shot had hit Petrov squarely in the shoulder. Tarus had seen his partner spin and fall. The second shot had come his way. Tarus lifted up his shirt to see the bloody graze mark that lined his right side. A flesh wound that would leave a scar. He laughed, soft and deep. A trivial blemish for a man who'd spent twenty years of his life with a disfigurement that sent women screaming and made children burst into tears. The wound barely registered with him anymore. But the fact that Petrov had blown the operation tore at his gut and ravaged his mind. And now that his comrade had been responsible for the loss of Svetlana, Tarus was beyond furious.

Petrov had allowed himself to be followed.

Petrov had argued against killing the girl.

Petrov had stalled Tarus's attempt to obtain the disk.

Petrov had hired an incompetent IT man to install a trap.

Petrov had allowed the girl to escape. Twice!

Tarus stopped and growled like a rabid timber wolf. When he had obtained the disk for his country, he would kill Petrov himself.

CHAPTER 16

The readout on the rearview mirror indicated they were heading south. They drove in silence, munching on the Oreos Lana graciously shared. Roughly an hour later, Lance pulled into the parking lot of a Best Western motel on the outskirts of Loveland. It was just after two a.m.

"There'll be little foot traffic at this hour," he explained. "I've been going over options, and this is the best one."

He'd slipped into his military mode again. Lana thought it was cute and annoying at the same time. "Whatever. I just need a shower and a bed."

"As I was saying, our best option is a single room with double beds and—"

"Woah there, Lieutenant," she interrupted. "Why can't I get my own room?"

"You can't get one by yourself because you don't have any ID or a credit card with you."

Lana had all but forgotten her purse was back at Poudre Valley Hospital. What he said made sense. Besides, she knew she could trust Lance to behave as she slept.

As if reading her mind, he said, "I will be a perfect gentleman. You have my word. I only need about four hours of deep sleep. You can take more if you need. I plan on reformulating my research first thing in the morning."

"Research?"

He rubbed the back of his neck before turning up the radio a smidge. "Yeah. Sorry, but at first, all I wanted was the disk. If my hunches are correct, it contains information that could save thousands—perhaps millions—of lives. That's really what I meant by it being potentially fatal."

"What are you going to research?"

His demeanor hardened as he stared forward without answering.

Lana huffed loudly. “Not this again! We agreed to work together, didn't we? You already know I don't know squat about any of this. And you saw that Scarface guy Tarus stab the back of my head, so clearly I'm not on their side.”

He turned to her. “Biological weapons of mass destruction.”

Lana frowned—both at his declaration and the fact that, knowing a bit of his history, she hadn't already guessed the subject of his research. But what about her father? Had he known what the disk contained?

“Is that what my dad was doing over there? In Eastern Europe?”

Lance looked up sharply. “Did he tell you he was there?”

She touched her rhodonite pendant. “Not really. He told me he got this in the Ural Mountains. I looked it up. Do *you* know why he was there?”

“He and his partner, Aaron Goodwell, and a UN team were tasked with finding evidence of nuclear development and proliferation.”

“What?” Lana frowned. “He wasn't a medic?”

“He was at first. He transferred to special ops because his aptitude-test scores in deductive reasoning were near perfect. That's why he was assigned to the unit seeking nuclear-testing evidence. But then his file suddenly ended—even though several loose ends remained—including the mention of Red Cicada. He was granted early retirement because of personal medical issues.”

Lana quickly aligned the facts. “Red Cicada. The disk. Does it hold military secrets?”

“I only have guesses.”

She thought hard. Of biggest concern was why was this the first time she'd ever heard such things about her father? “What medical issues caused my father's retirement?”

“The file didn't say. He received a Purple Heart from a gunshot in the abdomen as a medic in Kuwait but never had any residual issues from the wound.”

Lana remembered her dad sharing that story with her only once or twice. Whenever she'd asked about his scar, he'd said he got it “being stupid.” She nodded and softly said, “Thank you, Lance. Now, go get that room. We need sleep if we're going to get to the bottom of this.”

Δ

Lance helped Lana carry in her Walmart purchases and her small suitcase via a side staircase. Security cameras would record their brief journey, but there was little he could do about that. Their room was on the second floor. He told Lana to wear her ball cap and keep her head down, eyes staring at her feet while they passed under the small blackened camera domes.

They entered the room and quickly shut the door. Lance turned on the bathroom light and unplugged the phone. "Don't turn on any other lights," he said before doing a quick search of the room. "Are you hungry?"

"Starving. But it's late. I think I can wait until morning."

"I can't. I'll grab something while you get cleaned up."

"Nothing greasy."

"Noted," he said, heading to the door. "Use the security chain after I'm out."

"Affirmative," she answered, following on his heels.

Lance parked his SUV in the lot of an adjacent motel, then walked across the street to a twenty-four-hour Wendy's. The night air was warm and scented with sagebrush, cedar, and a hint of rain from some far-off storm. He ordered a burger meal for himself and a chicken salad for her.

"Late-night munchies?" the cashier asked while wearing the harried smile of a single mother pulling a graveyard shift to cover expenses.

"Just passing through," he said to the woman. "Gotta keep fueled. Better add a couple of large Cokes with that, please."

"You bet. You on a long haul?"

He chuffed. "I hope not."

Lance was running on spent energy; his adrenaline and natural stamina had given out long ago. But what he'd been through was nothing compared to what Lana had endured. Boy, had he misjudged her!

Memorizing Lana's file on the way to Colorado had been no problem. It was conspicuously thin. There was absolutely no data on her birth, no record that Deacon Baker had produced offspring or that he'd even been married. Lana's history began at age nine, with a well-child visit at an InstaCare clinic in Greenville, Kentucky. The clinic had sent notification to the Kentucky Public Health database of the child not having had standard state-required infant immunizations. After treating young Lana for a bronchial infection, the PA on staff had given her the first round of catch-up vaccinations. No record existed of a second round. Lance had been able to find her driver's license, Social Security number, school records, and a very vague work history, but not much more.

"Your food's ready," the woman at the Wendy's counter said.

Lance accepted the meals. "Thank you, ma'am."

"You hang in there," she said with a sincere smile.

"You do the same," he said, sliding a twenty toward her.

"Oh. Did you want something else?"

"For you to keep smiling."

He took a different route back to the motel. There weren't any indications he was being watched; he simply wanted to remain cautious. It might be overly vigilant, but the situation warranted it. Deacon Baker must have continually taken similar precautions, and Lance wondered if he had become so burned-out always looking over his shoulder that he'd gotten complacent.

Lance never could find anything on the soldier's medical discharge. His health records during service were outstanding. Deacon had had no medical limitations and had spent only two days in a hospital for his bullet wound. Nor did he have any documented mental-health challenges. So what were the "personal medical issues" that had granted him early retirement? And did they have anything to do with Lana? Lance was increasingly curious about what Deacon *had* told his daughter about his past. She was still under the impression he was only a medic, but Deacon's last job was investigative, which he clearly had not told her.

Lance stopped at the motel door and cased the area, looking for suspicious vehicles or nontypical pedestrians. All looked clear. He grabbed the doorknob and paused. How had Deacon Baker been able to keep so much from his daughter? Perhaps he *had* told her and she was simply very adept at keeping secrets. Or perhaps he'd answered all her questions with lies. No, not lies. *Deceits*, maybe. He'd used falsehoods to protect her. When dealing with the level of espionage Deacon had dealt with, he'd have needed to take every precaution—especially when safeguarding loved ones. So how much of Lana's past was real and how much was deception? What other delusions was she living under?

There was only one way to find out. And it went against all standard military protocol.

CHAPTER 17

Lana felt like she'd been reborn. She'd taken a steaming-hot shower, washed her hair twice just because it felt good, scrubbed her skin to the point that it had turned red, then turned the knobs to cold and briefly reveled in the brisk invigoration. She toweled off, feeling totally refreshed, and donned clean clothes. She didn't try to do anything creative with her hair—just untangled it and let it air-dry. Being rejuvenated—with a clear mind and wonderfully headache free—she realized how ravenous she was. But she also knew her enlivenment wouldn't last long. There were simply too many stressors tearing down her endurance.

When a knock sounded at the door, Lana peeked through the eyehole, and her heart sank. Lance's slumped shoulders and darkened eyes revealed his deep fatigue. He wasn't under the same stress she was, but it was wearing on him nonetheless.

"What's the secret password?" she asked lightly, retracting the security chain.

"I have food."

She opened the door. "Close enough."

He entered and set the Wendy's bags on the small desk. "So what *is* the password?" he asked, unsuccessfully trying to mask the weariness in his tone.

"There isn't one. I just wanted to see what you'd say."

"Sorry. I'm too tired to be creative."

Lance opened his burger and took a huge bite. Lana squirted a dressing packet over her salad. Swallowing a sip of soda, Lance said, "You know, that's actually not a bad idea. Having a password, I mean."

"You think?"

"Yes. In case we need a signal or code word. We should have two: one for 'I'm in trouble' and one for 'All is well.'"

Lana thought for a moment while chewing. "How about *migraine* and *tulips*?"

"Tulips?"

"Sure. I love tulips because they herald the end of winter and the beginning of spring." Unexpected emotions welled within Lana. "It was my dad's favorite season. He said it was the renewal of life, when things that appear dead come back to life." She swallowed hard. "It's a chance to start over."

"I can appreciate that. But what we need is a word that isn't *too* random, something that can be fitted into a sentence that doesn't come across as a signal. *Migraine* works because you've had them all your life. *Tulips* . . . probably not."

"What do you suggest?" She swallowed a couple of bites of salad.

"Do you have a favorite childhood memory or something you always wanted but never had?"

"I always wanted a puppy as a child, but dad said it was impractical."

Lance shrugged. "You could always train it as a guard dog."

She paused. "Dang. Why didn't I think of that?"

"Okay, I think that'll work. *Migraine* means 'I'm in trouble'; *puppy* or *puppies* means 'All is well.'" Lance finished off his burger.

She nodded. "Migraines and puppies."

He snorted. "Sounds like a cheesy Hallmark movie," he said, forcefully rubbing his eyes.

Lana laughed softly, but just as she had predicted, her renewed alertness was quickly seeping away. Her meal finished, she washed it down with a glass of water, brushed her teeth, and collapsed onto one of the beds.

"I claim this one," she said, curling into a fetal position. "Thanks for a wonderful dinner. Good night, Lieutenant."

Lance switched off the bathroom lights and quietly drew a bed cover to her shoulders. "G'night," he whispered before stepping away.

Lana felt a brief twinge of disappointment that he didn't kiss her forehead, then chastised herself for such a girlish desire. Still . . .

Listening to Lance shuffle around the hotel room brought back pleasant childhood memories. Soft footfalls on thin carpet. The rustle of papers. The squeak of a desk chair being used. The drawn-out breath of a yawn.

She felt herself drift back to a trailer home in rural Kentucky. She couldn't remember the town's name. Green-something. She was probably eight or nine.

It was night. She was nestled under a quilt on the living room sofa. Her mind felt feverish and foggy. The man at the clinic had given her some shots that had really hurt. But she'd been brave and hadn't cried. Dad said to always be brave—even if you were scared spitless inside. She smiled. The phrase 'scared spitless' always made her smile.

Dad was at their small kitchen table across the living room. The plastic seat cushion squeaked every time he moved. Before going to bed, she noticed he was studying a map of Wisconsin. That meant they were going to move again. Dad looked worried. He always got that look when he decided to move. His brood mood.

She wished she could do more for him, but she was just a kid. What Daddy needed was a mommy by his side. Mommies were great at helping people feel better. A mommy could help Dad make a decision about where to go. They always moved because of his work, but she wondered if the shots the doctor at the clinic had given her were the real reason they were moving again. The doctor had mentioned something about putting a record of her shots in a state database. She assumed that was some kind of internet file anyone could read. It had made Daddy upset. Not mad upset. Upset like he was very worried.

She also wondered if Dad missed Mommy as much as she did.

"Daddy?" she whispered.

He looked up. His soft smile looked heavy. "Hey, Lightning Bug. How come you're awake? Are your vaccinations hurting?"

"A little. But I'm okay," she said, stretching under the blanket.

"That's my girl. Go back to sleep now. I'll turn off the light in a moment."

Lana lay still for a few minutes, but concern for her dad kept her awake. "Do you miss Mommy?" she asked before she could stop herself, realizing her question might make him sadder.

Daddy got up slowly and walked to the sofa. He looked so tired. He sat beside her and gently stroked her hair. "What makes you ask that?"

"I don't know. I was just thinking about how she might help us."

"Help us how?"

"You know. Like maybe finding a new place to live."

He closed his eyes for a minute. "Yes, sweetheart. I miss Mommy too."

"Tell me about her again. Please?"

Daddy drew a large breath and let it out slowly. "She was very, very pretty. Just like you. She had dark-blonde hair and really blue eyes."

"They looked electric," she said, having heard the description many times before.

"That's right. She passed that on to you," he said, gently tapping the tip of her nose.

"Genetics."

"That's a big word. But you're right."

"My eyes are why you call me Lightning Bug."

"It's one of the reasons."

"Am I as pretty as Mommy?"

"You sure are."

She snuggled deeper into the quilt. "Tell me more."

"It's very late, Lana. You need your sleep."

"Please?"

He sighed. "Well, there's not much more to tell—except that she loved you very much."

"She loved you too, right?"

He sighed again. "Yes. I'm sure she did."

Dad seemed so sad that it made Lana's heart hurt.

She had learned a new word the other day. Melancholy. It meant feeling lonely and unhappy. That must be what she was feeling right now. Maybe it was because she'd been thinking a lot lately about not having a mother . . . and wondering why she didn't. "Daddy?"

"Yes?"

"Was Mommy sick?"

He looked away, but Lana saw him swallow several times. "I don't really know. She'd been in the hospital a long time . . ."

"Did . . . did I kill Mommy, being born?"

"What? No. Of course not, sweetheart."

"But you said she died the day after I was born. If I wasn't born, she wouldn't be dead." She felt a hot tear run down her cheek. Maybe that was part of being melancholy.

"Oh, sweetie, that wasn't your fault," he said as he wiped away the tear. "Mommy had other things happening to her that . . . well, they got in the way. She had what they call 'preexisting conditions.' But she was able to hold you and tell you how much she loved you many times before she died."

"But how do you know? You said you were deployed when I was born."

"You're right; I was." He pushed her hair back and kissed her forehead. "I know because she left a note."

CHAPTER 18

Lana jerked awake and bolted upright—but she couldn't remember why. Something in her dream? The sudden motion made her head swim. She clutched her rhodonite pendant, gaining stability from its familiarity. The hotel room was bright with morning sunlight. Lance's bed was made to military crispness, but he was not in the room. The bathroom door was open, revealing a dark, empty interior.

"Lance?" she called.

No answer.

Standing, she saw a handgun and a note on the desk.

> *Lana,*
>
> *I need to check on a few things. I'll be back with lunch. Do not leave the motel room. Do not answer the door. Use the dead bolt and chain. I'll use our password on my return. If you watch TV, keep the volume very low. Use the gun only as a last resort.*

The bedside clock read 10:41 a.m. She couldn't believe she'd slept in so late. It made her angry. She should have better self-control. Lana crumpled the note and threw it into the trash. She also couldn't believe Lance had already forgotten their pact to do everything together, to keep each other in the loop. Yet here he was, telling her what to do at every step without conferring with her first. *I need to check on a few things.* What few things? She clenched her fists and suppressed a growl. He could be the most infuriating man! She marched into the bathroom and splashed cold water onto her face. Looking into the mirror, she saw tangled hair, frown lines etched in her brow, and bags under her eyes. Even though she'd cleaned up last night, she felt like she needed to start over.

She appreciated that Lance was only trying to be helpful. He was probably used to working solo. But this situation was different—*her* circumstance was different. That alone should be reason enough to include her in *all* plans.

She took her time in the shower, allowing the hot water to scald the bitterness from her soul. She needed to step back, take a breath, and look at the bigger picture, the way Dad had taught her.

Sliding back the plastic curtain, she realized she'd forgotten to turn on the vent fan. The room was thick with steam. She peeked out into the living room. Finding it empty, she toweled off and changed into fresh clothes while the bathroom aired out. Then, returning, she wiped down the mirror and again considered her reflection.

The light caught her irises at such an angle that they fairly glowed, a dark-blue perimeter emphasizing nearly iridescent light-blue centers. They looked electric. "Lightning Bug," she whispered to her image.

Last night's dream instantly materialized in her mind, and her breath caught. Dad had known about Mom's love for her because *she had left a note.*

He'd never mentioned the note again after that night. That's why she'd forgotten about it. Was that note still around?

Lana removed the lockbox from her suitcase and sat on her bed. The interior of the box was sacred territory. She rarely opened it because of the bittersweet emotions sequestered inside. Opening the box was tantamount to reopening a scar. She occasionally built up enough courage to play with the Rubik's Cube, but she couldn't bring herself to touch anything else.

Steeling her resolve, Lana opened the box and removed the Rubik's Cube. Dad's death certificate sat atop a thick stack of papers. She stared at the document as a mental battle ensued. She knew it was just a piece of paper. Touching it wouldn't do anything to her . . . or her dad. He was gone. Handling it would not kill him again. The first time she'd read the certificate eleven months ago was difficult enough. The memories were still poignant, still surgically sharp.

Initially being in denial about Dad's death, she had asked to identify his remains. The coroner had suggested she not do so because the accident had disfigured his face and all but decapitated him. It was not a pretty sight. But she'd insisted on seeing something that identified him. She'd needed that confirmation to begin closure, and it'd give her a chance to say goodbye. The coroner had given an understanding nod, led her into the morgue, and slid out a tray from a large bank of refrigerated drawers. A body lay secured inside a zippered black plastic shroud. A clear bag sat at the foot of the shroud. Lana recognized Dad's watch, wallet, and marine corps ring with its rhodonite center stone.

"He had a tattoo," she'd said with great effort. "Inside right bicep: *Semper fi.*"

The coroner had unzipped the shroud and carefully withdrawn the dead person's right arm. It was flaccid and pale, but it had Dad's musculature. The coroner had gently rotated it, exposing the marine corps motto tattooed on the skin. Seeing it had been more than Lana could bear. She'd turned from the table and collapsed.

She remembered awaking in the coroner's office with a cold compress on her forehead. The doctor had sat at his desk, reading a file bristling with Post-it tabs. When she stirred, he'd looked up.

"Take it nice and slow, Lana. I'm sorry about the shock. I should have been more sensitive. Can I get you anything?"

"No, thank you. I'm okay, really."

A county official had soon joined them and led Lana through the documents she needed to sign. Dad had notarized a short will leaving everything to her. But he hadn't had much. His bank account had had a couple thousand in it. No hidden savings. No bequeathed military pension. Just a stack of five $10,000 federal bearer bonds. That had helped her start anew, but it wasn't enough to retire on. Lana would have to continue to work for her sustenance. But it was the best way to carry on and not fixate over her dad's death. It's what he would have wanted her to do.

Lana rubbed her eyes and took several deep breaths to clear her head. She removed the death certificate from the open security box and set it to one side. She couldn't resist wiping her hands on the bedspread afterward, even knowing how silly that was. Dad's marine corps ring was sealed in a small clear baggie. She took it out and let the light play over the rhodonite stone at its crest. She quickly set it aside. She couldn't handle the memories it triggered right now. Her quest was a manila envelope at the bottom of the box. She bypassed accolades and all other mementos and retrieved the thick envelope.

Inside were all Dad's personal papers: a number of military commendations, some college memorabilia, a number of receipts and old account numbers, and a few birthday cards Lana had made him as a child. For whatever reason, she had never read completely through any of the documents. She began sorting through them, setting aside all that were typed. She was seeking anything that looked like a woman's script. *A note*, Dad had said. That implied something short, handwritten. There were a number of pages folded in half, some in fourths. She opened each scrap of paper but found nothing revealing.

Disappointment formed a heavy lump in her chest, and Lana began putting the assorted paperwork back into the manila envelope. A note from her mother? What was she thinking? Dad had explained that all their correspondence and wedding photos had been destroyed in an apartment fire. He hadn't reproduced the images because he'd said it was too painful. She couldn't fault him for that.

Lana blinked away tears and continued repacking the envelope. Dad certainly would have shown her something her mother had written, if such an item had survived the fire. He'd talked about Mom with such love and admiration. Her dream last night had rekindled those happy moments.

She paused when she discovered a hand-colored crayon drawing she'd made of her dad, herself, and what she imagined her mom had looked like, all holding hands.

Tears formed and burned through Lana's resolve. She gave in to them for a moment, then wiped her face and forced herself to stop. *Stop dwelling on unchangeable things!*

As she picked up the last homemade birthday card, a time-yellowed slip of paper fell out. Folded in half, it was little bigger than a business card. Lana opened it and drew in a gasp. The delicate printing on it was in Cyrillic letters.

CHAPTER 19

Lance knocked lightly on the motel door.

"What's the password?" Lana asked from inside. Her tone sounded surprisingly upbeat.

"Puppies."

The dead bolt retracted and the door opened a crack. "What breed?"

He frowned. That wasn't part of the code. "Do you have a migraine?"

"No, not that." The security chain scraped along its channel and the door opened all the way. "I'm just curious what kind of dogs you like," Lana said, stepping to one side.

Lance entered, carrying a McDonald's bag that emitted a deep-fried-potato fragrance that prompted a Pavlovian response. He hoped Lana wouldn't smell on his breath the french fries he'd already snitched. "I don't know. Maybe a bloodhound. They're the best at sniffing out clues."

"Well, as much as I hate comparing myself to a dog," she said lightly, "I've sniffed out a doozy."

"Really?"

She thrust a folded piece of paper toward him. He set the bags on the small table, accepted the note, and opened it. The Cyrillic handwriting looked feminine and somewhat rushed.

He read it quickly and looked up. "Where did you get this?"

"It was in my dad's stuff. He once told me about the note, but I'd forgotten about it until this craziness began. I had a dream about it just last night. Dad said my mom left me a note. I just now found it in the security box."

"You mean you've never seen this before?"

"Never." She nodded toward the container on the bed. "That box holds a lot of things still too painful to be opened." A catch in her voice told Lance she spoke the truth. "But last night, I remembered my dad telling me my mom had left a note. He didn't say to whom, but he said it mentioned me and how much she . . ." Lana's voice weakened to a whisper. "How much she loved me."

Lance reread the delicate handwriting. His heart ached—both at what was written and for who it was written to.

"Can you read it?" Lana asked eagerly. "Is it for me?"

"Yes, it is."

"And?"

What should he say? Lana had been through so much heartache. Translating the note verbatim would only cause her more. Even so, he couldn't bring himself to make something up as her father had done so many times, nor did he want to. Lana deserved the truth. The trouble was the note didn't really answer much. Quite the contrary; it created more questions.

"Lana, what exactly do you remember about your mother?"

"Nothing. She died shortly after birthing me."

"Actually, no, she didn't."

Δ

Lana's legs weakened. The implications of what Lance said were piercing, heart-stopping. "Are you saying my father lied to me?"

"Not necessarily. What did he tell you?"

"That she only lived one day after childbirth. Is that what it says? That she knew she was going to die?"

"No. First, I believe this was written by your mother. But it seems to imply you were almost a toddler when you were taken from her."

"*Taken* from her?"

Lance nodded.

Lana felt like she'd been gut-punched by a prize fighter. Her knees gave out, and she sat hard on a chair. How could her father have kept that from her? Lana idolized her dad. The more she'd learned about how much he'd protected her from bad guys, the more she'd revered him. But she also had a building anger toward him for all the secrets. To keep such information from her as a child was understandable. But she'd been an adult for years before he passed away—before he was murdered. He should have mentioned . . . something! Anything!

"Please, Lance. What does it say? Word for word."

He softly cleared his throat.

"*Svetlana,*

You took your first steps today, so they will soon take you from me. I do not know what will become of you, but I want to believe it is for the good of the motherland. You are bound for greatness, my daughter. Know that I love you more than life itself."

The bittersweet words ripped Lana's heart in two. She felt the deep love of her mother, but now a whole new set of questions assaulted her. "Anything else?" she asked.

"No. I'm afraid that's it." He handed back the note. "But it does answer one thing: there's no doubt your real name is Svetlana."

"Just like Petrov said," she whispered, then huffed. "So far, he's the only one who's told the full truth about me."

Lance nodded solemnly, then peered out between the curtains. He was silent for a long time. His slumped posture revealed a troubled spirit. His frustrations seemed to match hers. At least they had that in common.

Lana fixated on the note, hearing the translation again and again in her mind, each time absorbing a different emotion from it. Her mother had loved her. That was the most important thing, wasn't it? But Mom hadn't seemed overly concerned that Lana—Svetlana—was going to be *taken* from her. If she loved Lana *more than life itself*, then how could she let someone take her? Who were *they*, and where had they taken her? And what did *bound for greatness* mean? *For the good of the motherland?* What in the world did that mean?

Tears covered her palms before she even knew she was crying. She heard Lance return to the table and sit. She looked up to see him staring at her with intense compassion.

"No more games," he said. "I'll tell you what I know. It's highly classified and has to stay between us, but I trust it will. And I can't promise you're going to like it."

CHAPTER 20

Lana watched Lance tap his index finger on the tabletop and felt his hesitation.

"First, do you want me to call you Lana or Svetlana?" he said.

"I don't know who Svetlana is," she said, then scoffed. "I'm not even sure who Lana is anymore. But that's the name I grew up with, so Lana."

"Okay. Let me start by saying I'm still not sure how much your father knew about the Red Cicada project. But I *am* convinced any mistruth your father told you was for your protection. The less you knew, the safer you'd be. But now we've crossed a bridge where I believe the opposite is true."

She nodded but found it strange that she was both excited and frightened at what Lance was about to share.

"Here's what I've unearthed over the past few years—"

"Wait. You've been investigating me for *years*?"

"Your father. You'll understand why in a minute. Deacon Baker was initially trained as a marine corps medic. In 1989, immediately after the fall of the Berlin Wall, he was given the rank of E-8 first sergeant and was transferred to a special-ops unit tasked with finding evidence of nuclear weapons development—mostly uranium and plutonium deposits. He was part of that team for about a year, going from one city to the next throughout former Communist bloc countries. At one point, sometime in the summer of 1990, they followed a lead to Kol'tsovo, Russia, in a rugged area just north of the Kazakhstan–Russia border."

"Near the Ural Mountains?"

Lance nodded. "There's a pretty thorough report from your dad's team regarding the Kol'tsovo investigation. They found evidence of gamma radioactive decay in a factory that made microwave ovens. They believed it was the weapons developers' attempt to hide their work since there's measurable radio frequency radiation in microwaves. While the team searched for hard evidence there, your dad and his partner, Aaron Goodwell, followed an invoice mentioning a shipment of 'sensitive material' to a science center in Novosibirsk, about twenty-four kilometers west of Kol'tsovo."

"Okay, but I still don't understand what any of this has to do with me," Lana grumbled.

"I'm getting to that. Your dad and Sgt. Goodwell filed a report saying they inspected a hospital research facility in an area called Akademgorodok. *That's* where they unearthed a project called Red Cicada."

Lana's hand involuntarily flew to her mouth. Several facts immediately fell into place. So many implications assailed her that she had to put her elbows on the table and cradle her head in her hands to keep from falling over. *Red Cicada* was printed in Russian on the disk in her skull. The note from her mother was handwritten in Russian, probably from that very research facility. So did that also mean her mom was . . . a spy? A secret agent? No. That couldn't be. Dad had said Mom was born in Greensboro, North Carolina. Lana herself was born in Atlanta, Georgia. And yet if her mom's note had anything to do with Red Cicada, then Lana had to have been near that science center.

They will soon take you from me. You are bound for greatness.

But who was to say that note wasn't written by someone else? For some other Svetlana?

Lana shook her head. Bile crept up her throat, and she choked it down. Her dad said the note was from *her* mother—not from some random woman. He said it had been written *to* Lana—well, Svetlana. And the note had been hidden in Dad's personal papers.

Deacon Baker. Dad. The bedrock of her life. The only person she'd trusted unreservedly, without question, had lied to her about . . . about everything! The more Lance explained, the more Lana recognized the delusions she'd been living under—a lifelong fallacy created and perpetuated by her father.

She didn't want to hear anymore, but there were too many loose ends to leave untethered. She needed to know what her dad had found. And what it had to do with her.

Lance gently touched her shoulder. "Are you okay, Lana?"

His voice was filled with concern. She appreciated that. But she didn't need pampering right now. She needed the truth. "Yes. Please, tell me everything."

He nodded and picked up where he'd left off. "After the Akademgorodok report, the records go fuzzy. When the Soviet Union collapsed, many government documents were shredded and burned. But, being an enormous country with countless government entities and more secret projects than you can shake a stick at, not all records were destroyed. Like I said, Sgts. Baker and Goodwell found a reference to the Red Cicada project at Akademgorodok hospital. But when they looked into it, they didn't find anything related to nuclear weapons or plutonium enrichment, so it's doubtful Red Cicada had anything to do with nuclear proliferation. However, Goodwell's report *did* mention evidence of pseudoscience experiments in viral manipulation."

"What were they? The experiments, I mean."

He turned up his palms. "I don't know. That's where the nuclear trail went cold. They weren't tasked to delve into other projects."

"And that's all their report said?"

"Just about. The stuff about the hospital and viral manipulation was briefly mentioned, as an addendum. I tried to find out whether any other agency followed up on the hospital, but I came up blank. The curious thing is that right after Goodwell and your father got back, Deacon opted out of the service. He requested immediate retirement due to personal medical issues. Since his tour was near completion and his service record was spotless, his paperwork sailed through, and less than a week later, he was out and basically disappeared."

"What do you mean he disappeared?"

Lance shrugged. "After he was debriefed, he turned in his gear and left without telling anyone where he was going. Didn't even say goodbye to his team members, which didn't go over very well. Ops teams are pretty tight. No one just up and leaves after barely a year of service unless they're carried out in a body bag."

Lana was silent for a long while. "How do you know all this?"

"My job is to clean up cold-case files from the former Soviet republic. About five years ago, one of my leads kept referring to a project called Red Cicada. But it was highly classified, and most of the records were destroyed when Communism fell. No one seems to know anything about it. But whatever it was, my leads included trigger words like *pandemic virulence* and *global impact*."

"Seriously?"

Lance nodded. "Hence my interest. In one communiqué, the names Red Cicada and Deacon Baker were linked."

Lana blinked hard.

"Here's where you come in. Initially, his name led me to the special-ops mission I just told you about. But, as I said, when he retired, his trail went cold—until four days ago. One of the web traps I put out tripped when your name was entered into a medical database in Colorado."

"But there must be hundreds of women in the US named Lana Baker."

"True, but only one with a disk in her skull with the words Red Cicada printed in Russian. When the emergency doctor sent out a web search looking for any facility that'd seen a similar patient presentation, my snares were sprung."

Lana stared blankly at the tabletop, as if she could find answers in the faux-wood pattern. "These reports of my dad's. There was no mention of head implants or what they do?"

"None. Yours is the only implant I know of."

She drew a stuttering breath and slowly released it. "So what does all this mean?"

"I believe the answer is inside the disk."

"No, I mean what does it mean for me?" She looked up at him, stinging tears falling without restraint.

"I'm not certain, other than you're still in danger."

"I know that." Her voice dropped to a frightened whisper. "But why is the disk in *my* head?"

"I don't know."

Lance was right; Mom's note delivered more questions than answers. Lana lined up what she'd just learned. "I think my mom knew about the experiment, about Red Cicada. And it looks like she was Russian. And that she had me sometime before my dad went on tour there. Which means that—" She stopped short and gawked at Lance. She had to force the next words from her mouth. "Was Deacon Baker my dad?"

"I believe he was," Lance said without hesitation. "He raised you, he cared for you, taught you, supported you, protected you. He loved you, Lana." In a very uncharacteristic move, Lance reached over and took her hand in both of his. "Any man can be a father, but it takes someone special to be a dad. I believe Deacon Baker was your dad in every sense of the word . . . except biologically."

CHAPTER 21

Lana grappled with her emotions, trying to rein them in to a point where she could handle them one at a time. The trouble was each emotion had so many side chains that a one-at-a-time approach wasn't doable. This whole experience was like being in a giant spider's web. The more she struggled, the more entangled her situation became. The end-all spider's bite was Lance saying Deacon Baker was not her biological father.

"How can we find out for sure?" she asked with an unmasked tremor.

"We look at every scrap of information we have and don't disregard any lead until we've exhausted all options. Nothing held back."

She nodded and resolutely wiped away her tears. "What do you need?"

"I'd like to start by looking in that security lockbox." He gestured at the container.

She paused only briefly. "Help yourself."

Sitting on the bed, Lance carefully sorted through the documents and knickknacks. While he did, Lana absently twisted the Rubik's Cube, trying to align the different faces. She recognized the marine corps crest with its bald eagle perched atop the earth, both images superimposed over a large roped anchor. *Semper Fidelis* spelled out the US Marine Corps motto.

Lana's heart swelled with pride in her father when she saw that emblem. But why did the man she thought was her father claim that title? Lance said he was her dad in every way but biologically. Deacon Baker had loved her unequivocally. In the end, he'd given his life to protect her. Wasn't *that* the important thing? Wasn't *that* truly being a dad?

She watched Lance make orderly piles of the paperwork he pulled from the box. Lana appreciated his tenacity, but she still dreaded the truths he might uncover. In many ways, having lived a life with no history left her blissfully unshackled to a past—be it good or bad.

"Let me know if you find any adoption papers," she said.

"Will do. But I doubt there'll be any. That was one of the many things I looked for when I made the connection between you and your father. Since there was no child's birth record connected to Deacon, the obvious assumption was adoption—which always carries with it a mountain of paperwork. But there isn't any record."

"Can you think of any reason why not?"

"Only three. You either had one and it was deleted from the database, or you never had one."

"Do either of those happen very often?" she jumped in.

"The first one? Not so much. We have pretty good records in the US. There are several websites with free genealogical records, including births and deaths. The second reason? Unfortunately, it happens more than you'd think. A shocking number of births are never reported because the birth mother abandons the newborn and it dies before it can get help. Most of those are listed as Baby John Doe or Baby Jane Doe."

Lana knew that was true. She cringed thinking of the times she'd heard about a deceased newborn found in a dumpster or a public bathroom. "That's horrible."

"That anyone could to do that to their own child is incomprehensible."

Lana frowned, all her instincts telling her the lieutenant was wrong. "Hang on. I have a copy of my birth certificate back in my apartment. It's notarized and everything," she argued passionately. "It says I was born in Atlanta, Georgia, on August 29, 1981. Seven pounds, seven ounces, twenty-one inches."

"Deacon probably forged it. I've already scoured all of Georgia's birth records for 1980 to 1990, just in case they got the year wrong. You're not there."

"Why would Dad do that—forge my birth certificate?"

"To get you into schools and get you a Social Security number, a driver's license, other stuff."

"Okay, so where *was* I born?"

"I don't know. The first real record we have of you starts in Greenville, Kentucky, when you were vaccinated."

Her eyebrows shot up. "I dreamed about that last night. How old was I then?"

"Nine. I believe if we can find your true birth certificate, it'll go a long way to solving this mystery." He held up the handwritten note, as if presenting evidence. "Then there's the third option. You were born in another country and brought here under the radar."

Lana froze, staring at the scrap of paper. *Impossible.* "How are we going to determine *that*?" she asked incredulously.

"Just keep following clues." He eyed the Rubik's Cube in her hand. "Let me see that."

She tossed it to him.

"Do you know what these images are?"

"No. I've never figured it out," Lana confessed. "There's the marine corps stuff, but none of the other images make sense to me."

"Some look like old photos." With a few deft twists, Lance aligned the marine corps side, but the other sides remained jumbled. After about five minutes of struggle, he stopped. "Lana," he said in a shocked tone. "Why would your father put photos on these other sides?"

"I don't know. It was his toy. I mean, he let me play with it occasionally, but he never really *gave* it to me."

"And you never asked?"

She thought hard. "Not really. I once asked him to teach me how to solve it. He said that one day I'd figure it all out."

The focused look in Lance's eyes grew so intense that it frightened her.

Speaking slowly, he echoed, "'One day you'd figure it *all* out.'" He made a couple more twists to the cube. "Lana. What if your dad wasn't simply referring to unscrambling this toy? What if he meant you'd figure *everything* out because of the toy? What if these aren't just random pictures? What if they're clues to who you are? A puzzle that unlocks your life?"

"That's a lot of what-ifs." Lana moved from the table to the bed and gawked at the Rubik's Cube. "Keep going."

Twisting the cube, he solved most of one side, but the squares were not perfectly aligned, and the remaining five sides were still jumbled. "I can probably get these sides one at a time, but the individual cubes may not line up correctly . . ." His words drifted off as he continued to unscramble random sections with only partial success. Then, suddenly, he stopped, as if coming to a realization.

"What is it?" she asked.

He showed her the cube face he'd nearly solved. Staring back at her from the cube was a face that had materialized from four aligned sections.

"Who is that?" Lana asked.

"Aaron Goodwell."

"Aaron Goodwell?" Lana said. "Dad's old partner?"

"The same."

"They must have been best buds for Dad to put his picture on the cube. Were they partners on other investigations?"

"A few."

"So does that mean something?" she asked, tipping her head toward the Rubik's Cube. "Or is it just a snapshot of an old friend?"

"If it was nothing more than a service memory, why put it on this puzzle?" Lance continued his attempt to align the Goodwell side of the cube. He made a few more turns and grumbled. "Gah! I wish I knew how to solve these things."

Lana glanced at the nightstand clock. 3:58 p.m. "I saw a gas station with a convenience store last night just up the road. At this hour, there're probably a few kids hanging out after school. I bet if we offer one some cash, they'll solve it for us."

Lance stood and surveyed the room. "It's best if we get moving again anyway. Staying in one place for too long isn't safe. Let's get packed and out of here. We'll fill up with gas and see if anyone can help." He held up the McDonald's bag. "You want any of this?"

"Pass."

"Me neither."

In a matter of minutes, they were on the road, heading east. They ignored a number of convenience stores that were too busy for Lance's comfort and finally found one with several bicycles parked out front but only one car. A Subway sandwich shop was part of the convenience center. Inside, four teenaged boys sat in a booth, each with a soda in front of them. They were sharing images on their phones and laughing uproariously.

"I got this," Lana said.

Lance stayed back as she walked up to the teens. She affected an easy smile and a flirty lilt to her voice. "Hiya, boys. How's it going?"

As a group, they immediately placed their phones facedown on the table. Their expressions ranged from guilty to thrilled.

"Howdy," a cocksure blond said.

"We being too loud?" another teen asked.

"No, not at all," she said with a chuckle. "I just need some help, and I'm . . . well, I'm a little embarrassed to ask."

They shared mischievous glances with each other.

"Help with what?" a slender ginger-haired boy asked.

She set the Rubik's Cube on the table. "You all look like smart boys to me. Can any of you solve this for me?"

They simultaneously reached for the cube, but the ginger won the grab. He adjusted his glasses and turned the cube in his hands, examining the individual blocks. "Did you make this?"

"A friend did," she said. Dropping her voice, she added, "It was sort of a challenge, so don't tell anyone I got help. If you do it quickly, I'll buy you all another round of sodas."

"And a sandwich?" the blond asked in a bargaining tone.

"Sure." Lana winked at him.

The blond slapped his palm on the table. "Jacob. Go."

In a flurry of twists and rotations, the bespectacled boy aligned all six faces in just over two minutes. He set it down and adjusted his glasses again. "I'm usually faster," he said, somewhat frustrated. "I'm just not familiar with these images, ya know? Not knowing what they're supposed to make makes it a little harder."

Lana examined the cube. "Wow. You did great."

"Thanks."

"Sandwiches are on me." She handed each boy a ten-dollar bill. "And for the smart one . . ." She leaned in quickly and gave the ginger a kiss on the cheek. The other three boys hooted loudly and offered their fists for him to knuckle-bump. Red-faced, he smacked the fists and flashed Lana a blush-filled smile.

As she walked away, she heard one of them say, "Man, she was hot!"

Another—the blond, she thought—said, "Did you check out her eyes?"

Another teased, "Dude, Jacob finally got kissed."

Lana couldn't help but smile at their banter.

Back in Lance's Cherokee, she looked closely at each picture while Lance drove. The marine corps emblem and motto had a bright-red background, but there were no other images on that face. The next side had a somewhat grainy picture of Aaron Goodwell, back then a young man with a military haircut. Digital photography hadn't been very refined when the shot was snapped. The sergeant stood in front of Novosibirsk Hospital, according to a posted sign, and pointed back at the building, smiling like a tourist. The next picture was a little clearer, and Lana recognized it immediately. Lake Julia, Rhinelander, Wisconsin. It had been taken from the west shore, probably from the same small pier she and her dad used to visit. When her eyes began to burn, she quickly turned the cube. The next side was divided into four quadrants, each one containing a section of a road map superimposed with three uppercase letters: TSE, BBU, LIS, and ATL. Lana had no idea what the letters meant, and the map images under the letters were too grainy for her to recognize landmarks or city names. The next side looked like a magnified image of a bacterium or virus. Lana had seen similar pictures in biology textbooks. The last side was a photograph of a random UPS Store in a strip mall. Location unknown.

"You get anything from all that?" Lance asked from the driver's seat.

"Not really. I recognize some of the pictures, but . . ."

She studied each side again, trying to make sense of the images.

Lance glanced at the cube, then back to the highway. "I think it's more than just a random photo album. Your dad was a genius at figuring things out, at solving puzzles. That's why he was chosen for investigative assignments with special ops. It stands to reason if he was good at solving puzzles, he was also good at making them. Are you sure none of the sides stirs a memory?"

Lana shook her head. "Just the marine corps emblem and this snapshot of Lake Julia in Wisconsin. Like I said, he let me play with this a couple of times, but he never said anything about it, and I never asked."

"Let me see that microscope image."

She handed him the cube. He looked at the picture for a moment, then handed it back. "That's some species of virus. Not sure which. The halo caused by the antigens surrounding it looks like a corona-type virus. Maybe a SARS variant."

When she favored him with a blank look, he said, "Microbiology degree. Remember?"

They traveled in silence for a while. The more Lana studied the cube, the more frustrated she became. She was smart. She should be able to figure such things out.

"Are you getting hungry?" Lance asked.

"I could eat," she replied, noticing the time was nearing seven p.m.

"Ogallala is an hour or so ahead. We'll stop for a bite, and I'll take a closer look at the cube. Hopefully, it'll tell us about the disk and what it contains."

Just then Lana noticed the windows were up and the radio was nothing more than background music. She whispered, "Aren't you afraid of others listening in?"

"Not anymore. We're bug-free. That's what I was doing this morning. I went to a self-serve car wash. When I sprayed the car down, I checked all the wheel wells, inside the engine compartment, any place a transmitter could be installed. I also did an extra-thorough job of going through the interior, pretending to be vacuuming but really checking every crevice for microphones. I'm pretty confident it's clean."

"Well, that's the first bit of good news I've heard in a while. Got any more?" she asked hopefully.

He smiled. "Yes, ma'am. I know where to find the next set of clues."

She stared hard at him. "And how, pray tell, do you know that?"

He reached over and turned the cube so that the picture of the strip-mall UPS Store was faceup.

"How in the world is this a clue? There are thousands of these stores across the country."

"True. But I'm guessing there're only a couple that have the St. Louis arch in the background."

It was only then that Lana saw the top portion of the famous landmark cresting over the top of the strip mall. Gateway Arch. She marveled at Lance's attention to detail.

"Aren't you the astute one," she commented appreciatively.

"Wait. Was that a compliment?" he teased.

"Sure, why not?" she shot back. "We're not being bugged, so if anyone ever asks, I can vehemently deny ever making such a generous remark."

CHAPTER 22

Lance paid cash for a twin queen room at a Travelodge in Ogallala. Over a meal of Chinese takeout, he examined the Rubik's Cube, making notes on a motel scratch pad and referencing his laptop computer. Some clues were obvious; others were not.

"Why do you suppose he'd include a picture of Lake Julia?" he asked.

"I don't know," Lana said softly. Lance could see the emotional strain it took for her to look at the picture. Her eyes glistened and her breaths shortened.

"I don't think there're any hidden clues in the photo." Holding the cube closer, he continued. "But there's got to be some subliminal significance to the shot."

Lana nodded and wiped at her eyes. "I think you're right. It was there that we felt safest. We stayed there almost three years. Dad may have included it to let me know there's hope. That all will be okay, just like it was in Rhinelander." She paused, then looked up quickly. "That was where he gave me this pendant. He basically told me it would help give me direction and comfort in stressful times."

"So your pendant may have more to it than just an endearment," Lance said, nodding. "Anything else?"

She shrugged.

"Okay, then. Let's move on. I've been looking over these maps and letters. I believe TSE, BBU, LIS, and ATL are airport designators." He turned his laptop so she could see and typed *TSE*. The main Google hit was a ticker symbol on the New York Stock Exchange for a plastics company. Other hits included the Toronto Stock Exchange and a reference to a creepy infection called transmissible spongiform encephalopathy—the malady that caused mad cow disease. "It's none of those," he said as he scrolled to the next page and selected a specific feed.

"TSE is the International Air Transport Association code for Tselinograd."

"Why is that airport significant?" she asked.

He took a sip of soda before continuing. "Bear with me. It's now the Astana International Airport, but they kept the old designator. The important fact is that it's the primary international airport serving Astana, the capital city of Kazakhstan."

"Okay . . ."

"BBU is the international code for Bucharest Băneasa Aurel Vlaicu International Airport in Romania; LIS is the international airport in Lisbon, Portugal; and ATL is Atlanta International Airport in Georgia."

"Those locations mean nothing to me."

"They didn't for me either at first. But I've been thinking a lot about this." Lance pulled up a map of Europe. "If you tie the airports together, from Atlanta to Lisbon to Bucharest to Astana, you'll see a definite trajectory. It's not a straight line, of course, but it does head in the right direction."

"Direction to where?"

"Novosibirsk Hospital, Akademgorodok, Russia."

She frowned. "Where Dad and Aaron Goodwell went."

"Exactly."

"But . . . why?"

Lance showed her the notepad he'd been scribbling on. "I'm not a hundred percent sure, but I think it's a clue about you."

"What clue?"

"Where you were born, Lana. Who you really are. Follow me on this. You say you were born in Atlanta. But, as I said, there aren't any state birth records with your name or your parents' names. As such, I believe you were born outside the US."

He pulled the handwritten Cyrillic note from his pocket and set it on the table. "If this note *is* from your mother—and I believe it is—then, in all likelihood, you were born somewhere in Russia or close to it—perhaps even Akademgorodok."

She scoffed, but it sounded dry and empty, without conviction.

"Think about it. Why else would Deacon put these pictures on this toy? Why would he suggest a line from Novosibirsk to Atlanta? I believe your father *told you* that you were born in Atlanta because that's where he brought you *into* the country. Your proxy birthplace, as it were."

Lana looked white as a sheet. Her eyes were fixated on the note on the table. Her hands trembled and fidgeted. In little more than a murmur, she said, "So I'm not American?"

"As far as anyone—including me—is concerned, yes, you are. You have a birth certificate, a Social Security number, a driver's license, and a history in several small towns throughout the Midwest."

"But I wasn't *born* here. I don't know where I'm from."

"Lana, at this point it doesn't matter where you're from, okay? You are an American citizen because no one else even knows about this stuff."

Her color returned so fast her face flushed crimson. She slapped the table, making him flinch. "Petrov knows. He knew my name was Svetlana even before you did. He also said he knows what's on the disk in my head. He said it contains information. I wonder what else he knows about my past."

"When I was checking the Jeep for bugs, I contacted my department and suggested they interrogate Petrov about the Red Cicada project. So far, he claims he knows nothing. Typical, but they're still working on him."

Lana's shoulders slumped. Lance's heart went out to her. Her tone revealed how deeply these revelations cut. In a matter of hours, she'd learned not only that her past was fiction but also that her parents weren't who she thought they were and that, in all likelihood, she'd been born in Communist Russia. How would he feel if *he* were in her shoes?

He took both of her hands in his and gave them a firm squeeze. "Lana, I promise you this: we will find the answers to all this."

"How?" she snapped. "Everyone I speak to tells me lies. You, Petrov, even my own fath—" Emotions choked off the word. She swallowed hard. "Who are we going to ask?"

"We don't have to *ask* anyone," he said with calm assurance. He released her hands and picked up the cube. "Deacon gave us a road map. All we need to do is follow it."

CHAPTER 23

It took a few minutes for Lana to mentally align all that Lance had divulged. The information was crippling. She wasn't who she thought she'd been all her life? She'd actually been born in Eastern Europe? The notion was absurd—like something out of a Hollywood movie. But she knew truth was often stranger than fiction. She wasn't ready to fully accept this crazy theory about her past, but could she accept it as a remote possibility? Even Lance had said he wasn't a hundred percent sure about his analysis, and yet it made sense. Mostly.

"I still don't see the connection between my da—between Deacon Baker and myself. Assuming he *isn't* my father."

"There's a definite blank spot in that association. I think he found you in the hospital and somehow arranged for you to come to the United States. He may have even brought you here himself."

"Why do you think that?"

"For starters, he didn't come home via military transport. Flight manifests prove it. Secondly, look at the airports. They're all large, international hubs. Thousands of people go through them every day. Back in the 1990s it wouldn't be hard for a man with proper military credentials to bring his own child back to the US. Children didn't need a passport as long as their parents had one. Remember that security was much more lax back then—9/11 changed all that."

"Why wouldn't he use military transport?"

"Exactly my point. It's a free ticket home, so why not take advantage of it? I believe it's because he couldn't do so with a previously undocumented child in tow. Bringing a child into the United States without proper credentialing is international kidnapping. It carries with it severe penalties, including court martial from the service and jail time. Deacon was special ops; his assignment was specifically to search for evidence relating to nuclear proliferation. It had nothing to do with child trafficking or medical experimentation."

"Medical experimentation? Is that what the disk is? Some jacked-up experiment?"

"Again, I'm not certain."

"Did my dad know about it?"

"Well, you said he told you never to get an X-ray, right? That's a good sign he knew about the disk."

Lana nodded. It made total sense. "So the question remains: why would he smuggle me into the United States?"

"I don't know."

She gasped in disbelief. "Was he working with the Russians?"

Lance gave a definitive headshake. "No. Not with his service record. Not with what he did to keep you away from them."

"Then, why?"

"Perhaps . . . he fell in love with you. Or with your mom. Who's to say? There's no proof he even met your mother, but what your dream revealed makes me think he might have."

"Is there any way to find out?"

He turned the Rubik's Cube slowly, examining each side again. "Follow the clues."

Lana nodded, but her mind was still awhirl. "I . . . I need a while to process all this before we go willy-nilly on some haphazard treasure hunt."

He gave a crooked smile—one filled with equal amounts of amusement and mock offense. "Ms. Baker, I never do anything willy-nilly or haphazardly."

"Never." She huffed. "Unless it involves kidnapping a key witness."

"Protecting, Lana. Protecting. Not kidnapping." His warm smile was genuine, and Lana couldn't help but believe him.

"Look," he said, standing. "We should both get a good night's sleep. Tomorrow's going to be another long day of travel. I'm going to have a quick rinse and brush my teeth while you take some time to process everything. If you think of any other clues, write them down, no matter how far-fetched they seem."

He moved to shut down his laptop, but Lana stayed his hand. "Wait. Can I use this to do some searching? I've got some ideas I want to chase."

He considered her with wary eyes. "I don't think that's a good idea. I can use a VPN to hide our location, but there's no telling how sophisticated the bad guys' tech is. And if you search for information that matches anything dealing with Red Cicada, you could clue them in to our whereabouts."

"Please? I'll be careful. I can't just sit here and do nothing. This will help keep my mind focused on stuff other than not knowing who I am."

Lance remained silent, but Lana could tell he was debating the pros and cons.

She said, "Look, memories are contextual. Most require some sort of trigger to come up. You know, like someone's anecdote sparking one of your own. Maybe I'll find another clue."

After a moment, Lance nodded. "Do not identify yourself on any site. Keep your searches brief and as random and nonspecific as possible. Don't search for *Red Cicada* or *Svetlana Baker*."

"I won't. I promise."

When Lance stepped into the bathroom, Lana looked up all the cities listed on the Rubik's Cube. She started with Lisbon. Nothing about the city or country sparked a memory. Neither did Bucharest nor Astana.

Atlanta was different. The images on the screen were mostly just pictures of the city—landmarks and such. She scrolled to another page of images, and one jumped out to her. A winter scene along a stretch of four-lane highway. The trees were frocked with a dusting of new snow.

Lana closed her eyes. A brief snippet came to mind.

Traffic suddenly slowed to a crawl. The tires made a strange hissing sound on the icy freeway. A car up ahead had slid into a shallow ditch and was now pointing in the wrong direction.

"You're going to need to know how to drive on snow and ice," Dad said as they passed the stranded vehicle.

"Dad, I'm fifteen."

"You've got your learner's permit. You won't always have good weather."

"I know."

"The key is anticipation. No sudden movements. That guy back there probably changed lanes too quickly or hit the brakes too hard. Anticipate having to slow down well before you actually do."

"I will."

Dad was a great guy—he was always teaching her one thing or another—but she was a young woman now. He needed to chill and let her figure things out.

They traveled a few more miles, passing road signs that indicated exits for various Olympic venues as well as the Atlanta International Airport.

"Is the airport far from Olympic Park?" Lana asked.

"Centennial Park. About twenty minutes away. Why?"

"I imagine a lot of people came through here over the summer."

"Tens of thousands, I'm certain."

"Traffic must have been crazy between the airport and there."

"It has been every time I've been through." He chuckled. "But it was probably worse then, no doubt."

"When did you go through Atlanta airport?"

"A few times in the service. You have too."

That surprised her. "Really? When?"

Dad glanced at her, then quickly glanced away. His jaw clenched as if in frustration. "A long time ago. You were too young to remember."

She smirked at him. "How young?"

"It's not important."

She recognized Dad's body language: a certain tenseness in his shoulders, a deepened crease between his eyebrows, a subtle agitation in his breathing. She used to call it his brood mood. She guessed that still fit. It was always best to let him just work through it on his own. If he said it wasn't important, then she should just forget about it.

The memory was gone as quickly as it'd come. Lana's mind buzzed as she lined up facts from Lance's comments and her memories. Her birth certificate said she'd *been* born in Atlanta in 1981. She was almost thirty years old, which matched an '81 birth date. Dad had said she'd been *through* the airport but was too young to remember. If she had been a toddler, then that meant she was actually closer to thirty-three or thirty-four. She tried not to care. Age was just a number, wasn't it? But even those few added years caused her shoulders to slump.

She then wondered if the airport would have a record of her and her dad passing through. Probably not. ATL was a major international hub. Even if she'd gone through as a five-year-old, it was doubtful their security cams would have captured a clear image of her and her dad . . . if they even still had the recordings. Deacon Baker, undoubtedly dressed in civilian clothes and accompanied by a child, would simply have been another dad in the crowd.

The mental fatigue brought on by new realizations, coupled with the physical fatigue from four solid days of trauma, instantly coalesced into an incapacitating force. The brief sleep Lana'd had last night was lifesaving but not long-lived.

She backed out of her search and closed the laptop. She wanted to brush her teeth and wash her face, but her energy level was suddenly empty. Instead, she took a swig from a water bottle on her bed stand, turned off the light, and curled up, facing away from the bathroom. She was too tired to even dream.

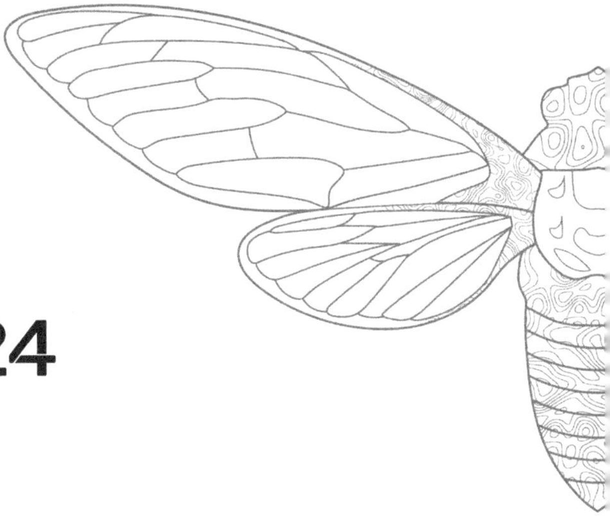

CHAPTER 24

Light spilled across the darkened room as Lance left the bathroom. He saw Lana curled on her bed, her back slowly rising and falling, indicating a deep sleep. He moved his laptop from beside her to the desk. The search history revealed searches for the airports he'd mentioned. Nothing else. Good.

He gently removed Lana's shoes and pulled a cover over her sleeping form. After a few moments, he realized he was still staring at her, thinking about how impressed he was with her resilience . . . and how pretty she was.

Lance shook the thoughts from his head and crawled into his own bed.

Δ

Lana woke to the sound of water running in the bathroom. Cloudless daylight blazed behind the room curtains. The clock read 7:05 a.m.

She sat up and knuckled the sleep from her eyes.

Lance stepped from the bathroom wearing jeans and a T-shirt that fit very well. He smiled at her as he wiped residual shaving cream from his face. It took a moment for Lana to realize her eyes were lingering a bit too long on his athletic build. When he walked past her, she detected a clean, soapy scent, along with the faint hint of cloves that she remembered from their meeting in the hospital. In the back of her mind, she heard Camry's voice: *Good! Glory! He smelled good enough to gobble up.*

Camry! In all the turmoil, Lana had completely forgotten about her friend. The excitable busybody must be going crazy not knowing what was happening. Camry had undoubtedly left a thousand messages on Lana's cell phone—which she no longer had. Had her friend gone so far as to file a missing person report? Was Lana now on some Amber Alert list? Camry would insist on it. The police *must* be looking for her. Unless . . . unless the police had assumed Lt. Lance Kipling had taken her into protective custody at some army facility, and had subsequently closed the file. So what had the hospital done with her phone and other personal belongings? In fact, what was happening with her apartment, her car, her job . . . everything? If anyone would know, it'd be Camry.

"We really should get moving," Lance said, sitting on his bed to put on his sneakers.

"Okay. Just give me five minutes to freshen up," she said, rolling out of bed.

"Fine. I need to brush my teeth first, and then the bathroom is yours."

"Perfect."

As Lance went back into the bathroom, Lana moved to the desk and opened his laptop. The VPN didn't autolink, so Lana opted to use the free hotel Wi-Fi. It'd be a fast message to her work account, so she figured it'd be safe.

She typed,

> *Cams. I am well. Please don't worry. Look after my stuff. Talk when I can.*

She paused, her fingers hovering over the keyboard. Should she type her name? No. Camry would know who it was. She pressed send and logged off.

When Lance stepped out of the bathroom, he asked, "Did you find anything in your internet searches?"

"I think so. I looked at the different cities from the cube and remembered my dad telling me I had been *through* Atlanta International, not just born in the city."

Lance looked up. "When?"

"He didn't say exactly, but the conversation took place December of 1996."

He blinked. "Wow, that's specific."

"It was the year of the Centennial Park bombing at the Atlanta Summer Olympics. I was fifteen. We were heading back home from SeaWorld in Orlando. We talked about the heavy traffic, and he said I had been to the airport. I asked him when, and all he said was 'A long time ago.'"

"Well, that confirms that you entered the US in Atlanta. Being a young child at the time is why you don't remember."

"My thoughts too. But here's the thing—if I was born in 1981, and my dad said I was very young when we went through ATL, which you say was in 1991, that'd make me ten—which I wasn't. So that means I was born sometime *after* 1981, right?"

His brows furrowed. "That makes sense." He smiled slyly. "But that also means you're not twenty-nine. You're probably twenty-five or twenty-six."

Lana couldn't help but smile from ear to ear. "That is the best news I've had since this ordeal began."

"Every cloud has a silver lining."

Lana quickly freshened up and then began packing her few belongings. "What do you think we'll find at the UPS Store in St. Louis?"

"Not sure."

"If it's something in a lockbox, would it still be there? I mean, when did he leave it? How long has it been there? I don't recall ever visiting St. Louis."

"He could have hidden something on one of his business trips. Those outlet stores have mailboxes and such you can lease. Perhaps he rented one."

"Could be. How will we know which mailbox it is?"

"I'm still working on that," Lance admitted, finishing his own packing. "Let's get moving. It's a good ten- to eleven-hour drive to St. Louis."

"I can take a turn driving if it helps."

"I might take you up on that," he said with a thankful grin.

Lana really wanted to do more to help. Lance was sacrificing so much for her. She sensed it was more than professional responsibility. She hoped the tone of his demeanor, the determination in his stance, the heartfelt concern in his eyes, were signs that he truly cared and that it wasn't simply about the case. He no longer seemed focused simply on national security; his emphasis was on helping her find out about her past, on helping her discover who Lana Baker really was. His attention to *her* needs touched her.

As he stepped toward the door, Lana grabbed his arm and turned him to face her. "Thank you, Lance," she said with a catch in her voice.

He nodded. "You're welcome. I appreciate your cooperation in this too."

"I know. But I also know you're crossing way outside your ethical boundaries." She tiptoed and gave him a quick kiss on the cheek. "It means a lot to me."

He stepped back and smiled warmly. "It's my pleasure, Lana."

Δ

The scarred Russian's phone emitted a soft ping. He swiped the screen. *"Da?"*

The male voice on the other side was gravelly and curt. "Petrov is still in custody."

"Petrov is a fool. He is soft."

"Yes, this is truth. Will he talk?"

"Nyet. His weakness is pretty women. But he hates America."

"This is good, Tarus. Is your location secure?"

"For now. There is yet much police activity, but I can operate."

"Svetlana. Can she identify you?"

"Da, is possible. She saw my punishment," Tarus said, referring to the severe scarring on half of his face. Years ago, he was involved in a revolutionary assault in Afghanistan in which, due to his carelessness, an incendiary device had prematurely detonated. Volatile jelly had sprayed across the left side of his face and torso and burst into flame. Reconstructive surgery could do only so much—especially when performed by black-market doctors. The subsequent infection had been even worse. Tissue scarring of such magnitude would always look hideous. In a perverse way, Tarus took pride in his appearance. It was punishment for his carelessness, but it also showed the depth of his commitment to the motherland. An emblem of courage, sacrifice, and commitment. And although his hypertrophic scars provoked instant mistrust in most people, he'd learned how to milk compassion out of those repulsed by his punishment.

"And the American lieutenant, Kipling?" the gritty voice asked.

"I do not know. He may have also seen my punishment."

"This is most unfortunate."

"Not so, comrade. I have never been captured," Tarus argued. "I have no record for comparison."

"See that it remains this way."

"Of course."

A pause emptied the line. Then, "Very well. We have a location on Svetlana. She sent email from a Travelodge hotel in Ogallala, Nebraska. Do you know this location?"

The scarred Russian was already on his computer. He Googled the city. "Yes. Is far but easy to reach."

"Go quickly. The target is probably moving. Do not fail again."

"Petrov got in the way—"

"I did not ask for excuse," the man interrupted.

Tarus clenched his jaw. "Yes, comrade. I will succeed."

"We need the disk. Red Cicada is overdue. But we can still create chaos, yes?"

"There are other ways," he said, then immediately regretted it.

"Do not tell me how to command!"

"Yes, comrade. Red Cicada will succeed. I will see to it."

"This is good. Svetlana is still with the lieutenant. It would be best to eliminate them both before retrieving the disk. You were sloppy last time. Do not repeat your error."

Tarus scowled fiercely. He felt the burnt tissue on his face making his expression grossly lopsided and gargoyle-like. "I will die before I fail."

CHAPTER 25

When Lance refueled his Cherokee in Ogallala, Lana assumed the driver's seat before he had a chance to climb behind the wheel. He figured she needed to focus on something other than the way her world had flipped upside down, so he didn't mind.

Four hours later, as they neared Lincoln, Nebraska, she said, "I have a question."

"Shoot," Lance said from the passenger seat.

"I've been going over every memory I have of my father, and I'm positive that at no time did he ever mention Red Cicada or its Russian translation."

"Krasnaya Tsikada."

"Whatever. My question—well, one of my questions—is did he know about it?"

Lance considered the query. "It's doubtful he knew before his assignment in Akademgorodok. And if he learned about it while inspecting Novosibirsk Hospital, he never mentioned it later on."

"But Goodwell did."

"Yes. He's the one who included the addendum in the report."

"What did it say?"

"It's classified informa—"

"Lance!"

He chuckled. "I was going to say it's classified information, so don't breathe a word of it to anyone."

She scowled at him.

He smiled and brushed a few errant strands of hair from her face, then gave her shoulder a gentle squeeze. It was a very tender gesture, and he wasn't altogether sure why he did it—other than it felt like a natural thing to do.

His smile broadened when he saw how the action caused Lana's scowl to vanish and her neck and face to glow. But he knew it'd be short-lived. What he was about to reveal would be sobering, heart-wrenching.

He continued. "Goodwell's addendum strongly suggested that human rights were being violated—especially those of children. He asked that an investigation be done on the research center. He said they found evidence of human experimentation on a microbial level. They documented BSL-4 clean rooms, genome splicers, numerous incubators, and an entire wing housing children from toddlers to late teens. The hospital staff said the kids were being quarantined because of smallpox, which made sense because those remote areas often don't have access to vaccines. Goodwell took pictures of several body bags labeled with biohazard stickers."

Lana frowned, not in anger but in sadness. "Did they die from smallpox?"

"He didn't specify that in the report."

"Did the morgue have other bodies besides . . ." She paused to steady her emotions. "Besides children?"

His voice hardened. "These weren't in the morgue. The special wing had its own incinerator."

Lana's eyes began to glisten. "Toddlers?" she whispered.

"Apparently all ages. Makes me sick to think about it."

They drove in silence for a few miles before Lana pulled into a rest area. Tears balancing on her lashes fell as she unbuckled her seat belt.

"You okay?" Lance asked.

"I need a minute," she said, opening her door.

"We can talk while we're still driving, or I can drive," he offered.

"I just need to sort this out." She clambered out of the SUV.

He quickly got out of the Jeep too. "Lana, wait. I really think we—"

"Leave me alone!" she yelled.

He flinched like he'd been slapped, but he persevered. "Hey, sorry. I was just trying to help—"

"You can help by letting me absorb this mountain of garbage you've dumped on me." A huge sob escaped her throat. When he took a step toward her, she waved him off.

"Just . . . just give me some space. Please. I'm sorry for snapping at you, but this is a lot of information that basically means my life is a fraud."

Not giving him a chance to reply, Lana walked quickly to a small visitors' center.

Lance felt terrible for what he'd revealed. But she had asked for full disclosure and he wasn't going to sugarcoat anything. Being forthright with each other was the only way they'd discover the truth. He knew the information he sought was on the disk, but the information she needed would be found only by following the clues left by Deacon Baker. If her father's Rubik's Cube clues led to a dead end, then Lance would be forced to make arrangements to retrieve the disk as soon as possible. The scarred Russian Tarus was clearly still after Lana. Lance knew how such agents operated. Tarus would redouble his efforts. And he would grow more ruthless.

CHAPTER 26

Tarus waited in his Lexus until the Ogallala Travelodge lobby was devoid of patrons, then entered with his gun hidden under his dark sport coat. The matronly receptionist looked up and gasped.

"Oh. I'm so terribly, terribly sorry," the woman gushed, holding her hand to her chest. "I shouldn't have reacted that way."

"I am used to this effect," Tarus said.

"Even so, I apologize. My name is Sarah. What can I do for you, sir?"

He pulled out a photo of Svetlana. "I am foreign attaché with CIA. I am looking for this woman. Have you seen her?"

Studiously avoiding his face, Sarah looked over the picture. "No, I'm afraid I don't recognize her."

"She was here this morning. She may have booked up last night."

"Booked up?"

"How you say . . . check in?"

"What's her name?"

"Svet—ah, Lana Baker."

"Baker. Well, let me see . . ." The woman tapped away at a keyboard and frowned. "No, sir. I don't have any record of a Lana Baker staying with us."

"An alias, perhaps?"

"I can't say. My shift started at six this morning. The night attendant went home hours ago, but he'll be back at ten this evening if you'd like to come back."

"I have not time. I need to see record of all check-in yesterday."

The woman hesitated. "I'm afraid I can't release that information, sir."

"You must."

The receptionist folded her arms. "I must?"

Tarus frowned deeply. "I am with CIA, you stupid woman. You must obey my command." He longed for the glory days of the USSR, when all he had to do was say he was KGB and people did anything he asked.

The woman met his scowl with a steely glare. "I am not stupid, sir. And I don't have to 'obey your command.' This is Nebraska, buddy. Where in the Sam Hill do you think you are?"

Tarus bit back a retort that probably would have come out in Russian anyway. He knew Svetlana had come to this motel with an army lieutenant named Kipling. What he really needed to know was whether they were still here. He quickly formulated another approach.

"I apologize, madam. My English is little good. I do not mean 'command.' What is proper word? Ask? Request? Require? Please. This is very important. Is international security matter."

Sarah's glare softened a bit, but she remained stone-faced.

"As you see in photo, she has beautiful blue eyes. Easy to remember, yes? She was possible with a man about her age." He used a brochure on the desk to cover the scarred half of his face. "A good-looking man, much like myself . . . on this side."

The woman's face instantly showed remorse and pity. "I'm sorry, hon. I got out of line. I just hate bullheaded men, is all. Used to be married to the most worthless piece of male flesh to ever walk this earth. Thought he was God's gift to women. Spawn of Satan, more like. Just gets my goat when men think they can push women around." She waved off her tirade and smiled at Tarus. "You're here on official business, so let's see what we can do for you. Do you have identification, please?"

"You are very kind," Tarus said, removing from his wallet a fake ID indicating he was a foreign agent with CIA-level clearance, just like he'd said. He had a collection of such IDs. "Please. What is name again?"

The receptionist pointed at her name badge. "Sarah."

Tarus drew a soft gasp. "This is Serafima in Russian," he lied. "It is beautiful name. It means princess. Is my daughter's name."

A soft glow colored Sarah's cheeks. She used her mouse to scroll through some information on her computer. "Do you know the name of the man Ms. Baker was with?"

"Kipling."

"First name?"

"He has many aliases. I do not know the one he currently uses."

"Could it be Lance?" she asked with raised eyebrows.

"Is possible."

"Then, I'm afraid you're too late, sir. They checked out more than four hours ago."

He cursed softly in Russian, his frustration rising quickly. "Do you know which way they travel?"

"I'm afraid not. People travel in and out of here all the time. It's not my business to see which way they go when they leave."

Tarus was tired of being nice. It wasn't in his nature. The more time he wasted here, the farther away Svetlana got. "Do you have camera on car park?"

"The parking lot? Well, yes, but I can't help you there, hon. I don't have permission to access them. You'd need my manager for that."

"Then, get him."

"He's not here at the moment. But I can leave a message if you'd like to come back."

In a flash, Tarus reached over the short counter and grabbed Sarah's hair. He yanked her forward while simultaneously pulling the gun from behind his back. She let out a scream but was silenced when he thrust the barrel into her mouth.

"Quiet, you stupid woman," he growled. "I need to see which way the lieutenant and the woman drive. Where is video equipment?"

With the gun barrel in her mouth, Sarah couldn't speak. She pointed a trembling finger to a small office behind her. Tarus dragged her along the counter until he could round the desktop, then shoved her into the back office. Slamming the door closed, he said, "Show me. Now."

"But I—"

Her words were cut short when he pistol-whipped her across her cheek. She collapsed into a chair with a yelp of pain. Cradling her face, blood seeped between her fingers.

Tarus leaned very close. "I promise I will make your face look like mine if you do not cooperate. Is this what you want?"

"No," she whimpered.

"Then, get video," he said, punctuating each word. "Now."

Sarah brought up the security feed from the previous night and ran it. Around noon, the camera captured a shot of a man and a woman leaving a room and getting into a dark-green Jeep Cherokee. A second camera showed the interstate in the background. The Jeep passed the westbound on-ramp and went under the bridge, out of the shot. It was easy to surmise they'd taken the eastbound on-ramp. The trouble with both cameras was that the images weren't very clear.

"Is that Kipling?" Tarus asked.

"I can't tell. Honest."

"Did they not book out?"

"No. But that's not uncommon. Lots of people prepay with a credit card so they can leave without stopping in. But they came out of the room that was reserved under his name, so it must be him."

"And the woman?"

Still cradling her lacerated cheek, Sarah said, "I honestly don't know. Like I said, the room was assigned before I got here. I never saw either of them in person."

Tarus grunted. "This is no good. Freeze camera on back of vehicle."

Sarah rewound the recording and stopped it as the Cherokee made a turn that revealed the back end. The license plate digits weren't readable, but the plate design was white with a strip along the base that showed a yellow-and-black checkerboard alternately patterned with a red-and-white Maltese cross design.

"You know this plate?" he asked as he threaded a silencer to his gun barrel behind her back.

"I think it's from Maryland. Those colors are on their state flag."

"This is good. Thank you, Serafima."

The shot was a muffled pop that no one outside the room would have heard. Tarus calmly donned some nitrile gloves, then used the computer mouse to access the lobby and parking lot feeds. With a few clicks, he erased the past five hours of recording while Sarah watched with lifeless eyes.

CHAPTER 27

Finding nothing to distract her in the visitors' center, Lana found a shady spot under a large elm tree and sat. She felt deeply vulnerable and alone. She shouldn't have blown up at Lance like she had. The shock of knowing Deacon Baker was not her real father was bad enough, but learning Deacon had discovered solid proof of experimentation on children tipped the scales on the craziness of the past few days. Her dad had always treated her with utmost respect. Growing up, she'd assumed all parents treated their kids the same way. But the older she got, the more she'd discovered that was not the case. Some parents were neglectful; some were downright cruel. Her own mother had allowed her to be taken away "for the good of the motherland." Now she had to reconcile the knowledge that innocent children had been used as guinea pigs. She needed time to step back—to sort and digest. She longed for peace and understanding.

Her mind rehearsed what the cashier in Laramie had said: Lana was the kind of woman who made her own luck. But every time she discovered something new about her past, that luck turned out to be anything but good. She berated herself for even starting this insane quest. Even the note from her mother—the only communication she'd ever received from the woman—had brought more sorrow than joy.

She clasped her rhodonite pendant with both hands and sought to bring back the cathartic memories of Lake Julia.

You have a sharp mind, and I know you have questions. There're a few things I need to tell you. You see, life comes down to a matter of trust.

Lana loved her dad with all her heart, but how could she trust anything he'd said now that she knew he'd fabricated her entire past? And what about

Lance? He'd shared a mountain of classified information with her, but how did she know he wasn't lying too? Where was the proof?

She shook her head but continued to clasp the pendant tightly. Dad's words wrapped around her like a thick blanket fresh from the dryer.

They say rhodonite lays bare emotional wounds and scars of the past, for healing, restoration, and reinvigoration. . . . They also say rhodonite empowers the holder to reach their full potential and can bring its owner back to center during stressful times. It's used for calming emotional shock and panic and provides grounding when dealing with painful issues.

Is that what you use it for?

As a matter of fact, I do, sweetheart.

She inhaled a deep cleansing breath and let it out slowly. Lana had taken a geology class in college. She'd learned the rosy gemstone was actually pink manganese inosilicate webbed throughout with black manganese oxide. It had no conclusive magical properties, and yet her pendant always brought a measurable feeling of calm when she clutched it. *A placebo effect?* she wondered. *Does it matter?*

"How're you doing, Lana?" Lance asked from a few feet away.

"I'll be all right."

"Does your chest hurt?"

She realized she was pressing her pendant firmly to her breastbone. "No. Just getting some grounding so I can get through this."

He glanced at his watch. "We still have about six and a half hours to go. If we push it, we could get to St. Louis around ten."

He held out his hand to help her stand. She looked up into his rich brown eyes. She knew the only way to truly trust him was to jump in with both feet. She needed to believe he wanted to help her, not just the project. She took his hand, stood, and didn't let go. Walking back to the Jeep, he didn't try to pull away, which made her happy.

After a few minutes on the freeway, Lana turned to Lance. "Why are you doing this?"

"The investigation?"

"It went way beyond a military investigation long ago," Lana said evenly.

His smile was a mix of resolution and compassion. "When I figured out Deacon Baker is probably not your real father, it um . . . it struck a chord."

"What chord?"

"I'm adopted. My mom raised me as a foster child before adopting me. I don't know who my father is either."

Lana ached with remorse for having yelled at Lance. He had to pursue all leads, and that included uncovering her past. She couldn't fault him for that. She softly cleared her throat. "I apologize for snapping at you back there."

"It's okay. I get it."

"I know you do. But I lashed out at you for something *I* asked for. That wasn't fair."

He gave her that soft smile that weakened her legs. "I can't blame you. I'm not sure I'd handle it as well as you have."

"Thank you." She leaned over and kissed his cheek.

They traveled in silence for a time. Sixty miles south of Lincoln, Nebraska, Lance said, "I have a question for you."

"Okay, shoot."

"How's your head?"

She touched the back of her skull. "You mean the disk? Fine, I guess. The incision seems to be healing okay."

"No, I mean your migraines."

"Well, there's always one lurking in the background, but they usually don't manifest until I think about them, so thanks for that."

Lance's face took on a look of contrition and Lana burst out laughing. "I'm just teasing. My migraines come mostly from stress. There are some triggers, like noise and bright lights, but they don't always come from those. The tension headache I was battling has almost entirely gone thanks to a good night's rest and a couple of hot showers. It's hard to keep stress-free, all things considered, but I'm trying. Why do you ask?"

"Because it dawned on me that no matter what we find in St. Louis, the fact remains that you have a disk in your skull that needs to be removed."

She gave a harsh chortle. "That *just* dawned on you?"

"No, what I mean is if we just get it out, then the bad guys will no longer be after you. You'll be in the clear."

She considered that possibility, then shook her head. "I don't think so. Petrov kept hinting they suspected not only that I know what was on the disk but that my dad shared all sorts of top-secret information with me."

"Oh. So even if the disk is out—"

"They'll still be after me. Who are these guys, anyway?"

Lance's jaw clenched a few times. "I don't know for sure. Honest. But there are numerous agencies that splintered off the KGB around the time of the wall collapse—especially speculative science groups, drug cartels, and black-market arms dealers. I think this is one of those."

"So it's not just a couple of guys wanting a new curio for their twisted collection."

"Not hardly." He chuckled. "I believe these guys want the disk so they can continue project Red Cicada."

"And the number nineteen?"

He cast a glance her way. "That one still has me stumped."

Δ

Just as Lance had calculated, it was a few minutes after ten when they passed though the outskirts of St. Louis. He searched on his phone for UPS Stores in the area near the Gateway Arch. There were three. They found the one pictured on the Rubik's Cube on the second try.

Lance parked on the opposite side of the street, a few yards from the store, and got out into the night air, still warm and humid. Lana quickly followed.

"I think you should wait in the Jeep," he said, scanning the neighborhood around them.

"No way. We've been driving for hours. My butt is numb and my legs are cramped. I need to walk it off." She looked around. "This place isn't chic downtown, but it's not a total ghetto either. Come on. Let's get some exercise."

A half block later, they stopped. Directly across the four-lane street stood the UPS Store. The sign above the door was illuminated, but the interior was sparsely lit. Behind the building, the tops of trees stood in dark silhouette against a backdrop of dazzling city lights. And centered directly above the store's rooftop stood the brightly lit stainless-steel apex of Gateway Arch. The image matched the photo on the cube perfectly.

"This appears to be the right place," Lance said.

"Looks pretty lifeless inside," Lana commented.

"Come on." He took her hand, and they jogged across the street.

A small neon sign next to the shop's entrance displayed the store hours:

Monday–Friday 9–9
Saturday 9–5
Sunday 10–4

"What time is it?" Lana asked.

Lance sighed. "Ten fifty-eight. Looks like we wait until tomorrow to see what your dad wanted to share with you."

They were able to find an express motel with twin queens a few miles up the street. The place wasn't five-star, but it wasn't roach-motel either. Lance was running low on cash. Among the gear stashed under the rear seat, he had an emergency credit card issued by the US government for travel expenses. It hadn't been used in years, but it was still in date, and he didn't think anyone could link it to his name. He hated using it now, but the banks were closed and he doubted the hotel would accept the gas card he used while on assignment. Besides, they were now a long way from Fort Collins. All the focus would still be in that area.

After checking in and getting settled, they sat on their respective beds, eating convenience-store burritos while watching a Midwest news channel. After headline stories and the weather, a reporter came on with a story for which the police were seeking help. A fatal shooting had occurred at a Travelodge in Ogallala, Nebraska, roughly six hours earlier.

Lance stopped chewing.

Lana did too. "Isn't that where—"

"Shh," Lance said, turning up the volume.

Stone-faced, the reporter announced, "Investigators say the fatal shooting took place around eleven o'clock this morning. Ballistics have recovered a nine-millimeter slug and are attempting to match it with police records. Security-camera footage of the lobby and parking area had been shut off and approximately six hours of footage prior to the event erased. Police are searching for anyone who has information regarding this incident."

"Do you think it's . . . ?" Lana asked in a dry voice.

Lance looked at her grimly. "Tarus."

CHAPTER 28

Lance and Lana had breakfast at a mom-and-pop restaurant next to their motel. Both ordered light meals and large coffees. Neither had slept well.

Lance kept glancing at his wristwatch and frowning. How close was Tarus? Would Lance be able to get the information he needed before he and Lana were found?

"You know, time's not going to go any faster by scowling at your watch," Lana quipped. "At least we're no longer driving through endless fields of corn."

He forced a quick smile and poked at his breakfast food. "I'm impressed you seem so unconcerned about what we'll find in the UPS place."

"Of course I'm concerned. But the your-life-is-a-total-lie bomb has already gone off. Whatever we find now can't make it any worse." She took a sip from her cup and stared out the window. "My dad was everything to me, Lance. He was my entire world. It sliced my heart open when he died, and it was just beginning to heal when all this started happening. Then, when Petrov said his team were the ones who killed him, the slice reopened, only deeper. Now, knowing he wasn't even my father, that he spent his life raising me in a fallacy . . ."

Lance reached across the table and placed his hand on hers, but she pulled away.

"You can't imagine the sense of betrayal I'm experiencing."

"You're right. I don't think I can."

"So until it's over, I'm blocking it out. Call it denial, I suppose, but I don't think I can take any more hurt. Maybe we'll find something new about my past at the UPS Store. Maybe it'll be about this stupid Red Cicada project. Maybe whatever Dad left isn't even there anymore. Frankly, I just want it to be over."

Lance could certainly understand her feelings. Solving these mysteries could help heal her broken heart, or it could rip it completely in two. He needed to work harder to keep a positive attitude—if only for her sake.

"Let's take a walk," he said, tipping his head to indicate the outdoors.

"Are you done eating?" she asked.

"No appetite, I'm afraid."

"Me neither."

When they exited the restaurant, Lance retrieved their ball caps from his vehicle, then took her hand and guided her down the street.

"Why aren't we going to drive?"

"Not a good idea." When she flashed him a questioning look, he continued. "Think about it. The news reporter said the security-camera recording had been erased. I bet that was done after Tarus got a good look at it. There's a high probability we were recorded driving away in the Cherokee."

"Oh. Man, you *are* good at this spy stuff."

"If I were good at it, I'd have figured it out by now and they'd be none the wiser."

A young clerk had just unlocked the door of the UPS Store when Lance and Lana walked up. The clerk held it open for them and offered a good morning.

"Thanks," they said at the same time.

"What can I do for you?" she asked when they were all inside.

Lance deferred to Lana.

"My name is Lana Baker. My father may have rented a lockbox of some kind here a number of years ago. I need to see inside it. I know it's a long shot, but how long do you keep them reserved?"

"If your dad paid in advance, as long as we're open. You can rent for a three-year block and then re-up it every three years. But box rentals have been really slow lately. No one needs them anymore because of the internet and next-day home delivery. Snail mail is almost obsolete." The clerk rounded her desk and tapped a few computer keys. "Can I call your father to verify you're allowed to access his security box?"

Lana softly cleared her throat. "He passed away eleven months ago."

The clerk put her hand to her mouth. "Oh, I am so sorry."

"Thank you. His name was Deacon Baker. I'm his only child."

"Oh man, that's rough. My dad left my mom two years ago. Left us with nothing but three months of delinquent rent payments and a stack of credit-card bills, so he can crash and burn for all I care. But if your dad was cool, then, man, him dying really blows. Deacon Baker, did you say? Let me see," she said as she pecked at the keyboard. "Oh, this might be it. You say your name's Lana?"

"Yes."

"Well, your name is one of the ones listed on those authorized to access the security box. Do you have some ID?"

When Lana's face blanched slightly, Lance stepped forward and removed his cap, giving what he hoped was a disarming smile. "Miss, I am Lt. Lance Kipling." He set his military ID on the countertop. "I'm with special investigations, and Deacon Baker is my top case. Ms. Baker here is, by default, under my province due to her father's death."

The young clerk hesitated, looking between the ID and his face.

Lance leaned his palms on the counter and said in a heartfelt tone, "We'd appreciate any help you could give us. It's really important for Lana to reconnect with her father. She never had a chance to say goodbye."

"Um . . . yeah, okay, I guess. Did he tell you what locker number he rented?"

"I don't believe he ever mentioned that," Lance said, scratching his ear to steal a glance at Lana.

Lana gave a hint of a shrug.

The clerk's eyes narrowed as she looked from Lance to Lana and back again. "Um, I really don't think I can unless you—"

"Nineteen," Lana blurted.

Lance immediately made the connection to Red Cicada 19 and smiled. "Yeah, that's right. I remember now. Box nineteen."

"Perfect. Be right back." The clerk stepped into a bank of secured lockers and used a master key to open number nineteen. She pulled a thin metal document box from the locker and set it on the counter. It was made of sturdy-gauge aluminum and had no markings or external hinges. The key slot was nothing more than a small hexagonal hole. Lance had hoped for a combination lock they could figure out. This box clearly needed a custom-made key to open it.

Lana reached for the box, but the clerk pulled it back.

"Wait. I'm still not sure I can let you take it without positive ID. According to the rental contract, Mr. Baker indicated that some form of positive proof was necessary to release this thing."

"My authority isn't good enough?" Lance said forcefully.

"It is for me but not for the company."

A silent, uncomfortable stalemate ensued. Lana examined the lock instead of engaging in the debate.

"Come on, guys, give me a break," the clerk finally said. "I could lose my job."

"I think I have some proof," Lana said, reaching behind her neck to unclasp her necklace. She aligned the rhodonite pendant to the keyhole. The hexagonal cut of the stone perfectly fit into the slot. She slowly inserted it until there was a metallic click, and the lid popped open.

"Is that proof enough?" Lana asked.

Lance was impressed and slightly irritated he hadn't connected the similarity between Lana's pendant and the shape of the keyhole.

"Yep. Good enough for me," the clerk said.

"Thank you so much," Lana said, sounding truly grateful as she closed the box.

The girl gave a warm smile. "So does this mean you're closing the account?"

"How much time remains on the lease?" Lance asked.

"It was renewed February of last year for three years, so . . . nineteen months. But the company charges a twenty percent cancellation fee, which is subtracted from your refund."

"Let it run out," Lance said, slipping his arm around Lana's shoulders and directing her toward the door. "Thank you for your help."

With the box in hand, Lana took two steps, then stopped and turned. "Hang on. You said my name was *one* of the ones on the authorized-access list," she said to the clerk. "What are the other names?"

"There're just three," the young woman said, reading off the screen. "Yours, your dad's, and some guy named Aaron Goodwell."

CHAPTER 29

THEY WALKED BACK TO THE Cherokee in silence. Lance desperately wanted to see what was inside the aluminum container, but he also wanted to allow Lana to progress at her own speed. It didn't take long. When they climbed into his SUV, Lana took a breath, inserted her pendant, and popped the lid open again. Inside sat an 8" x 14" manila envelope labeled **US Military Correspondence. TOP SECRET 1.4(e)**.

"What's the 1.4(e) mean?" she asked.

"It refers to highly sensitive scientific or technological information relating to national security, including terrorism."

She took a reflective moment. "I was hoping it'd be stuff about my background. Now I'm kind of afraid to open it."

"You want me to?"

She handed him the envelope. He unclasped it and pulled out two half-inch-thick reports, each secured with three brass brads. Both cover pages read

FINDINGS AT AKADEMGORODOK SCIENCE CENTER
NOVOSIBIRSK, RUSSIA
Submitted: 25 February 1991
Sgts. Aaron Goodwell and Deacon Baker,
301st Special Investigations unit, USMC

"Can you see any difference between them?" Lana asked.

"No, but one of them seems slightly thicker. This looks like the report I read when I first started investigating Red Cicada," Lance said, tapping both with his hands. "Their conclusions basically affirmed that no evidence of nuclear-arms development was found at the research center. There's a brief addendum that recommends experts in human-rights crimes investigate the same complex, but that's all."

"So why're there two reports in the envelope?"

"That's what I'm going to find out," he said, getting out of the driver's seat and stepping around to the passenger side. "You drive; I'll read."

Lana got behind the wheel and pushed the button to start the vehicle. "Where to?"

"Follow this road to Riverfront Drive. That should lead you to the junction to I-55 northbound."

"Destination?"

"We'll connect with I-39 north; then it's on to Bishop's Bay, Wisconsin."

She gave a slight frown. "Wisconsin? Why?"

"That's where Aaron Goodwell lives, last time I checked. I'll go through these reports, but I have a feeling I won't find much new material. If he's there, maybe he can fill in some blanks."

"I thought you already interviewed him back then."

"I did, but he was a closed book. Wouldn't budge when I asked about your dad or what they found."

"So . . . another road trip," she said without enthusiasm.

Lance couldn't blame her for being bored with all the travel. It was the part of his job he liked the least. But he'd found long ago that visiting a lead in person allowed him to pick up on clues that he would totally miss researching from a distance.

"I know it's another six hours in the car, but it's Sunday and traffic should be light. Here's the thing," he said, again patting the reports. "My last contact with Aaron was about a year and a half ago. He'd used his veteran's pension to finish his last year of college, then went to med school. Made it all the way through with high marks too. He practices somewhere in the Tri-Lakes area. I'll Google him in a minute."

"And?"

"And I want to ask him about Deacon again. Like I said, when I first contacted him, he said he didn't know where he was and that I would be hard-pressed to find him. When I asked what he meant, he said Deacon had gone into a self-made witness protection program. When I asked about *that*, he said 'no further comment.' I tried using my military status to force an answer, but he said he's a civilian now and wasn't about to incriminate himself or his friend."

"Incriminate himself how?"

"He wouldn't say."

Lana shook her head and pulled the SUV into traffic. She found the connection to I-55 and merged onto the freeway. Within minutes they were in Illinois, heading through rolling green countryside, but Lance was too busy reading to care.

When he finished going through both reports, he closed the pages and stared out the windshield, disbelief and deep concern heating his face.

"Are you okay?" Lana asked, trying to keep her eyes on the road.

"Just trying to put it all together."

"Are the reports that different?"

"Yes. Well, they say a lot of the same stuff, but this one is more complete," he said, patting one of the reports. He opened the glove box to retrieve a pen, with which he printed *Red Cicada* in the corner. "It documents a lot more of the stuff going on in the hospital. The other one is the copy on file with the military."

"Why the discrepancy?" she wondered.

"Not sure. But if I had to guess, someone was able to get to the original report and edit it to only *briefly* mention Red Cicada information. That's the one submitted to the investigations board—the 'official' report. But this one," he said, thumping the Red Cicada copy, "contains a lot of stuff completely chopped from the official report."

Lana frowned. "Why? I mean, who would do that?"

"Could be any number of upper-level administration personnel. Apparently, they didn't want anyone to know about what went on in that facility. Or it could be that your dad or Aaron Goodwell submitted the short version but your dad kept the honest version as evidence."

Lana gripped the steering wheel until her knuckles turned white. "Okay. So tell me what the longer version says."

"The Soviet scientists in Akademgorodok were experimenting with genetic modification of viruses and . . ." He paused and looked down at the report.

"And?"

"And they were testing their creations on children."

Lance evaluated Lana objectively, hoping she could handle what was written in the alternate report. It wasn't that it was graphic, but it'd be so easy to put two and two together and realize she had an intimate association with the document.

"The children my dad found in the morgue?"

"Among others. It really doesn't get very detailed—I assume because biology wasn't Aaron's or Deacon's field of expertise, although they were both medics before they joined special forces. But the gist of it plays pretty badly."

Lana took a deep breath. "Okay. Let's hear it."

He cleared his throat. "This is an extra page at the back of the report:

"Akademgorodok Hospital is part of the research complex in Novosibirsk. We found that not only is it a general-care hospital but it also takes part in drug studies, human drug trials, and genome studies (from hospital public info). When Sgt. Baker and I presented at the hospital, the staff were reluctant to let us in. We were allowed access to the first three levels but were not permitted to visit the basement or the north wing (which was a separate building joined by an aerial walkway). We showed proper documentation from the UN, the WHO, and US and Russian governments, which allows total access to research facilities. They argued that Akademgorodok was a hospital that only assisted in research. Then they claimed the north wing was in quarantine for smallpox infections. We threatened to call their local militsiya for arbitration, at which point they allowed us complete access. Sgt. Baker and I split up to cover more ground. I went to the basement; he went to the north wing. We communicated via walkie-talkies.

"I found a high-tech clean room with lab machines labeled as genome splicers, bacterial and viral incubators, several electron microscopes, and other such lab equipment (see list 1-A).

"I can read through the equipment list if you'd like, but it's pretty exhaustive."

"Is it relevant?" Lana asked.

"Not right now." He cleared his throat again. "Here's where it gets really sketchy:

"Sgt. Baker radioed for me to come to the north wing ASAP. I finished up and met him at the north-wing entrance. He had found ten undraped bodies in refrigerated storage, six of which were children.

(Note: This was not the hospital morgue, which is located on the first floor of the main complex.) The children's ages ranged from an estimated three years old to fifteen years old. There was no documentation on the bodies. The only identifier was a toe tag, each labeled with title Red Cicada and digits 02, 03, 05, 07, 11, and 13. The adult bodies found had no such identifiers on them."

"Prime numbers?" Lana asked.

"Exactly," he said with a leading tone.

She nodded and adjusted her grip on the steering wheel. Lance could almost see the battle raging in her mind. She breathed heavily a few times, as if struggling to maintain her composure. After a moment, she nodded again, resolutely. "Okay. So if they were sticking with prime numbers and I'm 19, that has to mean there's got to be a 17, and there may even be a 23 and so on."

"I think that's a definite possibility," Lance agreed.

"So . . . so why did primes 2 through 13 die?"

"Here's what Goodwell says:

"I do not know the meaning of the toe tags, and the hospital staff would not comment other than to say it was a project that had not seen success. No cause of death is listed anywhere. As far as I can tell, all documents on the project have been destroyed. I do not know what to make of my discovery, but I find it questionable and very disturbing. The fact that the only Red Cicada corpses were those of children, along with the similarity of their lack of identification, suggests illegal experimentation. If the same experiments were performed on adults, I saw no record of it, other than the fact that the incinerator in the main hospital had a large number of adult human bones in its ash bin. The presence of equipment used for bacterial and viral replication and the secrecy of the project brings the possibility of biological weapons development. I, therefore, highly recommend a human rights investigation be launched on this facility. Of paramount concern, however, was the number of children found in an adjacent isolation room."

Lance paused to access how Lana was taking it all in. He could tell she was trying to be stoic, but how long would she hold up to the possibility that she'd been part of those horrific experiments?

"Is there any more?"

"He recommended a thorough investigation of the entire facility and references several pictures taken. But there aren't any photos in the envelope. I suspect they've been destroyed. And that's all."

"What do you think about it?"

He reached over and gently squeezed her shoulder. "Honestly, I'm even more frustrated than before. We still have no idea exactly what Red Cicada is. But I have a guess about one thing."

She glanced at him, fear rimming her eyes.

"I don't know why Goodwell intentionally left this addendum out of his official report. But I suspect it has something to do with you."

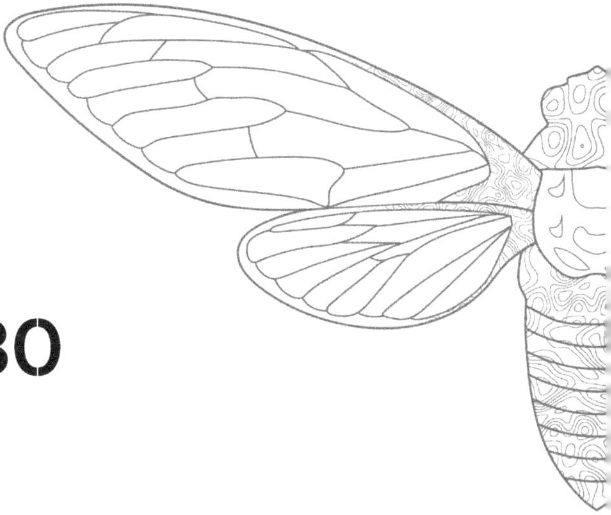

CHAPTER 30

"We have had hit on one of the lieutenant's credit cards."

Tarus was well familiar with the voice on the line. His contact was perpetually gruff and bitter. He'd come from the upper ranks of the KGB and was still outraged at Gorbachev for failing the motherland.

His contact continued. "He purchased a room at motel in St. Louis, Missouri, near Gateway Park. A traffic camera shows his vehicle in the parking lot this morning, but is gone now. We believe they are still in vicinity. You must go there quickly."

"This is good, comrade commander."

"There are many miles ahead. You can intercept?"

"Da. Is not a problem," he said through a yawn.

"When have you last had sleep?"

"I slept two hours in a rest area. Is no matter; it is enough for me. I will succeed."

"It is a matter!" the gruff man screamed. "You are sloppy. You kill a clerk in Nebraska for no reason. Is all over news."

"I was careful. I leave no evidence."

"There is always evidence, Tarus. You know this. Your face is unmistakable."

"My vehicle windows have very dark tint. I can drive without fear of identification." He exited the highway on a connection heading south. "Do you know why they go to St. Louis?"

"Nyet. We must assume is to gather information on Krasnaya Tsikada."

"This is impossible," Tarus argued. "All Krasnaya Tsikada information was destroyed."

"Do not be a fool. This what we assumed for many years. Then we found the man who kidnapped Svetlana. The knowledge he had was sealed by his death. But what Svetlana carries is information we need to seal. You know this! The disk you failed to obtain when she was in your hands is our future."

Tarus's jaw clenched in anger. He'd explained many times the events of that day. If Petrov hadn't been so soft, they would have the disk and would be well on their way to changing the world forever.

"I will not fail, comrade," Tarus growled. "This I promise."

There was dead silence on the cell line, but his superior had not disconnected. Tarus waited impatiently.

"We do not need promises, my friend. We need results."

After disconnecting, Tarus pushed his Lexus well over the speed limit. He had a high-grade radar detector that warned him of speed traps set by local highway patrol, and he kept a vigilant eye both ahead and behind him. His stereo blasted a Russian version of rage metal. The lead vocalist screamed in a hoarse bass voice about oppression and the need to rebel against authority. A large insulated mug filled with iced coffee and laced with vodka and methamphetamine sat in the center console. The perfect mix to keep him alert and energized yet focused enough to keep his mood in check. But the refreshment wasn't working as well as it usually did. American coffee wasn't nearly as strong as the blend he could get from a supplier in Saudi Arabia. When he got back home to New York, he'd order some.

His cell phone buzzed over the music. The caller ID was coded, but he recognized the cipher. He pressed a button on his steering wheel, and the call connected. "Da."

"Turn down that noise!" the caller yelled.

Tarus did.

"What do you even call that garbage?" The caller spoke English with just a hint of a Jersey accent. It was Tarus's annoying contact on the East Coast. Why they recruited the annoying foreigner, he'd never understand.

"Is Russian band Brain Melt."

"You can say that again. Listen, are you good?"

"I am alone," Tarus confirmed.

"Good. So it turns out you don't have to worry about Petrov anymore."

Tarus said nothing. The silence did not last long.

"Yeah, I was pretty excited to hear it about it myself," the caller said with heavy irony. "He was locked in a secured facility and ended up shooting himself in the head."

"He had gun?"

"I know, right? Like everyone in high security has access to a gun. No, you nincompoop. We had a guy on the inside who owed us a favor. He did the job with five inches of narrow conduit pipe, a bullet, and a nail. Not very accurate for distance, but put it against your skull and *bam!* Lobotomy on steroids. He left it in Petrov's hand to make it look like a suicide. They're investigating, no doubt, but they ain't gonna find nothing."

Tarus absorbed the information with a satisfied grin.

A few seconds passed before the caller said, "Hey, don't mention it. You're welcome." Then he disconnected the call.

Good. Tarus hated dealing with that American idiot. It was regrettable that they had to obtain such in-country contacts, but that was part of the game. They had to secure locals in order to play on their turf.

Tarus was very pleased to hear the news, but he was disappointed he wouldn't get the chance to eliminate Petrov himself. It would have been a challenge because of Petrov's imprisonment, but he would have found a way. This time, his superiors were one step ahead of him. Or so they thought.

Tarus had been recruited by a militant shadow division of the former KGB who called themselves Sovetskoye Dvizheniye Vosstanovleniya, the Soviet Recovery Movement.

The SDV had splintered from the KGB in 1988, but because not many people knew of their existence in the first place, not much fanfare was made of the split. That was exactly the way they'd wanted it. The SDV funded themselves by selling black-market drugs and weapons, orchestrating some human trafficking, and continuing defunct Soviet scientific research projects that showed promise of world domination. Anyone who'd known of the schism when it happened and hadn't signed a blood oath to the new faction had mysteriously disappeared. Tarus had seen to some of those cowards himself.

He smiled at the memories.

Now the SDV had ordered Tarus to retrieve the disk, eliminate all evidence and ties, and simply hand it over to them. But he had other plans. When he obtained the disk, he could sell it on the black market for millions—perhaps even billions. Then he could have any house he wanted, any car he wanted, even any woman he wanted. Women around the world always found a man with an eight-figure bank account very attractive regardless of his looks.

"No matter," he said aloud to no one, turning his stereo back on.

He'd have plenty of time to explore those possibilities after he'd killed the American lieutenant and carved the disk out of the back of Svetlana's pretty head.

CHAPTER 31

Tarus parked outside the motel in which the lieutenant's credit card was last used. He waited twenty minutes but saw no sign of the officer's green SUV. He glanced at his watch and feared they may have already moved on. But to where?

Lt. Kipling had done well not using anything that would reveal his location—a personal cell phone, credit cards, emails, and such. The fact that he *had* used his credit card on this discount motel meant he was running low on cash. Either that or he was intentionally luring Tarus into a trap.

The Russian slouched lower in the driver's seat and took in the area around him. He saw no sign of unusual activity. In fact, the streets seemed curiously devoid of people. He huffed. It was Sunday, and he knew many people in the Midwest had religious convictions that monopolized half their weekends. Such foolishness. The Communist way did not need an imaginary being to guide them to perfection. The people were their own gods. The people ruled themselves in perfect unanimity in which all things, all classes, all people were equal. They could achieve a perfect community without the silly superstitions of an all-forgiving god. Marx was right when he said that religion was the people's opium. They were addicted to their delusions. The more pious their devotion, the more addicted they became.

But Americans were also ruled by fear. And so many spent their Sundays cowering inside houses of worship, trying to appease their invented god.

Was the lieutenant such a person? No. He was cunning and scheming. A perfect soldier.

In the past few days, Tarus had developed a considerable respect for Lt. Lance Kipling. He could be a formidable presence, or he could be a ghost, changing his stance in the blink of an eye. He'd proved to be an expert at unearthing clues and was always a step or two ahead of the SDV on Red Cicada information. Tarus could not let Kipling or Svetlana get away again. He was determined to bring both of them down.

From his Lexus, Tarus scanned the motel for security cameras but found none. It was definitely a low-end facility for the United States. In Russia, it'd be a fairly nice place to stay. For most of his life, Tarus had stayed in much worse. But this motel looked to offer the minimum in comforts. He vowed that after he obtained the disk and sold it for a king's ransom, he would never have to stay in such a place again.

Tarus reached into the glove box of his car and removed a pouch that contained a collection of fake licenses and identification. He'd already used his CIA attaché in Nebraska. He was confident he'd left no clue about his identity at that motel, but one could never be too cautious. He traded out his CIA persona for a Belarusian embassy liaison identification.

He slipped on his dark glasses and entered the motel's tiny lobby. A bald man wearing a filthy T-shirt that strained over a beer belly sat behind an open-glass partition. He looked up from a newspaper and frowned. "Geez, buddy. What happened to you?"

"A traffic accident when I was little boy," Tarus said, adopting a nonchalant tone.

"That's too bad," the man said, not really seeming to care. "You need a room?"

"I need information."

The man folded his paper, placed a stubby smoldering cigar in his mouth, and chewed it reflectively. "A room will cost you less."

Tarus knew the kind of man he was dealing with in an instant. Neither seeking compassion nor using brute intimidation would work. This man was street-hardened, much like Tarus himself. He pulled out his wallet and laid a hundred-dollar bill on the countertop, along with Svetlana's photo.

"I am looking for this woman."

The bald man picked up the picture. "Wow, she's a looker, ain't she? She got a name?"

"She was with a tall man with short brown hair. Handsome. Very fit."

"Lucky him. Nah, I ain't seen either of them."

"Are you certain?"

He looked down at the hundred-dollar bill and back at Tarus. "Yeah, I'm certain."

Tarus laid a second hundred next to the first one.

"Oh yeah. Now I remember," the man said, tapping his cigar ash onto the floor. "Tall guy, just like you said. Looked like he just got outa boot camp. Could be a poster boy for the army."

"And the woman?"

The man rubbed his hand over his baldness a couple of times. "Seems to me all I remember is the guy."

Tarus pulled a third hundred from his wallet and held it over the other two.

"Hang on. It's coming to me now," the bald man said, taking another puff. "They didn't show up together, but I seen 'em leave together and get into a Jeep wagon. Cherokee, I think. Dark green. Maryland plates."

"Which way did they travel?"

"He asked the quickest route to I-55 northbound."

When the bald man reached for the bills, Tarus pulled the third one just out of reach.

"When?"

"It was around nine this morning," the man said eagerly. "Traveled light too. Just a small carry-on each."

Tarus set the third bill atop the other two and leaned forward. "You never see me, yes?"

"Nope, never. For all I know," he said, taking the money, "you're the bad result of one six-pack too many for breakfast."

CHAPTER 32

Madison, Wisconsin, was only two hundred or so miles ahead—a little over two hours of driving—but Lana suddenly felt drained of all energy. "Can you drive for a while?" she asked.

"Of course. Go ahead and take the next off-ramp. If there's a convenience store, we'll get caffeined up."

After filling the tank with gas, Lance eased behind the wheel and handed Lana a large soda from the store.

"How are you doing?" he asked.

"I've been better. I think another migraine's coming, but I'm trying to ignore it."

"Does that work?"

"Not usually."

"Here, maybe this will help," he said, handing her the soda. "I couldn't remember if you prefer Coke or Pepsi, so I made a daring choice and mixed half and half."

He flashed her that soft smile that made her feel that everything would soon be right in the world. She accepted the drink. "Thanks. I'm more of a Dr Pepper gal, but you know how I like a daring adventure."

"Sure do."

After a couple of sips, she said, "Lance, what am I going to do?"

"*We* are going to head to Madison and get ahold of Aaron Goodwell."

She looked down at her soft drink. "If he's still in the area."

"Pretty sure he is. I did a Google search from my phone. It shows he has a dermatology practice in Middleton, a suburb of Madison."

"Do you think he'll tell us anything? I mean, anything other than what's in his report?"

He took a sip. "I believe he will."

"And what am I supposed to do with the information once we have it?"

"That's entirely up to you," he said with caring finality in his tone. "But I promise to help in any way I can."

Δ

The area around Madison was urban but still exuded a rural charm. Lots of green, even in the heat of August. Lakes Waubesa and Monona were both teased into a light chop, which was perfect for the myriad sailboats plying their surfaces.

Lance noticed Lana gazing at the bucolic sight with intense longing. She sighed wistfully.

"Anything wrong?" he asked.

"I love sailboats."

"They do bring a feeling of peace. Are you a sailor?"

"Sort of. Dad took me several times in Rhinelander. Lake Julia. I remember it being cold but very fun. It was some of the only times my dad's brood mood was lifted."

"Brood mood?"

She nodded. "It seemed like he always had this weight on his shoulders. Sometimes it got really heavy, and he became withdrawn, even melancholy. Now I know why."

"I see. Did he teach you how to sail?" he asked, wanting to direct the conversation to happier things.

"Yes, but I never got the hang of going into the wind."

"Tacking."

"Yeah," she said, returning her gaze to the lake.

Lance could almost feel the pining in her voice. Her physical and mental stamina were clearly waning. She seemed near wit's end. She needed a distraction, something to take her mind off the nonstop madness of the past days. Yes, it was probably not the wisest venture, but the healing that could come from it was worth the risk. Besides, this was so out of character, even Tarus wouldn't guess what he was up to.

"Well then," he said, making a quick lane change to take the oncoming exit to Lake Monona.

"What are you doing?" she cried, grabbing the armrest for stability.

"There's still plenty of day left for a sail, and you need a serious diversion."

"Lance, wait. We can't do that," she said with a tone that indicated she felt otherwise. "We still have lots of investigating to do. What about the disk? What about Aaron Goodwell?"

"The disk isn't going anywhere without you. And Goodwell's probably on the lake himself." He gave her a resolute look edged with mirth. "Lana. It's Sunday. No way he'd be in his office today anyway."

Her mouth moved as if she were trying to articulate a thought that hadn't quite formed. "Well . . . maybe he's . . . you don't know for sure. Can't you call him?"

"Don't have his current number."

"Surely your secret spy connections can find it."

"Perhaps. But it can wait."

Lana gawked. "Okay, smarty-pants, where are we going to get a boat?"

He pointed to a billboard advertising sailboat rentals at Cap'n Rob's Sail Craft on the east-shore marina.

"We can grab a boat and maybe a couple of windbreakers and snacks and sail away from all our cares."

She scoffed. "Our cares will just be waiting for us when we get back."

"Perhaps. But by then we'll both be refreshed and ready to take them head-on. Trust me on this."

She shifted in her seat to face him directly. "Who are you, and what have you done with Lt. Kipling?"

"I gave him the day off. He needed some serious R & R himself." Lance pulled onto a frontage and headed for the large marina up ahead.

Cap'n Rob's was a quaint little operation that featured nothing with a gas motor. Paddleboards, windsurfing boards, and a fleet of small sailboats. Lance pulled into a parking spot near the shop and turned off the engine. He quickly exited and ran around the Jeep to open Lana's door for her.

"Thank you for your gallantry, kind sir," she teased, stepping out.

They went into the shack and were pleased to find it devoid of customers. A ship's bell announced their entrance with two bright *clangs*. A middle-aged man with wind-bleached blond hair sat behind a bamboo lattice counter, reading a paperback. Lana giggled and quickly brought her hand to her mouth. Lance followed her line of sight and smiled himself. The book was *Moby Dick*.

"Gotta love Melville," Lance said lightly.

"I do?" the man asked without looking up. "Why?"

"Well, I mean he's one of the great American novelists, right?"

"I guess," he said, placing a bookmark in the paperback. "The guy knows sailing, but he doesn't know jack about whales."

Lance didn't know what to say. "Um . . ." was all that came out.

The man stood and tossed the book onto the countertop. Lance was surprised to find he was as tall as—if not a couple of inches taller than—Lance. "Melville wrote a whole chapter on cetology," Cap'n Rob said.

"The study of whales and dolphins," Lana filled in.

The shopkeeper seemed impressed. "Exactly. He went into all sorts of facts and such and then came to the conclusion that they are fish, which any fifth grader can tell you is wrong."

"They're mammals." Lana nodded.

He smiled broadly at her. "The lady with sky-blue eyes knows her sea fauna. Now then, I'm Cap'n Rob. What can I do for you folks?"

"We'd like to rent a sailboat, please," Lance said, taking out his wallet.

"What size? We got eight-, twelve-, and sixteen-foot models. Most are dinghies, but the sixteen-footer is a daysailer. You know the difference?"

"Sure do," Lance said. "I cut my teeth on a Catalina 16.5 daysailer on Delaware Bay."

"Nice craft."

"Wait," Lana said, surprised. "You know how to sail?"

"Of course. I grew up taking lessons. I knew how to sail before I knew how to drive. No respectable Easterner can not know how to sail."

The captain narrowed his eyes. "Sounds like you two need to get to know each other a tad more. No place better than on a sailboat. So what'll it be?"

"I'm thinking either a twelve- or sixteen-foot model will do. Big enough not to get tossed by every little ripple but small enough for one person to manage."

"Good choice. Here," he said, rotating a clipboard with a rental form on it. "Fill this out. I need a photo ID and a form of payment to hold until you're back. I'll get my kid to prep the Hunter 16. You'll like her. She kisses the wind."

CHAPTER 33

Flashing blue and red lights in the rearview mirror caught Tarus's attention. He cursed loudly in Russian and pulled over to the shoulder. An Illinois police cruiser parked at a slight angle behind him. Tarus knew the drill. The less belligerent he acted, the better he was treated. Usually. It all came down to how he used his disfigurement, his punishment.

The officer approached on the right side of the Lexus and stopped just shy of the doorjamb. "Good afternoon, sir. May I see your license and registration, please?"

"Of course," Tarus said, handing his counterfeit driver's license and diplomatic identification card to the young man. The ID read *Valeri Kozlovsky*.

"You're from Belarus, Mr. Kozlovsky?" the officer asked as if delighted.

"Yes. Is country south of Russia."

The officer stepped forward and looked inside the sedan. Tarus turned with as much of a smile as he could form, knowing it created a twisted, disturbing visage. The young man paused ever so slightly, then removed his dark glasses for a better look. He compared what he saw with the photos on the IDs, which being face-forward, showed only a little of Tarus's scarring.

"Is okay, officer. I know I am ugly, even though I have woman's name," he said playfully.

"Thank you, sir," he said, squatting beside the open window and handing back the identification. "So you're with the Belarus government?"

"Yes, is true. Belarus and Russia."

With a curiously eager grin, the officer asked, "Listen, Mr. Kozlovsky, can I ask you something kinda odd?"

Caught off guard, Tarus shrugged.

"I served in the Peace Corps in the Moscow area about sixteen months ago."

"Is noble cause."

The young man looked up and down the highway, then said, "Listen. This is an official traffic stop, so it's okay if you don't want to, but can I practice my Russian with you? It's been a while since I had the chance."

Tarus felt himself frown. He had no idea where this was going, but the young officer did not look like the kind of man to play tricks. Tarus was itching to keep looking for his marks, but if he indulged this fool, maybe he'd get off with just a warning. "Is okay. Da."

"Awesome," the officer said, lightly tapping his fingers on the windowsill. He cleared his throat. "Okay. Do you know why I stopped you, Mr. Kozlovsky?" he asked in Tarus's native tongue.

"I was going too fast?" he replied likewise.

"Yes, that is correct. Twelve miles each hour over the posted limit."

"I apologize. My vehicle instruments are set to metric system. That is what I am used to in my country. I forget to calculate the difference. I am terribly sorry."

"I understand," the officer said, again tapping the sill. "I have some . . . discretion around nine miles each hour, so I can give you a spoken warning. May I ask where you are heading?"

Tarus wasn't sure how to answer without sounding suspicious. He quickly opted for a go-to story for situations like this. "Of course. Your accent is very good, by the way." He smiled in a way that didn't pull too much at his burn wounds. "I am looking for a man and a woman. We were to meet on official business."

"For what purpose, sir?"

"Is there a problem?"

"No, no. I mean, I know you have diplomatic privilege. Purpose wasn't the right word." The young officer struggled, taxing his memory. "I, um . . . I just want to know if I can help."

"This is very generous," Tarus said, "as is your verbal warning offer." The officer seemed very keen to attain an impromptu friendship, so Tarus decided to see how far he could get. "This man and woman used to work in the American embassy in Belarus. They are good friends. The vehicle they drive is a rental with Maryland plates: a dark-green Jeep utility vehicle. Very elegant. They were supposed to meet me at a rest stop in Bloomington, and I was to escort them to my office in Chicago." He chuckled. "You know how difficult Chicago streets are to navigate first time, yes?"

"Absolutely. I get lost every time I go there."

"My friends are almost two hours past time. I fear they may also be lost. Or perhaps in an accident. So I am driving the highway to find them."

The officer tipped his head to the side. "Can't you just call them?"

Tarus sighed in frustration. "I have tried, but they do not answer."

"What are their names?"

"The man is Lance Kipling. The woman is Svet—her name is Lana Baker."

The officer patted the windowsill a third time. "Hang on a moment." He stood and spoke into the two-way mic clipped to his epaulet. "Dispatch, this is Officer Hank Smith."

"Go, Officer Smith," a female voice crackled from the unit.

"Hey, Ginger. I need eyes on Interstate 39 north and south of Bloomington and vicinity. I need to locate a dark-green Jeep SUV with Maryland plates. There are two occupants: one male, one female. You got anything?"

"What is the nature of your request, Hank?" the dispatcher asked.

"It's a nonemergency. I have a Belarusian diplomat searching for a couple who used to work with his embassy overseas. They're late for their rendezvous. They are unfamiliar with the area and do not answer their phones, so he's anxious they're lost or hurt."

"Ten-four. Searching traffic cams."

Tarus understood most of what was said. He couldn't believe his gamble had paid off this well.

"Hank, I got a dark-green Jeep Cherokee with Maryland plates northbound, approximately one mile from the Wisconsin border on US 90. Do you want me to send intercept?"

"Is anyone close?"

"Timmons is twelve miles out."

Officer Smith leaned down. "They think they've found your friends. Do you want us to ask them to wait? I can try to contact Wisconsin highway patrol if you'd like, but unless it's an emergency or an active pursuit, I don't know if they can help."

Tarus thought for a second. If the police stopped them, Kipling and Svetlana would claim not to know anyone from Belarus, which would blow his cover. Kipling would know who was searching for him, which would ruin the element of surprise.

"No, thank you, my friend," he said in his kindest Russian. At least this fool of an officer had given him the basic location of his quarry. "I don't want to take any more of your time. I will contact my friends in the Wisconsin embassy for assistance. You have been very helpful. And your Russian is very good. Well done."

Smith nodded. "That's a negative, Ginger," he said into his mic. "Thanks anyway. Smith out." Then to Tarus he said, "It was a pleasure meeting you, Mr. Kozlovsky. Oh, and please try to keep it closer to the posted speed limit, okay?"

"Thank you, Officer Smith. I will."

CHAPTER 34

A GENTLE WIND BLEW STEADILY across Lake Monona, rippling the surface of the water and keeping the ambient temperature and humidity at an agreeable level. Lana reveled in how cathartic it felt. Lance had spent a small fortune on sailing gear: windbreakers, sunglasses, sunscreen, even boat shoes so their sneakers wouldn't get wet. The merchandise had far exceeded his cash reserves, so he'd put the rental deposit and purchases on his old credit card. Lana felt guilty for the huge expense, knowing he was doing this for her and without expectation of reimbursement. It seemed such a waste. Sure, it might be fun, but it wasn't necessary. Dad had always cautioned her about the gray area between wants and needs when it came to money. This little side trip was nothing short of extravagance.

The Hunter 16 was a beautiful midsize craft and was well kept for a rental. It had a broad mainsail amidships and a nice jib over the bow. It was big enough for four people but was still manageable with two. Lana felt they could have gotten by with a smaller boat—one that was less expensive—but that was Lance's decision.

Using an electric trolling motor, they glided slowly out of the small harbor's no-wake zone. Lance then raised the sails and got comfortable at the tiller. The wind was perfect, and Lance handled the craft like it was second nature. The steady breeze came from the northeast, which allowed them to run west for a while before they had to start their tack. He instructed Lana on handling the trim on the jib, which she found quite an easy job, but she suspected he could have handled both sails himself.

"Captain Rob was right; this thing kisses the wind," Lance said, his voice strong against the frequent gusts. "You ready to learn how to handle her?"

"I guess so," she said, still feeling that the whole idea was a waste of time but enjoyable nonetheless. "But I told you I don't know how to tack into the wind."

"That's totally fine," he said with a cheery smile. "Here, come sit next to me."

She did.

"Okay. Here're the basics. When you need to sail into the wind, you want to angle the boat so that the wind flows across the sail instead of filling it. It's kind of like how an airplane wing works. Air flowing over the sail creates lift, but because the sail is vertical instead of horizontal, the lift pulls the boat forward instead of upward."

"That's what my dad said." Lana smiled broadly at the memory. "I didn't get it then either."

"No worries. I'll show you what to look for to keep her in the sweet spot. Rule number one: don't spit into the wind." He winked at her.

"Gee, thanks, Captain Comedy."

"Rule number two: when you make a turn, watch out for the boom. If you're not sailing solo, call out your tack by saying, 'Coming about' so others aren't knocked overboard."

"What if you *want* that to happen?"

He smirked. "Rule number three: once you make your turn, trim your sail in tight to keep generating lift. If you point too much into the wind, the sail will begin to flutter. If it starts flapping like a bedsheet hanging out to dry, you've lost lift and the boat will stop. This is never a good thing unless you're tacking at the moment, in which case you want to turn through it as fast as possible to keep your momentum. A good tack is usually a ninety-degree arc. It's all in how you time your boom swing with your tiller turn."

Lana started laughing. Lance was so cute thinking he made perfect sense. She understood the mechanics of the maneuver. She even grasped the physics behind it. Her dad had drilled that into her. But as a child, she could never get the hang of it, and describing it in excruciating detail didn't help.

"Why are you laughing?" he said with a confused pout.

"I'm sorry, Lance, but it's like *telling* someone how to ride a bike," Lana said, still chuckling. "You just have to *do it* before you get it."

"You're absolutely right. Let's switch places, and you take the tiller."

She laughed some more. "Did I just hear a dominant alpha male admit that a *woman* was right?"

He rolled his eyes. "Yes, you did. Now, scoot over here and sail this thing."

"No, really, Lance. I'm fine just sitting here."

"No, you're not. You need this."

Before she could argue, he angled from his seat and pivoted under the boom, then bodily slid her to the tiller.

"Okay, okay." She continued to chuckle. "Aye, aye, Captain."

It took a few stall-outs, a couple of 360-degree turns, a few times of almost capsizing, and a number of curse words, but within an hour, Lana was able to steer the craft anywhere she wanted while still maintaining a good forward momentum. The nonstop demand of attention to roll and yaw were taxing but strangely rewarding. A tug on the mainsail, a nudge of the tiller, and the sixteen-foot craft cut through the water with comforting *swoosh* and *hiss* sounds.

Lana smiled to the point that her cheeks hurt, realizing that for the past two hours, she hadn't thought once about her past life, the disk in her head, or Russian spies. Even her impending migraine had vanished. She knew the troubles were still awaiting them on shore, but at that moment, she was free of all cares and nothing else mattered but holding to the sweet spot that heeled the sailboat at just the right angle to glide through the water like a dolphin.

She looked at Lance sitting toward the bow. He no longer kept his eyes on the trim of the sail or the posture of the boat. Instead, he cast his gaze about, taking in the other boats, the gorgeous shoreline, the waterfowl skimming just above the surface, and anything else that caught his attention. He was clearly in his element.

Lana sighed a deep cleansing breath. Lance had been so right about this. It was exactly what she'd needed. It was invigorating, liberating, even healing. For the first time in a long time, she felt happy. She felt at peace. And she owed it all to Lance Kipling.

CHAPTER 35

The sun was touching the horizon when Lance motored back into the harbor and docked at Cap'n Rob's in the east-shore marina. Lana's cheeks were crimson, her hair was wind-tossed despite the efforts of her scrunchie, and her countenance fairly beamed. Gone were the dark circles under her eyes and the weary pull on her face. She looked rejuvenated.

Lance smiled. He was very glad the side trip had had such a positive effect. He, too, felt more enlivened than he had in days. Cap'n Rob stood at the dock and helped secure the Hunter 16 to the mooring.

"How'd she handle?" he asked, helping Lana onto the pier.

"Like a dream," she said.

"She's a sweet boat in the right hands. I was watching you navigate your approach to the harbor inlet," he said, tapping the maritime binoculars dangling from his neck. "You're a natural, young lady."

She scoffed. "I'm neither a natural nor young, but I appreciate the compliment. I had a great teacher."

Lance leapt onto the platform. "I've seen people struggle for weeks to master the helm. Captain Rob's right. You *are* a natural."

Lance loved the deeper blush that came to her cheeks.

They watched as the proprietor quickly checked over the craft with a practiced routine. "All shipshape," he said, heading toward his office.

Inside, Cap'n Rob hung up their life vests and grabbed the clipboard holding their rental contract. "Okay, folks. So you signed up for by-the-hour charges and were out just a smidge over six hours."

Lana looked shocked. "Was it really that long?"

Lance shrugged. "Time flies . . ."

"Our half-day rental is five hours and the full day is ten," Cap'n Rob said. "You're just over the five, but the boat is in perfect condition and the young lady had a great time, so I'll just charge you for the half day."

"Much appreciated," Lance said, handing the man his credit card.

"Yes, thank you very much," Lana said.

Lance signed the electronic pad and accepted his receipt. They shook hands with the captain and headed for the Jeep. The evening had cooled significantly, and Lana hugged herself in an effort to stay warm. Lance was very familiar with how endurance-sapping being out on the water could be. He eased his arm around Lana and pulled her close as they walked. She nestled into him and briefly rested her head on his shoulder.

When he opened the passenger door for her, he was caught off guard when she wrapped her arms around him and gave him a lingering hug.

"Thank you," she said into his chest. "I needed that."

He warmly returned the embrace. "It was my pleasure. And we both needed it."

Lance didn't want to do anything inappropriate but found he couldn't resist kissing the top of her head. She hugged him tighter when he did. They stayed that way for too short a time, but he knew they should get moving. Night was upon them, and they had plans to make. When he slowly loosened his embrace, she slid her hand behind his neck and pulled him toward her while tipping her head up. Their lips met in a soft, brief, perfect kiss.

He felt his face warm. "Thank you," he whispered, wondering if that was the appropriate thing to say.

"Thank *you*, Lance. For everything."

"You're welcome."

Once they were buckled in, Lance said, "I just realized we haven't eaten anything substantial since this morning. Are you hungry?"

"Starving."

"Any preference?"

"Drive-through is fine. I look like a mess."

"Nah, you look great. We passed a KFC on the way here. That sound good?"

"Sounds delicious."

CHAPTER 36

Tarus's phone buzzed. He wiped his mouth with his sleeve. A nearly empty fast-food sack lay crumpled in the passenger seat of his Lexus. The caller ID sequence was authentic. He tapped the hands-free button on his steering wheel.

"Da."

"The lieutenant was careless," the gritty voice said with unusual lightness. "He used his credit card a few minutes ago at boat-rental business in Monona, Wisconsin."

"Boat rental?" Tarus said, quite surprised.

"Is business called Cap'n Rob's Sail Craft."

"Was Svetlana with him?"

"We do not know."

He quickly accessed Google Maps to locate Cap'n Rob's in Monona, Wisconsin. He cursed his misfortune. He'd passed through there just two hours ago.

"I will find them," Tarus growled, frustrated with himself.

"Time is running out, comrade. The longer Svetlana eludes us, the greater chance we lose Red Cicada forever."

"I know this," he said, struggling to hold back the fact that his superiors had been searching for her for over twenty years and had failed miserably. "I will obtain disk."

"Good."

Tarus was currently in a small town called Tomah, just off Highway 21, some one hundred miles north of Madison. He'd driven there on a hunch that the lieutenant would seek refuge at an old army base, Fort McCoy. Tarus hadn't decided how he would meet up with the lieutenant and Svetlana yet, but he'd come up with something. He worked best thinking on his feet, as the American saying went. Their first encounter in the warehouse had been a fluke. He would not be caught unawares again. He'd used his wits to outsmart the young highway patrolman in Illinois. He'd been prepared to shoot the man but had instead used his talents to help him locate his target.

"Such ignorance," he said aloud, both in belittlement of the foolish Officer Smith and at himself for overestimating his target by 160 kilometers. Admittedly, he'd been foolish himself—but not nearly as much as the lieutenant had. Using his credit card twice in as many days was very foolish indeed.

Tarus searched Google Maps for the address of Cap'n Rob's Sail Craft in Monona. Obtaining the info, he knew he'd get there well after dark. In all likelihood, the rental shop would be closed. But with any luck, he'd be able to break in and obtain information on his quarry. When he found them, he'd take immense pleasure extracting the disk from Svetlana. If the situation afforded it, he'd carve it from her skull while she was still conscious. Her screams would be a melody to him, much like those of his favorite death metal groups. Then he'd offer the disk on the black market and cash in—another American saying he liked.

He felt a shiver of excitement course down his spine. Once again, his mind cavorted with the potential exploits such money could buy. He queued up a Brain Melt mix and cranked up the volume. Smiling broadly, he turned his car and headed south.

When he arrived, the shops around the marina were surprisingly busy for it being so late, and he turned off his anarchy-inviting music so as not to draw attention. The gently cooling air invited a stroll along the well-lit docks or a libation at one of the local outdoor bars, but he didn't expect to see Svetlana or the lieutenant enjoying a beer at one of the breweries. Kipling had used his credit card for what was probably an expensive rental, but he wasn't foolish enough to keep Svetlana out in the open when he knew people were still after her.

Tarus drove his Lexus at a slow pace, grateful that his upscale car fit in with so many of those in the affluent area.

At length, he found Cap'n Rob's Sail Craft. The place had closed hours earlier; only a few security lights were on inside. People walked by the shop too frequently for a break-in to be a wise strategy. Better to wait and work his only lead. *Be patient*, he told himself.

He parked in an inconspicuous tree-covered area that allowed a view of the boat rental across a two-lane road. Tarus walked to a twenty-four-hour convenience store a few meters away that was currently devoid of patrons.

The clerk was an older Pakistani man who didn't seem to care what his customers looked like. He rang up Tarus's purchases and offered a standard thank-you. Tarus gave him a nod in reply and returned to his car.

He popped open a tall can of Red Bull and drank it dry. He popped open a second can and took a sip before peeling open a premade beef sandwich. He glanced over the other items he'd purchased—cookies, gum, candy, beef jerky—and scoffed at the excess available to any American who walked into the store. No wonder there was so much obesity in this country.

Remembering his childhood brought visions of long lines in the grip of winter just for a loaf of coarse rye bread. People had to use government-issued vouchers for everything. Hunger wasn't an occasional thing; it was an ever-present demon that gnawed his belly day and night. More than once he'd gone to bed weeping because of the severe cramping that had come from a stomach deprived of sustenance. Despite his malnourishment, Tarus had grown into a large teenager who looked for every opportunity to better his situation. That opportunity had soon come from comrades in the black market smuggling food, selling drugs, and compelling the repayment of delinquent loans. It had quickly become a way of life that provided what he'd needed to survive. When he was offered the chance to work for quadruple the sum on contraband runs outside his country, he'd jumped on it. The lessons he'd learned were sometimes painful, but he always used them to hone his skill set.

Yes, he would be patient. His car was comfortable. He'd slept in it many times before. He'd awake early and be the first visitor when the boat rental opened. He would gather the information he needed. And if he had to do what he'd done in Ogallala to get it, so be it.

CHAPTER 37

Lana and Lance were at Tri-Lakes Dermatology in Middleton, Wisconsin, a half hour before they opened. Middleton was a flourishing rural area on the west side of Lake Mendota, nestled between the affluent communities of Shorewood Hills and Bishops Bay. It was the perfect setting for a high-end medical complex. An orthodontist, an ob-gyn, and a cosmetic surgeon shared the same two-story building with the dermatology clinic.

"When do you want to go in?" Lana asked, watching Lance nibble a fruit tart they'd picked up from a bakery next to their motel.

"Right when they open. I want to see Goodwell before he gets too busy."

"Okay," she said, rubbing her hands together.

Lance looked over at her. "Are you nervous?"

"Very. What if he doesn't remember my father? Does he even know Deacon raised me? And you said the stuff they did while on assignment is still considered classified. What if he can't tell us anything?"

"That's a lot of what-ifs," he said with a smile.

Lana laughed. "Before you go anywhere, you need to do something with your teeth. They're all blue from that pastry."

"It's called a *pasty* here," he said before running his tongue over his upper teeth. "It's usually stuffed with meat, but I've had these fruit kinds before. These must be made with fresh blueberries."

"Well, they are raised here," Lana said, still snickering.

It felt good to laugh. It helped alleviate the apprehension she felt. Yesterday had been so needed, so filled with emotional release. Lance had performed nothing short of a miracle taking her sailing. She still felt embarrassed at her brazen actions afterward, but she'd acted on instinct and an irrepressible urge to show her appreciation. And it was so nice. That kiss was the ideal ending to a perfect outing.

Even so, since she'd awoken this morning, the familiar uncertainties and anxieties had returned. She had no idea who Aaron Goodwell was besides what Lance had told her. That info was merely surface data. What was he like on the inside? Would he be willing to help them solve some of the mysteries they'd unearthed? Or would he deny being involved in any fact-finding operation? Lance had broken protocol and a number of regulations by taking her on this witness-protection adventure. If Goodwell found out what he'd done, would he turn him in?

"Lana?" Lance said, interrupting her thoughts.

"Yeah?"

He gestured with a nod. "Someone's opening the clinic door."

"Okay. Let me see your teeth."

He smiled at her.

"Handsome as ever," she said, flicking a crumb off his shirt.

The clinic foyer offered several cushioned seats, a big-screen TV, reading material, and a children's play area. It was clean and tasteful but not to excess. A receptionist was busy organizing papers behind her counter.

"Good morning," Lance said, taking the lead. Lana was all too happy to let him.

"Good morning, sir. Do you have an appointment?" she said with a welcoming smile. She'd probably gotten a discount with the orthodontist next door.

"We'd like to see Aaron Goodwell as soon as possible, please."

"An appointment with Dr. Goodwell?"

"No, ma'am. We have an extenuating circumstance that should take only a minute." Lance pulled out his military ID and showed the receptionist. "I'm Lt. Lance Kipling with a special investigations branch of the army. This is my assistant, Lana Baker." He gestured toward Lana. "We just have one or two questions for Dr. Goodwell."

The receptionist couldn't hide a smirk as she took in their attire. Lance had on a polo shirt and jeans. Lana sported capris and a short-sleeve button-down. Both wore sneakers. "Um . . . ," the receptionist fudged.

"We're undercover," Lance said in a lowered voice.

The receptionist tapped a few keys on her computer. "I'm sorry, but it looks like Dr. Goodwell is booked solid today. I could make an appointment for you later in the week, if you'd like."

Lana stepped forward. "Please. I know how this must look. Dr. Goodwell is clearly a busy doctor and people are always trying to cut in line. This isn't about dermatology, I promise. I believe Dr. Goodwell was with my father in the service. They did one tour in particular that I need to ask him about. It's very important."

The woman was now frowning.

Lana pushed on. "You're probably thinking we have the wrong guy, but Aaron Goodwell isn't a very common name. There can't be more than a handful in the US. I'm sure he's the right man. Let me just say hello. If it's not him, we'll be out the door in a heartbeat."

"What is it you want to ask him?"

"My dad was killed eleven months ago. The highway patrol said it was a traffic accident, but I have reason to suspect otherwise." She swallowed back rising emotions. "My dad's name was Deacon Baker. If you'll just go back and ask him if he knew my dad, it'll only take a second. Please."

The receptionist softened a little. "I lost my dad last year too."

"I'm terribly sorry," Lana said.

"Thank you. If you'll have a seat, I'll see if he's in yet."

They moved to the waiting area, but Lana was too nervous to sit.

"You okay?" Lance asked.

"No. But I need to do this, even if it ends up being a dead end."

"That's my girl," he said, taking a seat and rubbing his hands together.

Lana smiled inwardly at his Freudian faux pas. What did he mean by "my girl"? She shook her head. Now was not the time for such thoughts.

"Can I help you?" a kind male voice sounded from a door beside the reception counter.

Aaron Goodwell stood in the doorway with his arms folded. He was of average height and build, but the shape of his face and the set of his eyes left no doubt this man was her father's former partner.

Lance and Lana stood.

"Dr. Goodwell. I'm Lt. Lance Kipling, army special investigations. We communicated a couple of years ago regarding your tour in the former Soviet Republic."

The doctor tipped his head to one side in evaluation. "I remember. I still can't say much more because our mission was classified, but—"

"Deacon Baker was my father," Lana blurted, cutting short Dr. Goodwell's words. She took a faltering step toward him.

Dr. Goodwell's mouth dropped open, and his arms fell to his sides. "It can't be," he said in a voice that was mostly air.

Lana took another step. Her legs barely had enough strength to do it. “Please,” she said tremulously, her emotions moments away from complete breakdown.

Dr. Goodwell cautiously moved toward her, as if approaching an injured animal. “You’re . . . you’re Svetlana.”

CHAPTER 38

TARUS WENT FOR A BRISK walk as the sky bore the brassy yellow of sunrise. A bracing wind coming off the lake invigorated him. He stopped at the convenience store for fresh coffee. The same old Pakistani man was behind the register. They exchanged nods.

At his car, Tarus opened his trunk and withdrew a white shirt and a conservative tie. Changing quickly, he donned his linen sport coat and tucked his gun into his shoulder holster. Then, leaning against his car, he sipped his coffee and watched the sun breach the horizon.

At seven thirty, a tall man opened the door to Cap'n Rob's Sail Craft. He was older, perhaps sixty, but he looked like he knew how to handle himself. Rather than directly confront the man, Tarus decided to try his foreign dignitary ruse again. Sometimes, the soft approach worked better than the violent one—but it wasn't nearly as fun. He tossed his cup into a trash receptacle and crossed the street. A ship's bell clanged twice as he entered.

"G'morning," the tall man greeted. "What can I do for you?"

"Good morning," Tarus said, intrigued that the man didn't flinch at his scars. "My name is Valeri Kozlovsky." He handed the man his counterfeit ID card. "I am with Belarus embassy in Chicago. I am looking for a man and this woman," he said, showing the man Svetlana's photo. "Perhaps you have seen her."

The man looked at the image with narrowed eyes. "Maybe. What makes you think they came here if they live in Chicago?"

"They tell everyone they take vacation to lake in Wisconsin. Please. They are very close friends of mine from Chicago. Is very important."

"You said a man and a woman. Do you have his picture?"

"I do not."

"Strange you only have her picture, even though they're very close friends."

"Do you have photograph of each of your friends?" Tarus asked with raised eyebrows.

The store owner's face remained impassive. He held eye contact without blinking. After a moment, he relaxed and smiled. "Okay. You got me there. Yes, I have seen them. They were here yesterday. Why?"

"I have critical information for them. They have friend in Belarus in hospital in Minsk. He have serious injury. I must contact them as soon as possible."

"And the friend can't contact them himself?"

"Is not possible. Is on—" He paused, thinking with a deep frown. "How you say . . . life-support machine."

"I see," the man said, then shook his head. "I'm sorry, but I can't give out personal information on my clients."

"Perhaps I can call his phone."

The tall man folded his arms. "They're close friends, but you don't have their phone numbers?"

"I am fool. I have new phone and is not entered yet. Perhaps I need smart child to teach me how, yes?" He chuckled, hiding his annoyance that this man was asking too many questions. When the shop owner didn't respond, Tarus selected a six-inch tapered stainless-steel spike from a tray by the register and toyed with it. "This is curious. Is for . . . ?"

"It's a marlinespike. It's used to untangle knots in rigging."

"Is beautiful in its simplicity."

The man cleared his throat and placed his hands on the bamboo countertop. "Look, Mr. Kozlovsky. Your story just isn't holding water. You say you don't have their phone number but you happen to have a picture of her. You say they took a vacation to a lake in Wisconsin. There are over 15,000 lakes in this state, and yet you come from Chicago to right here. You have an embassy ID card I've never seen before that may or may not have jurisdiction here in America's Dairyland. I'm a former coast guard, so I've seen a few." He shook his head. "I'm sorry, Mr. Kozlovsky. I just don't think I can assist you. Perhaps you should call local law enforcement. See if they can help."

Tarus moved as if to replace the marlinespike in the tray but instead rammed it into the man's left hand, pinning it to the countertop. The man howled behind clenched teeth and grappled at the spike. At the same time, Tarus pulled his gun from his holster and pointed it at the man's face.

"You should be more cooperative with your guests," Tarus growled. "I need to find Kipling and Baker. Now!"

"Look," the owner said, breathing heavily against the pain. "I just rented them a sailboat. I don't have any information on them."

"Show me the rental contract."

"It's in my files." He groaned, gesturing toward a wooden four-drawer cabinet.

Tarus stepped behind the counter as the man continued to work at freeing his pinned hand. Blood now slickened the spike, making it nearly impossible to grip the smooth surface. The files were organized according to the make and model of craft.

"Which boat?" Tarus asked.

"The Hunter 16."

Seeing the file, Tarus turned and clubbed the owner with the butt of his gun. The man collapsed to his knees, dangling by his pinned hand.

Tarus removed the file and opened it. Lance Kipling's name was printed clearly on the top form. The contract required numerous details from the renter, probably because such boats were expensive to repair or replace. Tarus found Kipling's cell phone number; his address in Maryland; his driver's license number; the make, model, and license plate of his SUV; and so much more. He folded the paperwork into his coat pocket and returned the file to the cabinet.

He turned and stared at the unconscious owner. What a fool. America claimed it was the land of opportunity. But the more time Tarus spent in the country, the more he considered it a land of weaklings. To succeed, one had to do what was necessary—even if what was necessary was considered wrong by the rest of the world.

As Tarus rounded the counter, he debated whether or not to finish the man off. He could simply leave and search for Svetlana and the lieutenant. But the owner had said he was former coast guard. He would call the authorities when he awoke and give a detailed description of his assailant. Tarus was more careful than that. He had to be. He fired a quick shot over the countertop. The lifeless man's head jerked back.

Tarus nodded once, then continued toward the door and exited to the double clang of the ship's bell.

CHAPTER 39

Lana and Lance sat in Dr. Aaron Goodwell's private office. They were offered bottles of water, and Lana had already downed half of hers. She couldn't tell if she was dehydrated from yesterday's sailing activities or if she was bone-dry from fear. She was so nervous, she was spitless.

In all outward appearances, Aaron Goodwell was an average man. Five ten or eleven, light-brown hair thinning in the back, healthy build. Even his hazel-green eyes were unremarkable except for when he looked directly into Lana's. Just beyond the common color was a deep intelligence that said this was not someone to engage in a battle of wits.

"I admit I'm in a bit of shock," the doctor said, sitting on the edge of his desk, his legs stretched out in front of him. "I didn't think I'd ever meet you again, Svetlana."

"Again?" Lana said.

"Well, yeah. But I doubt you'd remember me."

"You have me at a huge disadvantage, Dr. Goodwell."

"It's Aaron, please."

"And I go by Lana, not . . . not that other name."

"Of course."

"I have so many questions for you; I'm not sure where to start," Lana said with a tremor in her voice. She swallowed a dry lump and took another swig of water.

"I have a few for you too. But . . ." He paused and looked at Lance. "No offense, Lt. Kipling, but if you remember the last time we talked, I said I had nothing for you. That still holds true. If I say anything, it'll be for Lana and doesn't leave this room."

"Fair enough," Lance said. "I'm actually kind of freelancing now anyway."

Aaron nodded. "First of all, I am so sorry for your loss, Lana. Deacon was a good man—my best friend, really. I took the news of his death very hard, as I'm sure you did."

"Thank you," she whispered.

"I found out weeks after it happened. That's why I didn't attend the funeral."

"There wasn't a funeral. I . . . I couldn't bear one."

He acknowledged her statement with a slow blink and tip of his head.

"How did you recognize me?" Lana asked. "I was only a toddler back then."

"Your eyes, of course. That was one of the first things Deacon said to me that day at the hospital. He was watching you play with a doll. Your head was bandaged up, same as every other kid in there. He called me over and said, 'You've got to check out this girl's eyes.'" Aaron smiled. "They haven't changed a bit."

Lana turned to Lance, wanting to say he'd been right all along, but the look on his face indicated more surprise than confirmation. "You said you knew nothing about Deacon Baker ever having a child," he said to Aaron.

"You're right. I didn't know about it. And to be honest, I still don't. Look, Deacon never contacted me after that last tour. I can guess how it all went down, but I don't really want to know. It's safer for everyone that way. But the fact that you're both here means the secret is out, correct?"

"I wish it weren't," Lana said. "I've almost been killed a number of times because of it."

Aaron frowned.

"Let me catch you up to speed," Lance said. He quickly reviewed everything he'd found in his investigation, including knowing about the altered Akademgorodok report. He told Aaron about Lana's abduction and about following the clues Deacon had left. "The bad guys are still out there. They're part of some Russian splinter faction who think Lana knows more than she does. But they also know about the disk."

"Wow" was all the doctor said. He seemed concerned but not shocked—as if it weren't unexpected news. He stared at Lana, who stared back with equal intensity. "I'd almost forgotten about the disks."

"I just learned about mine last week," Lana revealed. "Dad never told me about it."

"That must have been a shock. I assume you still have it?"

Lana tried to answer, but her throat was again impossibly dry. She gulped down the rest of her water and nodded.

"Can I see it?"

Lana wiped her mouth on her sleeve. "It's still in me."

He blinked. "Why?"

"Because I was abducted before the doctors could remove it. The really frustrating part is I still don't know what the heck it even is."

"Nor do I," Aaron said apologetically. "Do you?" he asked Lance.

"No. But I have reason to believe it contains information that's extremely dangerous in the wrong hands. We were hoping you could tell us more."

Aaron stood and walked to a picture window, with his hands clasped behind his back. "I can tell you what I know."

"Please," Lana whispered.

The doctor seemed to struggle with inner turmoil as he continued to stare out the window. Lana was on the edge of her seat, both yearning for what he had to say and fearing it.

"First, I still maintain I have nothing for you, Lt. Kipling. What I'm about to share is strictly for Lana. Therefore, I'd like to ask you to wait outside, please."

"No!" Lana shouted, prompting the doctor to spin around. "Lance has been my savior through all this. He knows as much as I do. Anything you tell me I'm going to share with him anyway, so you might as well spit it out right here, right now."

Aaron took in his guests with his penetrating gaze. At length, he nodded, sat at his desk, and folded his hands in front of him. After a long moment of contemplation, he pressed a button on an intercom box on his desk.

"Liz, please bump my morning appointments."

"Which one, Doctor?" a voice squawked through the intercom.

"All of them."

CHAPTER 40

Cap'n Rob awoke to searing pain in his hand. When he tried to right himself, an equal pain ignited across his scalp. He opened his eyes to a pool of blood covering the floor. He also felt it caking his face and neck. Steeling himself against the pain, he saw his hand still pinned to the countertop by the marlinespike. Gingerly touching his scalp, he felt where the scarred man's bullet had gouged a deep channel as it glanced his skull. He had no idea how much blood he'd lost, but his lightheadedness told him it was significant.

Feeling under his counter, he located a pair of pliers. Carefully rising to his feet, the captain fitted the pliers to the head of the marlinespike. He took three quick breaths and yanked upward. The spike dislodged from the countertop and slid through his hand in one fluid motion, the burning pain so intense, he collapsed forward to his elbows. Scabs that had started to form tore off, and fresh blood seeped from the hole in his hand.

Hissing deep gulps of air between his teeth, he waited until the pain lessened a fraction, then put the countertop phone on speaker and dialed 911 to request an ambulance.

△

Tarus sat in his car studying the page of information he'd obtained. Everything was useful, but the data he needed most was the lieutenant's cell phone number. He should probably vacate the area immediately, lest anyone discover the owner's body while he was still around—a few people were already strolling through the area—but he needed to make a call first.

He dialed his superior's number. The man picked up on the first ring. "What have you got for me?"

"I am very close. I need location of cell phone. It belongs to Kipling. He is somewhere in or around Madison, Wisconsin." Tarus gave the number, then waited.

"We show the phone is currently in a city called Middleton. I am awaiting exact location. Is Svetlana still with him?"

"Da. I have confirmation."

"This is good, comrade."

The high-pitched ululation of sirens sounded in the distance. Tarus ignored it at first, but when a police cruiser screeched to a halt with its lights and siren on in front of the boat rental, he instinctively disconnected his phone and sat lower in his seat. Two officers exited the cruiser and cautiously approached the shop. Tarus frowned. Who could have alerted the police? He'd shot the proprietor in the head, and he'd made sure there were no security cameras in the tiny building. As before, his training urged him to leave the area before the authorities started looking around. But his curiosity compelled him to stay and see what panned out.

As one policeman entered the building with his gun drawn, the other stayed outside with his gun at the ready. A few seconds later, he too entered the shop. What was going on in there? Tarus's inquisitiveness was so strong that he almost got out of his car to check. But then an ambulance pulled into the lot with its siren blaring. It stopped directly in front of the doors, and two EMTs hopped out the back: one with a stretcher, the other with a large medical kit. They quickly ran into the building, seemingly without any reticence. That meant the shop owner was still alive. If he were dead, they wouldn't be in such a hurry.

Tarus cursed and smacked his steering wheel. So sloppy. He should have checked the man to be sure he was dead. His shot had been hasty, but he'd seen the man's head snap back, so he knew he'd hit him. Nonetheless, it was clear the man had survived. That meant there was a chance he could identify Tarus. A scar-faced man with a heavy Russian accent would not be difficult to find.

He started his car and backed out of his secluded spot. Putting his car into gear, he paused as a second police cruiser pulled adjacent to the first one. One officer went inside as the second one began casing the vicinity. Such rotten luck.

Even so, it didn't matter if the boatman could identify him. Svetlana was close. His own brilliance had obtained the information needed to locate her. Tarus slid on his dark glasses and slowly drove out of the area, taking his time so as not to draw undue attention.

Soon, he'd have the disk, and he'd be able to get a new face and a new life. If Svetlana lived through the disk removal, he might even take her as his wife. She was pretty. She was strong. But most important of all, she was a chosen daughter of the motherland.

CHAPTER 41

"Deacon and I searched the hospital top to bottom," Aaron Goodwell said to his two guests. He paused to rub his forehead, remembering every detail. "We found lots of evidence that most of their experimental records had been destroyed. The incinerators were full of paper ash. We got so we could tell what the original product was, but I won't get into that." He took a sip of water before continuing. "It took some doing, but they finally let us search the entire facility. I went to the basement; Deacon went to the north wing. I found a high-end clean room with all sorts of high-tech lab equipment: genome splicers, bacterial incubators, electron microscopes, you name it."

"The list in your report. Was it complete?" Lance asked.

Aaron nodded. "I was pretty pedantic over such stuff—always have been. Anyway, remember that we were tasked to find nuclear proliferation evidence—development, enrichment, and so forth—but I found nothing of the sort." He chuffed. "What we found was something even worse. There were leftover notes and such indicating tests on viral manipulation and virulence-factor amplification. My gut reaction was that they were trying to develop a superbug. But I didn't have the right equipment or smarts to verify that."

"The report said you found the bodies of children," Lana said softly.

"Deacon did. We had walkie-talkies, and he radioed that he'd found something disturbing, so as soon as I was done in the basement, I went to the north wing."

The memory triggered a darkness that filled Aaron's mind with sadness, causing him to pause. "He . . . he found the bodies of ten people, six of them children, in a refrigerated storage unit that was separate from the morgue. Ages three to fifteen, I think. One had been opened for autopsy. But all—" He paused and closed his eyes for a moment. "Each one had had their brain removed."

Lana brought her hand to her mouth but said nothing.

"Isn't that a normal part of an autopsy?" Lance asked.

"It depends. Regardless, there were no records of what had happened to them. The north wing also had its own incinerator, separate from the rest of the hospital. When we sifted through the ash, we found the bones of several more children." He stopped and frowned at his hands, feeling as if they were stained by the dark memory.

"The toe tags were prime numbers," Lana inserted.

"That's correct. We looked for any reference to what those numbers meant. As I mentioned before, all the research documents had been incinerated or otherwise destroyed. But then . . ."

Aaron's mind raced, trying to piece together memories he'd long since repressed. He'd disobeyed orders—had broken the law. But he'd done so as a favor to Deacon, his best friend. Some of the repression seemed complete; he recalled only snippets of what he'd seen. But one memory that was forever seared into his mind was the look on Deacon's face that day in the nursery.

"Aaron?" Lana prompted.

He nodded vigorously. "Yeah. Sorry. We found an adjacent room that housed eight more children, who were still alive. All of them were sitting in beds, with bandages encircling their heads, like they'd all had the same operation. Their beds were separated by about seven feet. A moment after we walked in, Deacon made a beeline for a pretty little blonde girl near the end of the room. You were the little girl, Lana. You were only five or six years old at the time. I'm not sure. I started reading the chart of the first kid on my right, a little boy about twelve years old. His name was Viktor. No last name. His number was 29. I asked him why he was there, but he said he didn't know. He said he had a serious brain disease and was required to stay in the hospital without any outside contact because he could infect others, but we found no documentation to support that claim."

"So no smallpox?" Lance asked.

"I found no documentation or evidence verifying that either. He said the doctors told him he was sick. Same with the other kids in the room."

"And my dad?" Lana asked.

"Deacon spent the whole time there with you while I checked out the other children. They all had similar stories. Their ID numbers were also prime: seventeen, nineteen, all the way up to forty-three, as I recall."

"I'm number nineteen," Lana said.

Aaron blinked at the declaration. "How do you know that?"

"It's printed on the disk in my head, right after the words Red Cicada in Cyrillic."

"You've seen it?"

"Just a picture, but yeah. The short version of the story is that a few days ago I was taken to the hospital because I passed out from a severe migraine with seizures. When they took a CT scan, they saw an object in my skull about the size of a nickel right here," she said, touching the area with her finger. "Because they didn't know if it was metal, they chose not to do an MRI. Instead, the doctor made a slit in my scalp and took a peek. She figured out it said *Red Cicada 19*."

"I am so sorry," Aaron said, again staring at his hands as he slowly clenched them into fists. He should have found Lana and said something earlier, told her the whole story so she wouldn't have to stumble onto the facts herself—if not before Deacon's death, then immediately after—if only to let Lana know she wasn't alone. But he'd made his friend a promise. He'd sworn to help Deacon and Lana disappear. Trying to contact her after he died would've dishonored that promise.

"Please, continue," Lance prompted.

Aaron again rubbed his forehead. "Deacon had also found scraps of hospital letters that had gone through a shredder, severely creased but not completely destroyed. They talked about biological testing. Most of the notes were handwritten, with the words *original viral strain* and a lot number. We could only find a few obscure references to project Red Cicada. The words *lethal viral strain* and *Red Cicada* seemed to be connected, but we couldn't prove it, and we were under a time constraint. That's why my report suggested further investigation by someone trained in that area."

"Virology?" Lana guessed.

"Biological warfare," Lance answered with a nod.

Aaron mirrored Lance's nod. "That's what we suspected."

"Did the children's parents know about this?"

"Don't know. Most of the kids couldn't even remember their parents. Maybe that was a result of the brain surgery. Anyway, nothing on the charts mentioned parents. In fact, one form we found crumpled behind a file cabinet listed each child as a volunteer."

"It's unconscionable a parent could do that," Lance said.

"And what about . . . me?" Lana asked with some hesitation.

He offered a weak smile. "This is where Sgts. Baker and Goodwell may or may not have done something against their directive."

Δ

"What do you mean 'against their directive'?" Lana asked the doctor, her mind grappling for an answer. "You mean something illegal?"

Aaron briefly chewed on his lower lip. "This may take a bit of explaining. When we questioned the hospital staff about the purpose of the restricted north wing and the roomful of children with head injuries, they didn't seem to know anything about it. And the only staff in the north wing at that time were support personnel. All the doctors and researchers were gone. We checked their IDs and everything. Those present were told exactly what the children had been told: that the children were sick, highly contagious, and needed isolation. So we compiled what evidence we could and returned to base."

"You just left them there?" Lana asked, incredulous.

"We had no choice," Aaron said. "We were out of time. If we found no evidence that the Red Cicada project dealt with nuclear development, we were to return to base. We collected all the information and files we could find. We even took a bunch of pictures to submit to specialists. We sent in everything we thought could help—"

"But you just walked away?" Lana cut across. "You left all those children to be experimented on like they were a batch of guinea pigs?"

The doctor's countenance fell. "I've been ashamed of my inaction ever since," he admitted. "But those were our orders. Sometimes a soldier has to do things he's not proud of to follow orders."

Her father's voice sounded in her mind: *Sometimes we're faced with decisions that don't seem fair. I did things I'm not proud of.*

"But those kids . . ." Lana groaned.

"I know. Believe me, Lana, it gnawed at my gut to walk away. But look at it from our perspective. Everyone in the hospital was convinced those kids had some kind of virulent smallpox infection. The caretakers did their best to make them comfortable. There was no direct evidence that the virus experiments were linked to those kids."

"You couldn't have sent someone else to rescue them?" Lance asked the former marine.

His shoulders slumped. "We should have insisted on it, but like I said, we had no way of proving what was or wasn't happening. The older kids knew they'd had something put into their heads. They were told it would help them get better. The twelve-year-old, Viktor, said his operation would help him heal the motherland."

Lana wiped her face and swallowed hard, remembering her mother's note that they were taking her away *for the good of the motherland.* That's what was happening. Those innocent children were being turned into experiments to save their collapsing government.

"Leaving them about killed both of us—but especially Deacon," Aaron said. He looked directly at Lana. "Especially when it came to you."

"Why was I so special?" she asked with tears pooling. "It can't just be because of my eye color."

"It wasn't," he admitted, a tender smile growing through his angst. "I asked him the same thing: what made you so special. He said when we entered the room, you two made eye contact. He said you smiled broadly, as if you were deliriously happy to see him. He told me he didn't remember walking over to you, but he was suddenly at your bedside. You looked up at him with such joy and hope that it about tore his heart in two. Then you said, *'Ty moy papa?'*"

Lana's eyebrows knit together in confusion. She turned to Lance.

"It means 'Are you my daddy?'" he said.

Aaron nodded, the smile on his face expressing profound happiness. "Deacon said yes, he was your papa. Then you said, 'I love you so much, Papa. Thank you for coming for me.'"

Tears fell from Lana's eyes. She didn't remember anything about the encounter, but something deep in her soul told her it was true. It had really happened.

"That's why he couldn't leave you, Lana," Aaron said softly. "In that moment, he not only fell in love with you, he became your father."

Suddenly, all the deception, all the subterfuge, all the lies Deacon Baker had used to keep her safe didn't matter. How could she be angry at him for saving her life? For becoming the father she'd otherwise never have had? For giving up a career that could have led to greatness and instead choosing a life of running and hiding? All for her?

"So what was it you did that was against your directive?" Lance questioned.

"We sent in all the evidence we had on the children . . . except one." Aaron again stared pointedly at Lana.

"Me?"

Aaron nodded.

Lana turned to Lance. "So you were right. I was at that hospital. I was one of those kids they were experimenting on. That was where Dad found me."

"It was a guess. I wish I'd guessed wrong," he said with a grimace.

Aaron continued. "Deacon convinced me not only to hide all documents referring to you but to help him smuggle you out of the hospital. That's where we broke the law, Lt. Kipling. It's called kidnapping. We intentionally took a young child across international lines without the permission of the parents or either government."

Δ

Lance sat back and folded his arms. "That's why you were so elusive when I first contacted you about this investigation two years ago."

Aaron again nodded. "But it wasn't just to save my skin or Deacon's." He pointed at Lana. "It was to save hers. I made Deacon a blood oath to do so."

"Hence the incomplete report," Lance mused aloud, his understanding growing. "Hence the breaks in history and documentation. Hence the bizarre route Deacon took home and the reason he suddenly left the service. I mean, I've seen his service record. He was up for some serious advancement in just a few months. His career was set. Then he just up and retired. And after that he became a phantom. Tracking his whereabouts proved nearly impossible. It was to hide the fact that he'd kidnapped Lana."

"And to protect her," Aaron added.

"That's also why—that's why there're two reports! The original one and the edited one that was submitted to the investigative board." Finally, years of puzzlement lined up into perfect clarity, much of which matched his suppositions. "Man, Deacon didn't just go against a directive. He broke international child trafficking laws. That's a felony. That's a court-martial offense. Life in prison."

He looked at Lana for confirmation and was surprised to see her scowling at him.

"I don't like to look at it that way," Aaron said.

"Of course not. You helped kidnap her," he said. "You're equally guilty."

Lana stood abruptly. "Stop it, Lance! You have no clue what you're talking about here. I have no idea who my real father is. And, frankly, I don't care. My own mother, in a twisted sense of love and patriotism, willingly gave me up for experimentation. It was a stroke of Providence that Deacon Baker saw me and we connected. He saved my life. Aaron Goodwell helped him. If they hadn't worked together, I'd likely be dead or have my brains scrambled 'for the good of the motherland.'" She sat heavily and wrapped her arms around herself as if suddenly cold. "If Aaron hadn't kept the secret that Deacon saved me, I *would* be dead right now. That's the *only* way to look at this."

Her chastisement struck Lance to the core. He was so excited about finally figuring out a decades-old mystery that he hadn't wanted anything to take it away. The letter of the law had overshadowed the spirit of the law, and he'd completely overlooked the emotional impact it would have on Lana. *I'm such a jerk.*

Humbled, he slowly rose to his feet. "You're both right. Sgt. Aaron Goodwell, I apologize for my hasty accusations. What you did was selfless and heroic. That's clear to me now." He looked down at Lana. "Lana, please accept my apologies for my thoughtless outburst and egocentrism. As I said earlier, as far as I'm concerned, Deacon Baker *is* your father and the only man worthy of that title."

Without hesitation, Lana stood again and wrapped him in a fierce hug. "Thank you," she whispered into his chest.

Aaron stepped up and placed a comforting hand on Lance's shoulder. "I also forgive you," he said with a bit of a chuckle. "But don't expect a hug."

After a few awkward moments, Aaron returned to his desk and cleared his throat. "So have I answered all your questions regarding this grand deception?"

Lana hesitated. "Did you find anything about my true past? My mother's name? Where I was really born?"

"Not anything conclusive. Back then, Soviet Russia referred to its people as a mass, not as individuals with a unique set of parents. All I can tell you is that your chart listed your name, gender, birth date, and your country of origin, Estonia."

"When is my real birth date?"

Aaron rubbed the back of his neck. "I honestly can't remember. But as I said, I think you were between five and six at the time . . . so maybe 1985?"

"That's okay," she said with a nod. "Somehow, even just knowing I'm from Estonia makes me feel better."

"I'm glad. Do you have any further questions, Lieutenant?"

Lance fidgeted a bit. "Yeah. What the heck is Red Cicada?"

"We never found out," Aaron admitted. "But there's one sure way to know."

"How?" Lana and Lance said at the same time.

"Remove the disk and examine it. It's what you want, isn't it, Lana?"

"You have no idea," she said with a roll of her eyes.

"The problem is," Lance argued, "I had arranged to take her to Peterson Air Force Base in Colorado, but my superior said some things to me that gave me pause. He seemed to know what I had just discovered, even though it was supposed to be a freshly opened cold-case file. If he was more up-to-date than I was, then who'd he get his intel from? Suffice it to say I don't know any surgeons I trust enough to remove the disk and keep it a secret."

The doctor held out his hands widely to either side and gestured to his numerous diplomas and certificates adorning the walls. "You're kidding, right?"

"*You* can do it?" Lana asked.

"Of course. You said it's just under the skin. I'm a dermatologist. I do skin."

"Not just skin," Lana said. "It's hidden under the muscles that form the dent under that bump on the back of the head."

"Just under the trapezius, proximal to the occipital protuberance," the doctor clarified.

Lana gave an exasperated huff. "If you *have* to put it that way, I guess. You can still see the scar from the original incision."

Aaron had Lana move to a chair so he could examine her. He parted her hair and probed the area. "Yep, there it is. Looks like it's healing nicely except for this one spot."

"That's where a Russian operative tried to remove it with a switchblade," she said with a growl. "Lance stopped him just in time."

"Well done, Lieutenant. Now, you said your doctor was able to see the disk from this incision?"

"Yes. That's how she took a picture of it so I could see it."

"That means it's not very deep under the muscle. Probably just at the edge."

Lance joined in. "There was some concern that the disk might contain elements that are attached to her brain tissue."

"Not to worry. I'll be careful. Can I get an X-ray for reference?"

Lana flinched at the request. Warning bells rang through her head. But she pushed aside the anxiety, reasoning that she now understood that her father's cautions against such tests had been to keep her hidden from the world and, more importantly, from those wanting to find the disk.

"I'm not a fan of X-rays, but yeah, if it'll help. Just no MRIs."

"No problem. I have a new 3D imager that brings out amazing details up to three inches below the skin. I use it to see how deep melanomas go."

Lana floated Lance a questioning glance. He gave her a thumbs-up.

"Do we need to make an appointment?" she asked Aaron.

"Are you kidding? My entire morning is free thanks to you two. Let's just do this and lay this mystery to rest."

CHAPTER 42

Tarus's phone buzzed. He turned down his death metal music and pulled into a Shopko parking lot. "Da."

"We have pinpointed location of the lieutenant's phone. They are at a doctor's office in Middleton, Wisconsin. This is near your location?"

"Da."

The scratchy-voiced man then gave the address. Tarus used Google Maps to find the quickest route to the doctor's office. It was mere minutes away.

"Is this man surgeon?" Tarus wondered.

"Nyet. He is dermatologist. A doctor who squeezes pimples for a living," the man said with a sneer.

"What is his relation to Lt. Kipling?"

"None that we can find, but he might have connection with Svetlana."

"How so?"

"He was Deacon Baker's comrade. His partner. Aaron Goodwell."

Tarus thought back over the files his people had sent on Deacon Baker. He remembered seeing the name Aaron Goodwell, but he didn't recall much else about the man. He'd been more focused on finding Svetlana, and he wasn't one for memorizing information or analyzing evidence. He was a man of action. He didn't sit at a desk creating assignments from random bits of data. He got assignments done, preferring to think on his feet, altering his approach as the situation required. Even if that alteration meant doing dirty work.

He still cursed himself for being careless with the boat-rental man. But Tarus was certain he'd shot the man's head. If he wasn't dead immediately, he likely would be soon. He was old, and he was American, which meant he was weak. And when this was all over and Tarus had obtained the disk, he might just revisit the old boatman to finish off the job, if the man was still alive, and not because it was required. Simply because he wanted to be sure.

"You should go quickly, before they have chance to escape again," the man on the phone said, just shy of an order. Tarus took it as such regardless.

"I will."

CHAPTER 43

Lana stood in a machine that looked like something out of a *Star Trek* film. It was sleek and stylish and glimmered pearlescent white in the small room. She was instructed by a bubbly technician named Ashley to place her chin in a cradle and focus on a bright-red ellipse on a plate in front of her.

"Should I put my hair in a ponytail or something?"

"Nope. Just hold as still as you can. Use the handholds in front of you to help," Ashley said while securing a wide strap over Lana's head to hold it in place. "The machine will revolve around you and do all the work. It's supercool."

Lana latched on to the spongy grips and held tight. She felt herself trembling and tried to focus on pleasant images: Lake Julia in the fall. The love she felt from her dad's encouraging words. Lance's warm smile. She had nothing to fear. She knew this would be a painless experience, but the old warnings of her father kept niggling at the back of her mind. The red ellipse looked like an evil eye staring back at her.

"Do I have to keep my eyes open, or can I close them?" she asked.

"It's best to keep them focused on the red oval to help you hold still. This will only take a couple of minutes."

"Okay, I'll try."

"Okey dokey. Now, take a deep breath and let it out slowly."

Lana did.

"Do it once more, and then just breathe nice and easy. No quick gasps or holding your breath. Can you do that for me?"

"Yes."

She took and released another lungful of air, then concentrated on breathing normally while fixating on the red eye staring back at her.

"Okey dokey. Here goes."

The noise of the machine was almost nonexistent. A narrow arm about two feet long orbited around her head while another arm rotated over and under it. The machine repeated the motion several times over the next two minutes, pausing every so often as if to recalibrate its position. A soft whir sounded with each movement. Lana didn't really know what it was doing. But at least it didn't hurt.

As soon as it began, it was over.

"All done. You did great, Lana," Ashley said, removing the strap from Lana's head.

"How long before I can see the results?"

"Dr. Goodwell will show them to you in your room. Come this way," she said, leading Lana down a hallway to a tastefully appointed procedure room. The generous space felt clean and antiseptic without being overly sterilized. It was brightly lit but not headache inducing. She appreciated that. A wide table in the center of the room had a padded circle at one end, just like the one in Poudre Hospital. Two chairs stood against one wall. "Take a chair. I'll go get the doctor."

Aaron and Lance soon entered the room together. Lance sat next to Lana in the chairs as Aaron booted up a computer image on a wall-mounted flat-screen. The 3D image was astounding. She wondered why they didn't have a system like this back in Fort Collins.

"There it is," Aaron said, making some adjustments to sharpen the picture.

"Wow, that's incredible," she said, seeing details down to half a millimeter. "How much does a system like this cost?"

"Enough to feed a large third-world country for a year."

That's probably why Fort Collins doesn't have one, she mused.

The disk was clearly visible underneath a sheath of muscle connective tissue. It was a bit larger than a nickel and had a very smooth surface. The machine didn't pick up the writing on the disk, but that didn't mean it wasn't there. Red Cicada 19. Three words she wished she'd never heard together.

"So that's what it looks like," Lance said in wonderment.

Aaron looked closely at the image. "I've never seen anything like it before. What do you suppose it is?"

"I believe it's data storage of sorts."

"Like a microchip?"

"A very early one," Lance affirmed.

"What do data does it contain?"

Lance huffed. "I've spent more research time than I care to admit on that question. It clearly contains information on project Red Cicada, but I only have a guess what *that* is."

"Okay, then. Let's get it out and put it under a microscope. You all set, Lana?"

"No," she blurted before she could stop herself. "Sorry. I'm just really nervous."

She hated going through this again, but she drew comfort in knowing this would be the last time.

"How are you with needles?" Aaron asked.

"Hate them."

"You're not alone there," he said in a soothing tone. "Most people do. Here, climb onto the table. I need to insert an IV and wrap a blood-pressure cuff around your arm. But I'll give you a tiny shot of something that'll calm your nerves."

"I don't want to be knocked out. I hate the feeling of being drugged."

"Not to worry. This stuff's called Versed. We use it for conscious sedation, and I'll use a very small dose. I call it 'getting a dose of I don't care.'"

Lana appreciated the doctor's attempts to assure her. *It'll be okay*, she coached herself. *You're trusting him to cut into your skull. Might as well trust him with everything. It's like Dad used to say: it all comes down to a matter of trust.* If Dad had trusted Aaron Goodwell enough to include his picture in the set of clues he'd left, Lana would too. She lay facedown on the table as instructed. "Okay," she mumbled. "I'm ready."

She looked away and felt a quick sting in the crook of her elbow. The doctor then slid a blood-pressure cuff on Lana's arm and helped her lie facedown on the table. Lance whispered something to Aaron, but she couldn't hear what it was. The two shared a brief conversation while the drug kicked in.

"All right. I got the IV drip going. I'm going to put this clip on your finger to monitor your pulse and oxygen level." She felt him attach the equipment. "Now I need to strap you in so you don't move," Aaron said, pulling a wide band across the back of her head.

"Is that necessary? I hate being strapped down."

"It's for your own safety, Lana. I won't make the restraints too tight. I promise."

Memories of the operation when Dr. Perkes exposed the disk flashed through her brain. It wasn't something she cared to repeat, but she wanted the disk out, and she trusted Aaron. Besides, the medicine was calming her just as he had promised.

She liked Aaron Goodwell. A lot of his mannerisms reminded her of her dad. She drew comfort from picturing her dad's smiling eyes and gentle demeanor. They were just like Aaron's.

"Okay," she whispered, "go ahead and strap me in."

"I already did. Drugs must be working. I also need to put one across your back, but again, I'll not go too tight."

"Where's Lance?" she asked, hating that she sounded so weak.

"I'm right here, Lana. I'm not going anywhere."

"Will you hold my hand?"

There was a brief silence. She assumed the two men were looking at each other.

"That's fine by me," Aaron said. "Here, just wear this mask."

She heard Lance slide his chair to the side of the table opposite the doctor. He took her hand and gave it a reassuring squeeze. She really liked the feel of her hand in his. It made her feel safe.

"Right, then," Aaron said. "Let's do this."

CHAPTER 44

It was 11:48 a.m. when Tarus found the dermatologist's office. It was a midsize building in a simple collection of conjoined suites. He was glad it wasn't a large medical complex. An isolated suite with a single entrance would reduce his visibility.

The parking lot was filled with cars. He recognized Kipling's Jeep Cherokee and parked in the slot next to it. He got out and slid on his linen sport coat, concealing his shoulder holster and weapon, and quickly strode to a shaded area under a huge red maple. He kept his dark glasses on to conceal what he could of his face and surveyed the area. He saw no law enforcement of any kind. The traffic in the area rapidly increased as he watched. Americans took their afternoon mealtime seriously. Within minutes the streets would be packed with vehicles.

White vinyl lettering on the glass office door revealed that the only providers within were Aaron Goodwell, DO, FAAD, and Heidi Anderton, PA-C. There was undoubtedly some support staff too. It didn't matter. Tarus would do whatever was necessary to obtain the disk. He would not fail, regardless of the collateral damage.

He entered the office and quickly assessed his options. The reception room had five people of various ages awaiting one of the providers. The patients who looked up quickly looked away with expressions of embarrassment for having looked at all. He was used to that. Lt. Kipling and Svetlana were not among those waiting. The receptionist was a middle-aged woman named Candice.

"Good morning, sir. How can I help you?" she said with a pleasant smile.

Tarus was impressed that she didn't flinch at his scars. But then, this was a dermatology office. She'd probably seen worse.

"Good morning," he said, returning her smile. "Please forgive, my English is little good."

"Sounds fine to me," Candice said. "Do you have an appointment?"

"No. I was recommended to Dr. Goodwell by my doctor. I came for exam. No—is wrong word. How you say . . . consultation?"

"And your name?"

He took out his fake embassy ID. "Valeri Kozlovsky."

"Which doctor referred you?"

Tarus's stomach clenched. He'd thought for sure his embassy card would put him in the front of the line without question. America had much to learn about respect for government leaders. From the corner of his eye he saw some of the waiting patients look his way. He didn't want to make a scene without first securing the area.

"My doctor said to come. Perhaps I can wait for opening."

"Again, I'm sorry, sir. Dr. Goodwell has an emergency procedure this morning and has had to push all his appointments back."

"An emergency procedure" could mean the doctor was removing the disk from Svetlana. If that happened, the lieutenant would protect it. It would be much more difficult for Tarus to take it from the military man than a frightened woman. He needed to act immediately.

"I cannot wait long time," he said with more force.

"I understand, Mr. Kozlovsky. Honestly, if I thought there were a chance to sneak you in, I'd put you on the schedule, but it's doubtful the doctor will even get a lunch today. How about first thing tomorrow morning?"

What little smile Tarus held on to vanished from his face. He had not anticipated this delay. "I will try to wait."

Without further word, he chose a seat directly adjacent to the door and sat. He needed to formulate a plan quickly that would not create a scene of panic. Too much noise would alert the other offices.

Δ

Lana felt no pain, for which she was very grateful. Aaron had injected a numbing agent and had opened the site using the computer scan to guide his scalpel.

"And there it is," he announced. "Yep, it says *Krasnaya Tsikada 19*, just like you said."

"Can you remove it?" Lance asked, his voice slightly muffled because of the mask he wore.

"The scan shows it's nestled against the dura mater, but it doesn't look like it goes through to the brain, so I'm confident it's safe. But it will leave a hole in your skull we'll have to address," he told Lana.

"Great. I really will have a ragged hole in my head." Lana felt giddy from the drugs. "That'll give Camry ammunition for years," she said, remembering her friend's comment in the hospital.

"Camry?" Aaron asked.

"Her friend," Lance clarified. "Kind of a loon."

"She sure had the hots for you though," Lana said, giggling. "So maybe you're right."

"Okay, you two. Let's keep the laughter down while I'm operating. Lana, you need to hold perfectly still so I can figure out what this is."

"Yes, Doctor."

"Okay, you'll feel some tugging. I'm going to see how firmly this is in here."

Lana's head ticked from side to side, but the restraint strap prevented significant movement.

"You in any pain?" Aaron asked.

"Just uncomfortable being tethered. Makes me feel out of control. I guess it's my claustrophobia."

"Well, hopefully this won't take much longer," Aaron said.

Lana grabbed Lance's hand tighter as the doctor increased his tugging.

"You okay, Lana?" Lance asked.

"Fine."

Aaron grunted a few times as his efforts increased. "It appears your skull has knitted with the perimeter of the disk."

"Is that bad?" Lance asked.

"Not really . . . *ugh*!" Aaron grunted at the end of a lost tug-of-war with her skull. "Rats. It's not budging. I'm going to get the bone scalpel."

"I do *not* like the sound of that," Lana said, her own voice seeming strangely distant.

"It's a superfine chisel that oscillates at over 22,000 times a second. Cuts through bone like going through butter. Makes a slit less than a millimeter in width. We used to use a Dremel tool to shave obstructing bone, but that created a lot of uneven surfaces and bone fragments. And the smell! Have you ever smelled bone dust? It's like the smell when a dentist drills your teeth, only with a meaty overtone. I'll cut around the edge of the disk and it should pop right out."

“The graphics don’t help,” Lana mumbled.

“Sorry.” He rummaged through a cabinet and returned to his pneumatic stool.

Lance held Lana’s hand a bit tighter. “It’ll be okay, sweetie.”

She appreciated his encouragement and the endearment and, well, everything he’d done for her.

A very high-pitched trill filled the air. It wasn’t as nerve-cringing as a dentist’s drill or fingernails on a chalkboard, but it was still unsettling. Lana again felt a mild pressure against the back of her skull but, gratefully, no pain. Less than a minute later, the trill stopped.

“That worked like a charm,” Aaron said. “Now for the moment of truth.”

CHAPTER 45

A FEMALE MEDICAL ASSISTANT WITH coppery red hair came through the door to the exam rooms. "Amber?"

A teenaged girl across from Tarus stood and went with the redhead.

"How're you doing today?" the assistant asked as they passed through the door.

Tarus noted that the door handle had a locking mechanism. Good. He waited a moment, then stood and approached the receptionist Candice again.

"Please excuse me. I need use restroom. May I?"

Candice eyed him as if annoyed that he would interrupt her desk work but virtuous enough that she couldn't turn him down. "Of course. It's through the door and straight down the hall, first door on the right."

"Thank you," he said with a fake sigh of relief.

Passing through the entryway, Tarus closed the door and silently locked it. There were six rooms along the hallway; the only one with an open door was the restroom. He stepped into the restroom and closed the door, then pulled his handgun from its harness and checked the magazine, which he didn't *need* to do. He knew it was full. There was even a round in the chamber. The sound of the mag sliding into the custom-fit grip and locking into place gave him confidence. He removed a silencer from his coat pocket and threaded it onto the barrel of the handgun. Then he nestled the suppressed gun loosely in its shoulder holster and removed a switchblade from another pocket. Clicking it open, he admired the gleam of the fluorescent light off the polished blade. He would use this weapon the most. He loved its understated power, its silent whisper as it entered flesh, and its promise of a slow death. It was what he would use to carve the disk from Svetlana's skull.

Lance continued to gently caress the back of Lana's hand with his thumb. In spite of the excitement, she seemed to have drifted off. Either that or she was fully in the "I don't care" state Goodwell had mentioned.

The doctor used a pair of fine curve-tipped forceps to grip the edges of the disk.

"I'm going to try twisting it counterclockwise to see if it's free of the skull," Goodwell said, angling his arm for better torque.

Lance involuntarily held his breath. There was a soft snapping sound as the doctor's hand jerked to the left.

"That got it."

"Can you tell if it's attached to anything?" Lance asked.

"Not yet. It feels like there's something holding it in place, but the scan didn't show anything artificial, like a wire or something. Could just be scar tissue on the dura mater."

"Is there any danger in breaking it?"

"Shouldn't be," he said, gently rocking the pliers back and forth. "Just some bleeding. Maybe a little CSF loss."

"CSF?"

"Cerebrospinal fluid. The liquid that basically floats the brain inside the skull and creates homeostasis up and down the spinal cord. You can lose a little without much effect. Too much loss, and you've got a seriously bad day."

"Can you stop the leak if removing the disk causes CSF loss?"

"Yep. No problem." He stood to get a better angle. "The disk is pretty loose now. There's minimal bleeding. How're you doing, Lana?"

She mumbled something that made no sense. The two men shared a confused look over their paper masks.

"I'll take that as A-OK."

Lance gave her hand three quick squeezes. Lana squeezed back three times. *Good*, he thought. *She's still with me.*

A crash sounded outside the door. A woman's scream instantly followed. Aaron's hand pulled away from the surgical site as he looked toward the door.

"What do you suppose that's about?" Lance asked.

"No clue."

"You want me to check it out?"

Another scream sounded, then was immediately muffled.

"Yes, please. I shouldn't leave an open wound like this."

Lance gave Lana's hand one more squeeze, then let go. He removed his mask, then moved to the door and opened it a crack to peek outside. The hallway was barren as far as he could see, but he heard a woman whimpering close by. Easing the door further open, he angled his line of sight until he saw a young woman with copper-colored hair sitting on the floor with her back against the wall. A tray of metal instruments lay scattered beside her. Crying softly, she held her stomach as if in pain.

Lance returned to the doctor and whispered, "One of your nurses seems to have hurt herself. I'll go check it out."

"Thanks," Aaron said. "I'll keep going here."

Lance stepped into the hall. "Are you—"

The look in the woman's eyes stopped him midsentence. She wasn't just in pain. She was terrified.

The woman pointed to a room across from her. Her hand and abdomen were covered in blood. Lance's reflexes kicked into high gear, full military mode. He didn't know what was happening, but it wasn't hard to guess. He reached for his sidearm but came up empty. His gun was in the Jeep. Quickly returning to the procedure room, he said in an urgent tone, "I need a weapon."

"What the heck?" the doctor asked.

"Intruder," Lance said. "Close her up quickly."

"But I haven't extracted the disk yet."

"There may not be time. Do you have a gun?"

"In my top desk drawer, behind a false back."

Lance calculated the time needed to get to Aaron's office, arm himself, and return to the procedure room. It was an unknown quantity. Too many variables. The intruder had to be Tarus. Was he alone? How heavily was he armed? What assault training did he have? The only detail Lance was certain of was that Tarus was after Lana and the disk. He grabbed the scalpel Aaron had used to open Lana's skin.

"That's not sterile," the doctor said.

"Like I care," Lance countered. "Does this door have a lock?"

"Yes."

Lance scanned the room, looking for anything heavy to brace against the door as added security. There was nothing of significant weight. He took a step toward the doctor. "Protect Lana at all costs. Please."

Aaron Goodwell's eyes crinkled as he smiled under his mask. "It's what I've been doing for over twenty years."

Lance nodded and turned.

"Lieutenant," the doctor said. "Do your worst."

"Hoorah," he replied.

"Hoorah," Goodwell echoed.

CHAPTER 46

Lance heard voices in the hall. He peeked out and saw the back of a large man in leisure slacks and a summer sport coat. He recognized Tarus's huge frame immediately.

"Where is Svetlana Baker?" Tarus growled at the woman on the floor. His Russian accent was the linchpin in identifying the assailant.

"I swear I don't know who that is," the woman cried.

Tarus brandished a narrow blade tarnished with a red sheen. "I will kill you without question."

Lance entered the hallway and stepped as lightly as possible toward the big man, but the woman betrayed his position by looking at him pleadingly. Tarus spun in a crouch and stopped short. A twisted smile grew across half his face while the other half took on the visage of a vengeful ghoul. "Lt. Kipling," he sneered.

"Tarus," he replied. "The coward who fled the warehouse in Fort Collins."

The Russian chuckled. "A man who hides with running woman calls man chasing them a coward. Which is truth?"

"You really need to work on your English, Tarus. But don't worry. You'll have plenty of time to learn in prison."

Tarus's eyes flitted to the scalpel in Lance's hand. "This is what you bring?" He laughed loudly. "Is not enough."

"Try me."

Tarus calmly closed his switchblade and placed it inside his sport coat. Then, opening the opposite lapel, he withdrew his gun. He leveled the weapon at Lance's chest. "Is Svetlana in room?" he asked, nodding toward the door next to Lance.

"Yes. But the disk is out and on its way to marine headquarters in Fort Detrick. You're too late."

"Is lie. But no matter." The Russian adjusted his stance and set his aim.

Knowing a moving target was harder to hit, Lance leapt to one side and sprinted forward. Tarus fired, but at the same instant, the nurse on the floor kicked him behind his right knee. His shot grazed Lance's shoulder, sending a jolt of hot pain through his arm, causing him to drop the scalpel, but he kept sprinting forward. Slamming into the Russian, both men buckled to the floor. Lance rolled to his knees and tried to pin Tarus with his body. Glancing at the nurse, he yelled, "Run! Get help!"

She struggled to her feet, clearly in pain, while holding the bloody spot on her abdomen. She staggered down the hall, leaning against the wall for support. From underneath Lance, Tarus raised his gun and fired, hitting the woman in the leg. She crumpled to the floor with a cry of agony.

Lance grabbed Tarus's wrist and smashed the man's knuckles into the floor, causing the Russian to lose his grip. The gun bounced just out of reach. Lance tried righting himself to better attack, but he misjudged the location of his opponent's hands. Tarus smashed his fist into the side of Lance's face, sending him reeling. Darkness infused the corners of his vision. He grappled for focus as he rose to his elbows and shook his head, but as he did, Tarus straddled his back, making it difficult to breathe. There was a metallic click just before a sharp pain plunged into his back. His lungs spasmed reflexively, causing blood-tinged foam to spray from Lance's mouth.

He heard Tarus grunt with exertion and felt the intense pain deepen in his lungs. Lance's strength waned quicker than he thought possible. He couldn't wrest himself from the overwhelming weight of the Russian. He coughed and gasped as a thick wetness filled his airway. Tarus pushed again, sending white-hot agony through Lance's entire body.

The encroaching darkness ebbed across his vision. He felt his body give out and go limp. Despite his efforts not to succumb to the darkness, he slid helplessly into the silent black void.

CHAPTER 47

Tarus experienced the elation of victory even before the lieutenant stopped struggling. It was an intense feeling of satisfaction, of supreme power. Kipling had shown his bravery, but he was no match for Tarus's strength or skills.

The Russian stood, pulled his switchblade from Kipling's back, and wiped it on the lieutenant's shirt. He stepped over the lifeless man to retrieve his gun, then moved down the hall. Casting a glance at the empty lab passage, he turned to the closed door he was certain Svetlana was behind. He tried the door and found it locked. He stepped back and kicked the knob. A splintering crack resulted, but the door did not open. Reestablishing his footing, he kicked it again, even harder. The door swung open and banged against an inside wall.

He gave the room a quick scan. A woman lay facedown on an operating table in the center of the room. No one else was inside. The woman wore regular street clothing and was secured to the table with two nylon straps. An IV tree stood beside her, the clear tubing dangling free, dripping a colorless liquid onto the floor. A strip of cloth tape held a large square of gauze padding atop the disk site. This was indeed Svetlana.

Stepping to the woman's side, he tapped her back with the silencer.

She moaned, as if coming out of a deep sleep. "Whaaat's that baaanging?" she mumbled through the donut her face was in.

Tarus smiled and patted her shoulder gently. "Shh," he coaxed, wondering if even his shushing had an accent.

"Laaance?" She groaned. "Is it donnne?"

Tarus holstered his gun and covered his mouth with a spare gauze square. "Almost," he said in his best American accent.

"Good."

Tarus tenderly rubbed his hand back and forth across her shoulders and upper back. His eyes wandered down the length of her body and legs. Such a shame. Svetlana had grown into a beautiful woman—the kind of desirable woman who could bring Tarus much satisfaction. But that was not why he was here. She was merely a pawn in a much greater game, and he must finish the game.

He pulled at the tape on her head, bringing with it some fine hairs.

"Ooouch!" Svetlana complained.

"Shh," he intoned again. "Is okay."

He felt her body tense. "What did you say?"

He cursed himself for letting his accent slip but then figured it wouldn't matter in the end. He finished removing the tape and gauze despite her protests. The incision had been freshly opened and closed. There were no stitches; instead, the slit was secured with four small strips of surgical tape. He yanked them free and used his thumb and forefinger to open the wound.

"Ooouch, take it easy," Svetlana cried. "The numbness is wearing off."

There was a small hole in the back of her skull. Beyond the hole was grayish-pink tissue webbed with blood-filled capillaries. But the disk was gone.

Tarus cursed between clenched teeth, wishing he had something to throw across the room.

"What was that?" Svetlana asked. "Aaron? You sound strange. Lance? Are you still here?"

He filtered his mouth again. "I am sorry. I . . . cut my finger," he said, again trying to subdue his thick accent by speaking in a nasally tone.

He took out his switchblade and clicked it open. He placed the tip to the hole in her skull, then stopped. His superiors swore Svetlana knew more than she claimed she did about Red Cicada. Perhaps if he asked the right questions, in her semidrugged state, she'd reveal more.

"Oh, ouch," she said, sounding more lucid with each passing second. Whatever drug she'd been on must be wearing off. "Why have you stopped holding my hand?"

Tarus pulled the wheeled stool to her side and took hold of her left hand with his. She squeezed his tightly, then let go. She then shifted her head and arched her upper back, as if testing the restraints.

"Can you remove these straps, please?" she asked.

"Not yet," Tarus answered. He cleared his throat and said, "What did fath—*your* father tell you . . . about krasn—about Red Cicada?"

She paused for a few seconds, then said, "More information than you can imagine. Remove the straps and I'll tell you."

Tarus was thrilled his plan had worked so easily. He undid the Velcro fasteners and let the straps fall to the sides of the table.

Svetlana reached up and felt the hole on the back of her head. "Is it out?"

"Yes."

"Good. My throat is very dry. Will you get me some water, please? Then I'll tell you everything."

Tarus saw a dispenser with paper cups next to a utility sink. He stood and pulled a cup from the plastic tube and turned on the faucet. He would still have to find the disk, but he figured the doctor had it. He'd give Svetlana's interrogation another minute or two before he sought him out.

When he filled the cup and turned the water off, a high-pitched trilling hum sounded behind him. Turning, he had no time to react as Svetlana swiped something across his neck. It was too quick a motion to feel any pain but almost instantly the front of his shirt was soaked in blood. His blood. He looked up in confusion. Svetlana, the woman he'd spent years searching for, the former Soviet with vividly blue eyes, stood gripping a wand with a blood-covered tip.

He was shocked, then outraged, then extremely light-headed. He tried to pull his gun from its holster but didn't have the strength. The room started to tip and sway.

Tarus angrily tried to roar, "What have you done?" but it came out in a gurgle.

She held up the wand. "It's called a bone scalpel."

Δ

Three seconds after the Russian dropped face-first to the floor, Aaron burst through the doorway with his gun at the ready. His eyes were filled with determination and focused wrath.

Lana dropped the bone scalpel and raised her hands in surrender. She pointed at Tarus. "That's Tarus. A Russian spy."

Aaron's eyes jerked to the man on the floor. Tarus lay twitching, a pool of blood growing under his throat.

He dropped to a knee and felt the man's neck for a pulse. Pulling his fingers away, he rolled Tarus over. Reaching into a drawer, he pulled out a roll of cotton and pressed it against the Russian's wound. Within seconds, it turned bright red and couldn't absorb any more. He put his ear against the man's chest, then stood, shaking his head. His gaze moved from the man to the bone scalpel on the floor to Lana.

"Are you okay?"

"Mostly. Where's Lance?"

"He's stable for now."

"What do you mean he's stable?" she cried. "What happened?"

"This man attacked one of my employees. Lance stepped in to stop him and got shot in the shoulder. He also got stabbed in the back. He has a pierced lung, but I don't think any arteries were cut. He's coughing up blood but not a lot. An ambulance is en route."

"And your employee?"

His eyes misted. "She was stabbed in the abdomen and shot in the leg. I've got her bandaged and drugged up. I hope she isn't bleeding internally too much."

Lana felt the air surge out of her chest. The adrenaline rush she'd received from the terror of the moment instantly vanished. She leaned against the table, put her face in her hands, and started to cry. She didn't care that Aaron was watching. She was traumatized and frightened, and she felt strangely guilty. Everything associated with her life and the stupid disk came crashing down, smothering her as if she'd been covered in six feet of sand. Every breath, every movement, every thought was gritty, acrid, painful. Her father was dead because of her. He'd spent his life protecting her and died doing so. Lance was critically injured because of her. He'd jumped into a fight—*again!*—to protect her. If he died too, it would be her fault. It'd be as if she'd plunged the knife into his back, just as surely as she'd slit the Russian's throat.

Lana tried to breathe in, but her lungs refused to fill. A moment later she crumpled to the floor but didn't black out. Instead, the smothering misery and guilt continued to press down, crushing her soul.

Aaron picked her up and laid her on the table. "Just breathe, Lana," he said in a practiced mix of command and compassion. "Are you hurt?"

She curled into a fetal position, unable to respond to him. She shook violently, as if she were suddenly freezing, but she felt no chill. Her mind whirled and flared and buckled as her nerves short-circuited. She prayed to be allowed to slip into that dark void of unconsciousness.

"Lana, you're going into shock. Concentrate on taking deep, slow breaths. I'm going to rehook your IV and give you a sedative."

She tried to scream *No!* but couldn't. She shook her head fiercely but wasn't sure the doctor would understand. She didn't feel the bite of the needle, but in a matter of seconds, her mind slowed and began organizing cohesive thoughts . . . a warm tingle comforted her nerves . . . the thought of Lance's warm smile filled her mind.

CHAPTER 48

When Lana awoke, she was still on the operating table in the procedure room. She had pillows on both sides of her head and a blanket covering her from the neck down. The room lights were low but not off.

She rose to her elbows and looked at the floor. The Russian was no longer there. The tile had been mopped, but a dark blotch still sullied a large area where he'd bled out. A woman sat in a chair near the broken door.

"Oh. You're awake," she said, looking up from a tablet. "How do you feel, Lana?"

"Where's Lance?"

"He's at University Hospital. I hear he's doing very well. Dr. Goodwell checks up on him every hour."

"Every hour? How long have I been here? What time is it?" Lana felt her heart rate increase with every question. A monitor attached to her finger verified her pulse spike.

The woman stood and gently coaxed Lana's shoulders back to the table. "Shh, you shouldn't get worked up. Dr. Goodwell has taken care of everything. You're safe now. I promise. Are you in any pain?"

"I don't know," she answered, not trusting her own feelings. She reached behind her head. A thick gauze pad was taped over the disk site.

"Dr. Goodwell got you stitched back up. He says everything looks good. You should just try to rest."

"Where's the disk?"

The woman gave a slight frown. "Disk?"

Lana guessed Aaron hadn't told any of his staff about Red Cicada. She berated herself. Of course he hadn't. It was safer that way, for everyone's sake.

"I mean the piece of bone he said was damaged," Lana fudged.

She patted Lana's knee. "I'll get the doctor."

It took only a few minutes before Aaron walked into the room. He shut the kicked-in door as much as it would go and smiled at her. "How're you feeling?"

"Like I've been hit by a truck."

"That's understandable. Does your head hurt?"

"Surprisingly, no. The back feels more like a bruise than anything else. Can we take out this IV now?"

"Sure," he said, attending to the task.

"How is Lance?" she asked while he worked.

"He insists on being released, in typical army-grunt fashion."

Lana smiled, greatly relieved. "So he'll be okay?"

"He's fine, Lana. The lung puncture was clean and didn't hit anything critical. He's very lucky—as are you. The disk came out with only a bit of fascia but no meninges or dura mater."

She reached back again and pressed against the thick bandage. "What about the hole in my skull?"

"We have a couple of options there. Because there was no significant bleeding, I feel it'll heal over quite well on its own. We'll just have to monitor for infection and leakage for a while."

"You mean the bone will grow back?"

"That's unlikely. But the hole is only 2.3 centimeters across. What usually happens is a thick layer of fascia forms a kind of skin covering the empty space. Because it's on a fairly inaccessible part of the skull, there's little danger of puncturing the tissue later on. That's option number one."

"And number two?"

"Have a 3D-printed implant made that we secure in place."

Lana shook her head. "Why is that option two? That seems like the safer route to take."

"Normally, I'd agree. In your case, I'd like to try an experiment."

"What?" Lana cried. "Forget it! I'm done with being someone's lab rat."

Aaron held up his hands defensively. "No, no. That was a bad word choice," he said with an embarrassed chuckle. "Here's the thing. Lance told me about your history of migraines, so I read the charts created at Poudre Hospital and UCHealth. I can't believe your migraines caused seizures and you never saw anyone about them."

"You've been busy sticking your nose into my life." Her tone betrayed her current lack of humor.

His eyes lowered, and he sighed. "Lana, I apologize if that sounded like an accusation. It wasn't meant that way."

Lana rubbed her eyes. "Why are you telling me this?"

"Because there're also a couple of observational studies done on patients with skull damage. In a few patients with severe head trauma, they've found that not replacing all bone fragments lessened the incidence of migraines in those previously afflicted by them."

"Is that safe?" The thought of intentionally not having a complete skull didn't seem wise.

"Mostly. In emergency medicine, they often drill a hole into the skull to relieve intracranial pressure." He waved his hand to one side. "I digress. Letting your skull self-heal might not work because migraines typically present in the front of the head, but your meninges are nice and thick and there is no evidence of leakage, so I thought you might want to try it."

Lana considered the proposal. A life without headaches would be a dream come true. It was worth trying even if it wasn't a guarantee. "Why not?" she said with finality.

"Excellent."

She rubbed her face and stifled a yawn. "What time is it anyway?"

"It's a little after eight."

"In the evening? Have I been asleep that long?"

Aaron shrugged. "There was a lot of work to do: Get Lance and my MA stabilized and off to the hospital. Get you cleaned and stitched up. Get the Russian to the morgue. Fill out a police report. I also just finished up with my last patient."

"This late?"

"There was a distraction. I had to bump some patients back," he said with a wink.

"And on top of all that, you still managed to remove the disk," she said, trying to organize the events in her head.

"I'm a natural multitasker."

She felt the back of her head again. She couldn't believe the disk was finally out. She scoffed. She couldn't believe it had been in there in the first place. "So what happened to the disk?"

Aaron hesitated briefly before answering. "It's safe."

Lana didn't know why his curt answer triggered suspicion in her, but she couldn't push it away. It was more his tone than his words. "That's good," she said, wondering if it truly was. "May I see it?"

"I . . . don't think that's a good idea," he hedged.

"Why not?"

He rubbed his chin and gave an apologetic eyebrow raise. "Frankly, the less you know about it, the better."

She couldn't argue with that.

Within a few minutes Lana sat on the edge of the table, her head much clearer now that her IV had been removed and Aaron had given her a cold Dr Pepper. She tried standing and was able to balance but felt untrusting of her footing.

"Just take it slow, Lana," Aaron advised.

There was a small mirror over the sink in the room. She shuffled to it and took in her reflection. Fluorescent-pink Coban wrapped her head, holding the surgical site compress in place. Considering all she'd been through, she didn't look horrible. But she wouldn't win any beauty contests either, nor did she care to be seen in public this way. But she felt trapped in the small room. Bad things had happened here. She needed to get moving, to get away.

She turned to Aaron. "Can I get out of here? Out of this room, please?"

"Of course." He opened the door to a partially lit hallway and paused. "There's no need to feel guilty about what you did. It was undeniably self-defense."

She wasn't surprised he'd intuited her feelings about the room. Aaron was so much like her dad. They were both compassionate, sensitive to others' feelings, intelligent, and fiercely patriotic. They both had a conviction of what was right and what was wrong and were willing to do all that was necessary to uphold those principles.

"Thanks," she said, stepping into the hall.

He offered his arm for support, and she gladly took it. Toward the end of the hall, she saw some deep, dark stains on the carpet.

Noting her line of sight, Aaron said, "Sorry. We should have gone through the lab."

"It's okay," she replied, trying to remain stoic.

Aaron led her to his office. She sat in a comfortable chair while he wheeled his desk chair in front of her. "Can I get you anything?" he asked.

She met his gaze with wistful intensity. Just as she'd determined since meeting the friendly cashier in Laramie, she wasn't going to beat around the bush anymore. But she currently found her resolve shaky. She wanted answers. Sure, she was grateful the disk was out, but no matter how hard she tried, she couldn't simply walk away. The disk had drastically changed the course of her life. She needed to know why.

"Yes," she said. "You can get me the truth." When Aaron looked like he was about to argue, she added, "Look, I suspect you didn't tell us everything. I know you don't fully trust Lance, but I do. What is it you're still hiding from me? Exactly what was the promise you made to my father?"

Aaron leaned forward and broodingly rubbed his hands together. *Just like Dad*, she mused with a smile.

"That night, after our inspection of Akademgorodok, Deacon outlined his plan to go back to sneak you out and back to the States. I told him he was crazy, that he was breaking more laws then he could count, and that he risked court-martial and prison. He didn't care. He told me about your instant connection, about you calling him papa, and he couldn't be dissuaded." He smiled. "Can't say I blamed him. You were devastating in your innocence. Anyway," he said, talking to his hands instead of meeting her eyes, "he asked me to help. And I did—without hesitation."

"Why? You could have gotten into the same amount of trouble being an accomplice."

He stood and walked to his window to gaze out into the dusky evening. Lana could tell this weighed heavily on him. But she also sensed his need to finally get it off his chest.

His shoulders rose and dropped with a cleansing breath. "Did he ever tell you that he saved my life?"

"No. He did?"

"He risked his own life in doing so. I was pinned down in a firefight on a previous op in Kuwait. I'd been sloppy and was about to pay dearly for it. He intentionally used himself as a target so I could break free. Took three bullets for his stunt. Did he tell you he'd been shot?"

"No. I saw his Purple Heart medal and asked how he earned it." She smiled. "He said, 'Being stupid.'"

"I was the stupid one. And I owed him big time. Yet he never asked anything of me. Not until you."

Lana couldn't believe she'd never heard that story before—but then, she'd learned so much about her past in the last couple of days; nothing really surprised her anymore.

Still gazing out the window, Aaron continued. "Deacon's plan to get you free had a few wrinkles in it. We worked on it for almost a week, looking at every angle to make it foolproof."

"Like not using military transport and jumping from one major airport to the next," she filled in.

He turned to face her, a slight smile playing on his face. "Exactly. The one thing we forgot was that there were still people associated with the research facility's less-than-reputable experiments who might want the information you carried. And rather than blowing the whistle and risk not only losing you to US authorities but also having you killed by Russian moles, Deacon said he wanted to just disappear."

"Which explains our unusual lifestyle."

"Yes. I knew of all his plans, but he made me promise never to reveal the details to anyone. Even you. When he entered the States with you, he did just what he said he'd do. The two of you went dark." He returned to his chair. "But that didn't stop the bad guys from searching. When I learned of Deacon's accident eleven months ago, I . . . well, I should have reached out to you. I am so sorry I didn't, Lana."

"You kept your promise. That would mean more to my dad than anything else." She leaned forward. "And his death wasn't an accident. I can't prove it other than to say the Russian who kidnapped me told me his team had killed my dad and made it look like an accident."

Aaron's face paled. "That should have come out in the autopsy. Which makes me wonder how deeply these guys are entrenched in our system."

"Here's what I can't figure out: if they know what's on the disk, why bother getting it back?"

Aaron rubbed his hands together and brooded some more. It made Lana smile despite the seriousness of the situation. He was so much like her dad.

After a minute, Aaron said, "My only conclusion is that they don't want anyone else to have the information."

"Why?"

"I don't know. But I suspect Lance might."

CHAPTER 49

THE EVENING SKY GLOWED A cool indigo, even an hour after sunset. Traffic was heavy but not congested. Lana's thoughts filled with concern and dread, but they no longer gnawed at her, because she was free of the disk. Red Cicada was still a part of her past, but it was no longer part of *her*. Not knowing a thing about the contents of the implant, she could simply run away and hope the bad guys would concentrate on the disk rather than her. But she owed it to Lance to help him follow through on his investigation. He'd helped her accomplish her goal; now she needed to help him. She owed Aaron too.

Having removed the pink Coban wrap, she ran a finger across the stitches on the back of her head.

"You should avoid touching it for a couple of days," Aaron advised, keeping his eyes on the road. "Without a bandage, it's easier to accidently open the site."

"Sorry," she said, clasping her hands together. "It's starting to itch."

"I'll get you some ointment to dab on. That'll help."

"Thanks. And thanks again for letting me get cleaned up."

He smiled. "I have a feeling Lance will like what he sees regardless of how you look."

"No, not that." She laughed. "Well, maybe a little. No, I mean so I don't stick out like a sore thumb."

His smile grew. "Your eyes do that already. What was it your dad used to call you?"

"Lightning Bug."

He laughed warmly. "Yeah, that's it. Aptly named, I must say. And not just because of your electric eyes. You have a palpable energy, Lana, a power that truly radiates."

"I don't feel like I do—especially lately—but thanks."

She pressed her pendant against her chest. Logically, she knew it had no supernatural powers. But the comfort she drew from it was immeasurable.

At the hospital, Aaron led Lana through the emergency entrance. Either the place was unusually slow, or their timing was just right. There were six employees of various ages chatting in the bullpen area.

"Hey, Dr. Goodwell," a younger man in green scrubs called out. His smarmy grin and cocksure posture identified him as the office jokester. "Did you get an emergency call to pop a massive zit?"

"I tried that last time, Colby, but your head's still attached to your shoulders," Aaron shot back.

The other staff members all laughed. Even the young man leaned over the counter to give Aaron a congratulatory high five for his quick comeback.

"We're here to check on a patient. Can you buzz us through?" Aaron asked, gesturing at the double security doors.

"Sure," he said. "Who's the pretty lady?"

"This is Gretchen. She's my new MA."

"You sure know how to pick 'em, Doc." The young man turned up the charm. "Hey there, good-looking. Welcome to my hospital. They call me Colby," he said, gesturing at his name badge.

Lana estimated he was at least nine years younger than her.

"Well, this is Wisconsin," she said with a small shrug. "Why not be named after a cheese?"

"I'm a cheddar-head through and through, baby," Colby bragged without missing a beat. "When you and Dr. Blemish leave, why not slip me your digits? What do you say?"

Lana rolled her eyes. "Maybe if I were closer to your age and still making mistakes. I've since moved on."

The nurses gave her double thumbs-ups and a little applause. The young man blushed and seemed crestfallen enough that Lana felt sorry for him.

She leaned closer and said, "But you're kinda cute, so keep trying. One day, those lines just might work." She gave him a wink before following Aaron through the restricted admittance doors.

They stopped in front of an elevator, and Aaron pressed the call button. "You were pretty smooth back there," he said as they stepped inside the car.

"It's the new me."

"Really? What was the former you like?"

"Unsure. Somewhat timid."

"Huh. Since I never met the former you, I can only comment on the present one." He paused and tilted his head to one side, as if in appraisal. "I admire your fortitude."

She lowered her eyes and felt her cheeks redden. "Thanks, Aaron. I see why you and my dad were best friends."

"Blood brothers."

The elevator doors opened on the fourth floor. Aaron led her through a few turns, then walked into a two-person room. Only one bed was occupied. When Lana saw Lance, all her gathered stoicism and fortitude evaporated. She ran to him and wrapped her arms around his torso, pressing her face into his chest. He winced a bit but didn't push her away. Instead, he warmly returned the embrace. Lana's tears came without warning. She cried as he tenderly caressed her back.

"Whoa, hey. What's all this?" he whispered into her hair.

How could she answer that question without fully dissolving into a blubbering mess? In a matter of days, Lance had become her friend, her protector, her safe harbor. She finally admitted to herself that she had fallen for him. Not because he was good-looking or even because of all he had done for her. It was because he had a good heart.

He continued to lightly run his hand across her back until she composed herself, and then he gently pushed her into a sitting position. "Are you okay?"

Lana wiped her eyes, hoping her tears hadn't transformed her makeup from understated highlights to demonic raccoon. "I'm fine. Really. How are you?"

"I think I'll live," he said with a shrug.

She burst into tears again.

"Wow. Okay, let me rephrase that," he backpedaled. "I feel great knowing you're okay."

That didn't help either. Why did he have to be so nice? Why couldn't he just give her a playful punch on the chin and say something macho like "Kid, you're a brick"? Why was he sacrificing his time, maybe even his career, to help her? Why was he willing to risk his life for her?

"Seriously, Lana. I just want to get out of here. We have a lot of work to do."

She turned to Aaron.

"Not my call, I'm afraid," the doctor said. "I can put a bug in the attending's ear, but it's unlikely with a wound like yours."

"So a full night in captivity?" Lance grumbled.

"Afraid so, buddy. But hey," Aaron said, nodding to the empty bed, "I don't see why Lana can't keep you company."

"Yes, please," Lance and Lana said at the same time. They silenced abruptly and gawped at each other for a moment before bursting into laughter.

"Excellent. I'll be by first thing in the morning to break you out. You two try to get some sleep, but if you're up talking all night, at least keep it down so the other patients can."

Lance extended his hand to the doctor. "*Thanks* isn't enough for what you did for Lana and me. I hope we didn't put you at risk, personally or professionally."

Aaron accepted the handshake firmly. "As I mentioned before," he said with a grin, "I didn't do this for you. I did it for Deacon and Lana. But if you got what you needed out of it, then I'm happy for that too."

Lana stood and gave Aaron a fierce hug. She whispered, "I think I would have been just as happy if I'd had you as a papa."

"No, you wouldn't," he whispered back. "The bond between you and Deacon was something irrefutable and impenetrable. He was your papa, Lana, and he always will be."

When Aaron left them alone, Lana sat back on the edge of Lance's bed and held his hand. "What happens now?"

"I guess we get a good night's sleep and then figure out what Red Cicada really is."

"Aaron seems to think you already know."

"Like I said before, I have my guesses. But I need to do a lot more investigating before I make a conclusion."

She lowered her eyes. "I was kind of hoping to just run away."

"I totally get that. After what you've been through, it makes perfect sense. I can help with that, but I need to finish what I started. I hope you understand."

She did. But that didn't stop her from dreaming. She gave a determined nod. "How can I help?"

"Just stay by my side. You have your father's knack for puzzles. Plus," he said, pausing to secure a lock of hair that was threatening to fall across her face. "I kind of like having you around, Baker."

She smiled playfully. "Just try getting rid of me, Kipling."

With his hand still behind her head, careful to avoid the fresh surgical site, he drew her toward him until their lips met. Any heartache, discomfort, or worry Lana was experiencing vanished in an instant. All that mattered anymore was right here in this room.

CHAPTER 50

Lana awoke before Lance did. She rolled off her hospital bed and gazed at his sleeping form. Her heart was so full she could have sat there for hours, but her head overrode her emotions with sensibility. He had a job to do, and she was going to help all she could. They needed to get going.

She stepped into the small bathroom and freshened up as best as she could with the guest toiletries offered, all the while thinking of what could be done to solve the Red Cicada mystery. When she walked out, Lance was sitting up in bed. He looked up and smiled that warm smile that made her tingle. With his hair askew and his face with a day of scruff, the effect was amplified.

"Good morning, sleepyhead," she said.

"Good morning," he echoed with a huge yawn.

"How'd you sleep?"

He raked his fingers through his hair and looked around. "Not bad. But I can't stay here another minute."

"I'm sure Aaron will be here soon."

"I don't want to wait that long. Let's just go. Legally, they can't stop me."

Lana started snickering.

"What's funny?"

"I was just admiring our role reversal here. Wasn't it just over a week ago I was the one in the hospital bed insisting on being released and you were visiting me?"

He chuffed. "Interrogating, more like. I must have come across as a real jerk."

"Yep, you did." She sat on the edge of his bed. "But you were just doing your job. And now we need to finish it. Does Aaron still have the disk?"

"No. He said he wants nothing more to do with it. He feels the less he knows, the safer he'll be." He reached inside his pillowcase and pulled out the disk. "After being shot at twice, punched in the face, and stabbed in the back, I tend to agree with him."

Lana forced herself to reach for the disk. Like Aaron, she wanted nothing more to do with it. But her curiosity overrode her trepidation, and she accepted the unit from Lance. Just as the X-rays showed, it was a lightweight metal roughly the size and shape of a nickel, only a bit thicker. She recognized the Cyrillic letters from Dr. Perkes's picture.

"Krasnaya Tsikada," she said softly.

"Your Russian is getting better," Lance said with a grin.

"I was born with it," she replied without humor. "But I guarantee I don't want to learn any more."

"Too bad. It's really a beautiful language."

She huffed. She couldn't believe this thing had been inside her head—*implanted in her skull!*—for over twenty years. But to what end? "Why stick something like that inside a child's head?" she asked.

"I've been thinking about that. The way I figure, the high-ranking Soviet officials probably knew of the collapse of the Republic well before it happened. I mean, it's not like Mikhail Gorbachev just got out of bed one day and said, 'We're done.'"

"Maybe he did," she said with a laugh.

He shrugged. "Even though Communism fell, Russia was and is still a world superpower. Most of their research and technology remains hidden. But a few things were opened to UN investigators as a sign of goodwill. I'm guessing a few agencies were instructed to hide their more questionable research for a number of years until they could revisit it under less scrutiny. What better place to hide it than inside the innocent children they were testing it on? I mean, they undoubtedly thought you'd remain in-country the rest of your life, so why not?"

She shuddered. "So that's what you think is inside this? The formulas used in their testing?" she asked, holding up the disk.

"No other possibility works for me. It's too small to be a dirty bomb or a transmitter."

"Lt. Kipling!" Aaron barked from the doorway. "I was hoping Lana would never see that thing again. And me either, for that matter."

"Sorry," Lana said, cupping the disk in her palm. "I asked Lance about it, and he can't say no to me."

"Any luck with my release?" Lance asked.

"It's all taken care of. Here're your car keys," he said, tossing them to Lance. "It's parked in the west lot, all washed, gassed up, and ready to go. Nice ride, by the way. Oh—and you won't be receiving a call for a follow-up visit or a bill for services rendered."

"I can't let you do that," Lance argued.

"It's already done, my friend. I've filed a report with the police and have several witnesses—aka office staff who just got huge raises—who corroborate my story. I just came to say goodbye and tell you I hope never to see either of you again." He gave a lighthearted wink.

Lana stepped up to Aaron and gave him a prolonged hug. She kissed his cheek before ending the embrace. "I have something for you," she said, bringing up her hand.

He immediately raised his palms. "I told you I don't want that thing."

Embarrassed, Lana slipped the disk into her jeans pocket and reached up behind her neck. She unclasped her rhodonite pendant and extended it to Aaron. "I want you to have this."

He frowned at the stone. "Is . . . is that rhodonite?" He drew a sharp breath. "No way! Is this the same stone Deacon bought in Kazakhstan?"

"Yes. Dad said he got it when he was on an op in the Ural Mountains. He had it made into this pendant for me." She swallowed back a growing lump of emotion and continued. "He gave it to me to bring me comfort and assurance. There's no link to the disk, but there is to your *former* partner. I know one of the reasons he gave it to me was as a clue to my past. But I now know all I want to know about that. Please, I know my dad would want you to have it."

Aaron stared at it without moving. His eyes glistened as he looked from the stone to Lana and back again.

"I know how close you two were. I know how news of his death affected you. And I saw your reaction when I told you it was a murder, not an accident. You said my dad was your former partner. If you take this gift, it'll be like a direct link with him, and you'll be able to drop the 'former' from that partnership."

He slowly reached out to accept the pendant. She placed it in his hand and gently guided his fingers into a fist around it. She then stepped back and sat on Lance's bed. Her hands were trembling, but they stopped when Lance took them in his. The air in the room was heavy with unspoken respect and love. With shining eyes, Aaron smiled at them, then turned and walked out of the room.

CHAPTER 51

True to Aaron's word, Lana and Lance discovered the Jeep was gassed up and spotless. There was even a large gift basket filled with bottled water, fresh fruit, and tubes of high-end sunscreen and moisturizers.

"Only from a dermatologist." Lana chuckled as she fastened her seat belt.

"I'll take one of those waters, please," Lance said. Lana complied.

Twisting off the cap, Lance downed several gulps. He wiped his mouth and said, "You ready for another road trip?"

"Where to?"

"Maryland. I know an IT guy at HQ in Frederick I can trust. I want to see what he can do with the disk before I hand it over to army intelligence."

Lana's brows knit. "Why? Don't you trust the US Army?"

"I do, but I've met some researchers I'm leery of. If the disk contains what I'm afraid it contains, I have to give some serious thought to turning it over to people who spend their careers looking for the best way to covertly kill the enemy."

"That's harsh."

"That's reality. Are you in?"

"Of course. Where you go, I go. I want to see this nightmare over and done with."

Lance ran the back of his fingers across her cheek. The look in his eyes was tender, caring. "Can I share another thought with you?"

Lana's heart raced with the expectation that something romantic was forthcoming. But her heart stopped short when Lance said, "I strongly suspect Petrov and Tarus were not working alone. This may never be over and done with."

Lana's stomach twisted. "But surely whoever they worked for is going to know the disk was removed, right?"

"Perhaps in time. But they still suspect you know something more about Red Cicada than you're admitting. They may keep coming."

Now she wanted to throw up. Why was this still happening? What did she do to deserve this horrible life? How come she couldn't simply lean back and enjoy a life of leisure for once? How would she ever be able to function normally and head in the direction she wanted?

Then, as soon as she had that thought, the memory of her sitting at the helm of a sixteen-foot sailboat filled her soul. She'd found the sweet spot between too much and too little wind resistance that had propelled them over the water. The key was resistance. Without the wind's action against the sail, they would get nowhere. There were always resistances in life—some more harsh than others. But her father had taught her how to be strong. Lance had added his own lessons on how to sail with adversity. Resistance was what propelled a person forward if they looked for the sweet spots.

She could do this. "Thanks for the warning, I guess," she said.

"I said they *may* keep coming. I'll keep my internet traps open to follow any chatter, but I'm hoping there won't be much. If the disk turns out to contain sensitive material, I may have to do more digging."

She shrugged. Lance would find out what was on the disk and decide the best course to take. She trusted his judgment. She trusted him. "It's your job," she said matter-of-factly.

"Yes, it is. Depending on what's on the disk, I may just turn it over to another investigative department since my job is mostly looking at cold-case files to determine if they're still viable." He took her hand in his. "I am so glad I looked into yours."

Lana leaned over for a quick kiss that ended up lasting a little longer than she expected. And she was not the least bit upset by that.

EPILOGUE

Lance took the disk to his tech friend in the IT department at Fort Detrick. The tech looked it over using a modeler's magnifying glass. Applying various staining techniques, he discovered the disk was actually two halves joined top to bottom with an epoxy compression seal. He dissolved the epoxy with an acid compound that wouldn't damage other materials. Using suction cups, he gently lifted the top from the disk.

Nestled in a silicone matrix was a thick plastic square with a row of eight tiny gold strips at one end, each a millimeter in width. It was labeled with a set of numbers that made no sense to anyone. The tech thought it looked like an SSD card, but he had no connector that would mate with it, so he set about making his own. Within a few days, he was able to connect a reader to the tiny card, but it came across as a confusing string of alphanumeric code that included Cyrillic characters. He referenced computer languages back to 1975 but found nothing that would work on the strange cipher. It wasn't until he dredged up an old Soviet version of software pirated from a first-generation Unix language that he was able to piece together the code. To his surprise, it wasn't a program at all. It was a scientific essay written in Russian. It wasn't long—only about 280 KB in volume, which was max capacity for an early-model SSD. Not speaking the language, he printed it out and returned everything to Lance. True to his agreement with Lance, no one else knew about the project.

When Lance translated it into English, his stomach twisted at the inhumanity it contained. The essay documented a history of experiments on viral manipulation—a newly emerging field back in the 1980s. It outlined laboratory processes used to convert known strains of Ebola, rabies, and SARS into more virulent substrains. Most variations had proved either to be noncompatible to human hosts or were susceptible to common antibodies in the human immune system. The few strains that had proved viable in the lab were introduced into adult prisoners of the State and children whose parents had volunteered them into the service of the government for the greater good of the motherland.

The project was called Red Cicada. *Cicada* because the life cycle of the insect was hidden from view for most of its life—it emerged only every seventeen years for a few days, then went back underground to repeat the cycle. The researchers figured a new viral strain could be released into the world every seventeen years without anyone thinking it was a man-made occurrence. And *Red* because, well, it was Russian.

The substrains were developed in Russia but sent to other countries for public release. Less chance of tracking it back to the lab of origin. The mutations were assigned prime numbers for identification. Red Cicada 19 was a new strain of SARS-CoV—a novel coronavirus that infected everyone it came into contact with. However, the strain did not attack with the same deadly virulence across a population. For some reason, children seemed to develop antibodies more quickly than adults or those with preexisting health conditions. So they sent samples to China for further testing. Then Communism collapsed and the project went dark.

Lance immediately turned everything over to army intelligence, the biological warfare division. Now that he'd supplied facts and somewhat of a paper trail, they could take over the investigation. He did, however, make sure to eliminate all possible references to Svetlana before handing it over. Like Deacon, he knew the best way to protect Lana was to keep her off the radar.

Δ

While Lance was investigating the contents of the disk, Lana reorganized her life. She opted not to learn what the disk contained. The less she knew, the better. Sitting in a new apartment, she used a burner phone to call the county auditor's office in Fort Collins. Apologizing profusely, she gave her resignation, citing personal medical issues. Having witnessed her seizure, they were surprisingly accepting of it and even gave her a small severance despite her short tenure. A call to Poudre Hospital revealed they still had all her personal effects in storage. They were happy to mail them to a temporary postbox she'd rented.

The last phone call was the longest. When Camry answered, she yelled, "It's about time!" then went on for over an hour about the hot doctor she had met at Poudre while awaiting news on Lana's predicament. He looked like Ryan Reynolds—but with a better body. They were already dating, he drove a Hummer, he was totally into her, and he was divorced with one kid—but that was totally cool because he was an adorable little boy. Camry was still angry that Lana had "left the planet," but in the end, she couldn't be happier with her life. Oh—and she was glad Lana was okay.

Eleven months later, Lance and Lana were sailing on Lake Winnebago, a massive lake in the heart of Wisconsin. Their boat was a Sage 17, a fast, maneuverable craft with generous galley and bunk accommodations that was still small enough for two people to handle.

When they were in the middle of the lake, Lance turned into the wind and let the sail fall slack.

"That was a rookie mistake, babe," Lana said from her jib seat near the cabin.

"It was intentional. We have some unfinished business."

She loosened the jib line on its cleat and moved back to Lance's spot at the tiller. "What are you talking about?"

From his fanny pack he pulled out a small block of cement about the size of a Rubik's Cube. Firmly secured within one face was the Red Cicada disk shell.

Lana simply gawked, unable to utter the thousand questions she had.

"I know I told you I destroyed this," Lance explained, "and I basically did. I microwaved it dozens of times to erase any secrets it may still hold. You asked me never to tell you what it contained, and I never will. The disk itself is worthless, but it is evidence and needs to be destroyed. I could have done it myself, but I felt you needed to have a physical part in ridding the world of this monstrosity to get full closure. This is the last hard evidence of your connection to project Red Cicada. So I want to hand it to you, and I want you to—"

Quick as a snake strike, Lana grabbed the cement block and hurled it over the side of the boat. It made a small splash and was gone.

Lance laughed. "Didn't you want to say a few words first?"

"Yes. I'm grateful I've only had one migraine since that thing was removed." She then pushed Lance away from the tiller and took the pilot position. "You man the jib," she said firmly. "I'm sailing this craft away from this spot faster than you ever dreamed it'd go."

He gave a quick salute and moved to his new assignment.

Lana did not want to say another word about the disk. And she never did.

ABOUT THE AUTHOR

Gregg Luke, RPh, spent his childhood and young-adult life in Santa Barbara, California. He pursued his formal education in biologic sciences at SBCC, UCSB, and BYU. He completed his schooling at the University of Utah College of Pharmacy, including a rotation with the Utah Poison Control Center. He currently practices clinical pharmacy in Logan, Utah.

Gregg is a lover of all things science. He is a prolific reader, writer, and lecturer. He has eleven published novels, seven of which are Whitney Award finalists, and two novellas. You can find out more about Gregg's novels at gregglule.com.